THE CITY OF SNOW & STARS

To Maimona,
Thank you for all
your support!

THE CITY OF SNOW & STARS

CITIES OF WINTENAETH - BOOK ONE

S. D. HOWARD

NEW DEGREE PRESS

THE CITY OF SNOW & STARS

Cities of Wintenaeth - Book One

ISBN

978-1-63676-625-6 *Paperback*

978-1-63676-307-1 *Kindle Ebook*

978-1-63676-308-8 *Digital Ebook*

*To God, for giving me writing as an outlet for my
pain and a story of hope and healing.*

God hears.

God redeems.

CONTENTS

NOTE FROM
THE AUTHOR

———

Why does God let bad things happen?

This is a something I've been asked many times and a question I've asked myself more times than I can count. There are no easy answers to that question, and I would walk away feeling like I had failed the person asking in some way. I didn't have an answer for myself, so how on earth could I speak for someone else's life? Through writing this book, however, God showed me something that answered the question:

God is bringing something beautiful from the bad, the ugly, and the trauma.

Now, this is not an umbrella answer for all of life's pains. It is simply the answer He gave to my insistent questioning (and whining, if I'm being honest). Did I like it? Hell no, I didn't like it! I was hurting! I wanted the pain to stop and I didn't care about anything else.

As a child, I was sexually abused by my grandfather from the time I was four until I was thirteen. These memories were repressed until the summer of 2016 when they came roaring back to the surface. I relived one of the moments in vivid detail that shook me to my core. It was like being violated all over again and I was filled with a consuming rage at my innocence having been stripped from me. Truly, I didn't know such hatred could exist.

During my teen years, I became addicted to pornography and it was, looking back, a way to cope with what was done to me. Porn was how I could regain feeling from the perpetual numbness that settled into my soul, even though with every video I felt myself slip farther into a shame cycle. I had been a believer in Jesus since I was six, but here I was, trapped in the midst of pain and addiction, unable to escape. No matter how hard I prayed or read my Bible, I would find myself falling deeper into addiction.

When I was eighteen, I sat on the edge of my bed with my pistol, ready to end my life because I thought I didn't have any value. My first girlfriend had dumped me. I was ashamed of my addiction. I felt like there was no way God could love me when I was constantly backsliding to porn. I was empty, broken, and numb.

I felt alone in the middle of a crowd. I wasn't though. To say God rescued me from myself would not be an understatement. In that moment when I was ready to pull the trigger, He stepped in and said, "I have more for you than this."

You would think that everything got better, but I had a long way to go.

When I sat down in January of 2019 and pounded out fifty thousand words in twenty-nine days, I had no idea where this book would take me. Heck, I didn't even have a plot when I started writing it. I just wrote. As Trinia, one of the main characters in the book, took shape, I poured my traumatic past into her to more fully explore what it looks like before someone breaks from the weight of it all.

More than that, I wrote her for all of those who, like me, have dealt with the shame of sexual abuse—feeling dirty, unwanted, unloved, and alone in their silence. Trinia is meant to show what happens when you don't heal, when you stuff it down, hide it, or hold onto the hate that is so justly held against your abuser. I wrote her to show how that same hate hollows you out inside until nothing is left.

That's not even touching on all the issues Údar has! Good grief, that dude has issues. If Trinia shows how the hate can kill you on the inside, Údar wrestling with God reflects my own relationship with Him. The questioning of "Why! *Why me?*" is reflected in him, and I believe it echoes in the lives of others, too.

Because I believe so many have gone through similar things, and have never spoken about it, I wanted to continue with these themes. I wanted to give voice to how victims of abuse may feel because that was how I felt and still feel at times. They deserve to be heard. If that means I bare my soul before the world, I will do so. They are worth it.

While my dearest hope is that many will read this book and fall in love with the characters and the world, this book is for those who, like me, went through darkness. Some made it; others are trapped in it; many succumbed to it. Entering into the world of being an adult is something no one can ever truly prepare for because it affects us all differently based upon our experiences. And for those who have trauma (remembered or not), it colors our view of life.

It took until 2015 for me to join an addiction recovery group and begin to see the patterns of brokenness in my life and why I was using porn to cope with my pain. The year 2016 brought with it the first of the trauma memories relating to my grandfather and so much hatred. In 2018, more memories resurfaced, putting a new start date to the sexual abuse at age four. Not to mention my wife getting sick, injuring my shoulder at work, and having to move in with my in-laws (which was about the only blessing I could see at the time).

In 2019, we moved to Baker City, Oregon, and with it came a feeling of peace I'd not known since I was a teen going to our vacation spot at Wallowa Lake, Oregon. I had a feeling of finally being home.

But amid all the good things happening with me starting a business, my wife's health improving, and building friendships, I was still ungrateful. It was because I resented God. I didn't trust Him to take care of me and my family. I was bitter and angry with Him because of what He allowed to happen to me. I asked Him over and over again, "Why?"

You know those moments when you stop in your tracks because a thought strikes you? That's kinda how it happened with me.

In the blink of an eye, God showed me all the beautiful things that have come out of my pain because I was willing to let Him heal my soul. The people I met, the lives I've touched, the friendships forged—none of it would have happened without that pain. He didn't cause it to happen. He could have stopped it from happening. Now looking back, I'm really glad He didn't because He took what was meant for evil and used it to help other people through me. And that's a gift I never would have thought could happen.

This is only my life experience, and I don't know what things you have gone through before getting to this point in your life where you are holding my book in your hands. But no matter where you are right now, we know that life has a way of throwing things at us we didn't expect that can shake us to the core—whether abuse, the loss of a loved one, a disease with no treatment, or an act of violence.

I don't know where you are as you start this journey with me, just know that there is healing for you. There is more to learn, to love, and to be grateful for. We are on the same path, you and I, and we shall walk it together.

Wherever you are, thank you. Thank you for reading this; it is a piece of my heart and soul, a canvas of the pains and triumphs I've lived, and a call to those hurting as well as the healed. As you join Trinia and Údar on their journey, my prayer is that you will see how much God loves you, no matter the past you may have lived. No height, no depth, nor length, or width can keep His deep, abiding love for you away.

If you, my dear reader, are the only person to ever read this book, and it touches your life in some way, I shall count all the hours poured into this manuscript worth it. You are worth it.

May God rain down His love on you,

S.D. Howard

ACKNOWLEDGMENTS

I cannot thank enough everyone who supported this book along the way. It has been my dream since I was sixteen years old to publish a book, and a part of me was never really sure if it would happen. Thanks to everyone listed here, it will be.

But I would be remiss if I were not to list first the most important person in my life who helped me. My wife, Staci Howard.

Without her support and understanding, her words of encouragement, her ideas, her feedback, and pulling me back from the emotional ledge, this book would still be nothing more than a dream. Thank you.

To my children, I love you. Your sacrifice and understanding are not things I take for granted, and I hope you will always, without fail, pursue the dreams God has placed on your heart.

To my wonderful editor, Kristy Carter, whose emotions I wrecked several times: THANK YOU! This book contains some seriously difficult topics, and I'm grateful to you for all your insights and feedback during this process. You're the best!

A huge thanks to Brian Bies, the head of New Degree Press, for accepting my book and working with me. I truly believe that this book would not have been published without you guys.

To Gjorgji and Josip, the cover designers who made this exquisite cover that fit my vision perfectly. You are amazing at what you do!

I'd also like to gratefully thank my family:

Tracy Howard, McKenzie Schoen, Julie Cordahl, Rick Howard, Kim Saull, Melissa Lambert, Sherry Duncan

I want to express my deepest gratitude to my former clients and students whose books I have had the privilege of editing. Your support in my book means to the world:

Bridget Smith, Carla Durbach, Monica Street, Jen Hale Carly, Newberg Yasmeen, Sayyah Jenn Majus, Natalie Sanchez, Peter Fargo

To the best Jewish grandmother a person could ask for:

MarkliAnn Johnston

To all of you who heard my personal story and supported this book, you will forever have my thanks:

Kimberly Angell Dalton	Sean Denhart
Crystal Santoro	Chris Payne
Bridget F Trice	Marlana LaFountain
Rachel Arnold	Diego Vazquez Valenzuela
Renee M Oakland	Sarah Day
Samantha Harris	Andrew Hawk
James Leon & Gina Ann Bennett	Eric Koester
Stacey Hay	Lindsay Noll Branting
Kathryn A. Frazier	Ashley Meyers
Sherri Oswald	Christopher Conger
	Patricia Giramma

Lori Parker

Steve Flecken

Katelyn Frederickson

Brianna De Man

Bobbie Sam

Cassi LeTourneau

Jennifer Cikanek

Christine Vassos

Kay Em Ellis*

Nicholas Spurlock

Jen Brockett

Matt Diaz

Cheyenne van Langevelde

K&C Robbins

Casey Johnson

Shannon Simmons

Weber Salz

Megan Kendall

Makayla Hobbs

Mallory Brumfield

Jonathan Baer

Randy Blair

Cass Lauer

Linda Mcdonald

Karen Skodak

Heidi Nelson

Silas Moe

Anne Osborn

Mark Schmidt

Emma Hailey

Annabeth Istvan

Julianne Bieron

Zac Pierce

Elizabeth Ellis

Bethany Adkinson

Melodie Maertens

Joseph Tolonen

Verity Buchanan

Madisyn Auch

Jane Vega

Janina Flanagan

Jessica McCarter

Tim Undheim

Megan Wagemaker

Melissa Little*

ChandaElaine Spurlock

Nadine Tronnes

Lauren Sevier

Deborah O'Carroll

Shamsi Ruhe

Ida B O'neill

Katie Schwab

Ashley Deleon

Maimona Shafir

The Empty Sea

The Ancient Lands

Thydu

Sīphē Flats

Canämor

Forest of Nex

The Barren Coast

Ungäar

X'phos

The Great Southern Forest

The Endless Ocean

S.D. Howard, "Map of Wintenaeth", Wonderdraft, 10/02/2020

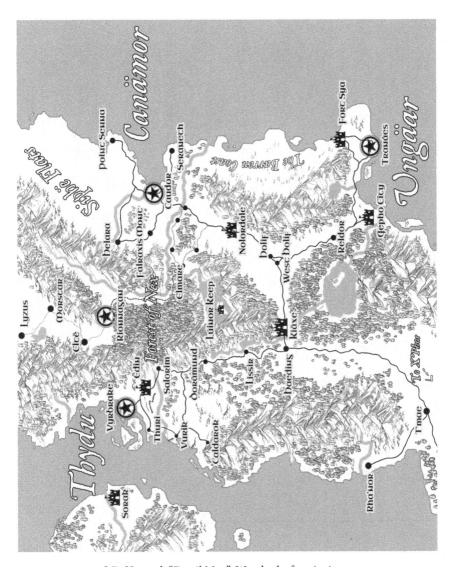

S.D. Howard, "Detail Map", Wonderdraft, 10/02/2020

MAP · 21

CONTENT WARNING

The City of Snow and Stars tackles some heavy content, such as physical, mental, emotional, and sexual abuse, rape, and human trafficking. While not graphic, these themes can be triggering for people who have gone through them. The author, having gone through many of these same experiences, understands and wants to be sensitive to this fact.

CHAPTER 1

There would only be one chance. If she failed tonight and got caught, the past beatings her father had given her would be light compared to what he'd do to her. Trinia shivered as she stuffed the rest of her belongings into her pack and tied the straps. *It'll work*, she told herself, taking a calming breath. *It'll work.*

Shouldering her pack, she threw her midnight blue cloak over her shoulders, pinning it in place with a silver broach in the shape of a wolf—the symbol of Vyrni, goddess of protection. Next, she moved to the mirror and quickly braided her silver strands to keep them out of the way. She leaned on the small table, gripping the sides until her knuckles turned white. *This is madness, sheer madness.* Looking at her reflection, she wondered if the girl looking back at her had what it took to stop a man as powerful as her father?

She sighed. "I've got to try. Prophecy be damned!"

Grabbing her daggers, she slid them into the sheaths on her belt and pulled up her hood. Opening the door, she peered into the dark hallway lit by sparse torchlight. Not a soul in sight. Creeping out of her room, Trinia moved swiftly down the hall toward her first stop before she headed out into the deepening night. She took a left, staying against the walls as best she could, all senses alert.

Coming to an opening in the wall, she checked around the corner to see the shrine empty. Rushing over to the altar, she kneeled before it. "I'm sorry, Vyrni. I have no offering," she whispered. "Please forgive this insult and protect me as I go out."

Trinia moved back to the hall and continued through the endless maze of passageways until at last she reached the Grand Stair, the only way in or out the palace proper. She looked up, seeing the endless night sky with the countless stars above her and relishing in its beauty. Then she took the steps down two at a time.

When she reached the bottom, she turned and looked back at the mouth of the palace carved into the side of the mountain, sitting like an open maw. Maybe one day it would be restored to its former glory and receive dignitaries like it had during the Old Empire. Just not at the cost of her people's lives.

She shook her head, making her way down toward the southern gate, the only real obstacle standing between her and her goal of reaching Canämor to speak with their king about fighting her father. Surely they would want to save their people from certain destruction?

Voices ahead drew her out of her thoughts, and she dove behind an ox cart, wrapping her cloak about her and holding her breath. Two guards appeared, talking casually as they patrolled the Upper Quarter. When they were far enough away, she crept from her hiding place and picked up her pace.

As she moved through the Upper Quarter, she wondered what Rionnagan, or the City of Snow and Stars as it was once called, would have looked like in all its glory. Precious few paintings or tapestries were left after the thousand years since the fall of the Old Empire and they were severely damaged, not unlike the real thing. After some unnamed god had sent a devastating winter upon the whole of the Empire, followed by flooding and other disasters, it had collapsed in the span of two hundred years.

While she wanted to see her home restored, she wouldn't do it at the cost of her people, unlike her father. Trinia grimaced at the thought of him. *Focus on the task at hand. We'll take care of him later.*

The Mid-Quarter came and went with only the decline in housing to show that she was nearing the Lower Quarter. Homes were cobbled together, and the roofs were a combination of stout moss and thatching while others were a patchwork of stones chiseled and shaped from the ruins. Typically, the area would bustle with the market and traders from the other Airgíd clans, though with the approach of winter, trade was slowing down.

Moving to the edge of Market Square, Trinia waited in the shadows and took everything in: Padrig's hammer was ringing through the night as he worked in the back of his smithy; Roparzh's honey stall outside her shop sat empty and dark; Niren standing watch by the gate.

She did a double take. *Hells, it is Niren!* The last thing she needed was him asking her questions. He could always tell when she was lying. Though, that was why he was one of her closest friends. *How in the name of Madol am I going to get past him? Are there more guards in the barracks?* She strained her ears but couldn't hear anything over Niren's soft singing.

Maybe if she got his attention somehow, she could talk to him and convince him to help her... No, that would only put him at risk. Looking around, Trinia spotted a bucket a couple of feet away. *That will have to do.* Picking it up, she crouched down and gave a low whistle, one he would recognize as hers.

Niren looked up and glanced around a moment before returning the call. Letting out another whistle, Trinia readied herself as his gaze turned to her hiding spot and he started walking toward her, as if he were out on a stroll. He sat down on the edge of a barrel, back turned to her, picking at his nails. "What on earth are you doing here?" he whispered.

Trinia brought the bucket down on his head hard. "I'm so sorry," she replied, dragging him back behind the barrels. Once she'd set him in place, she unsheathed his sword and put it in his hand. Hopefully, it would look like he was attacked. She kneeled and gave him a kiss. "You wouldn't understand, but I hope you don't hold this against me," she murmured.

She crossed the square and pressed her back against the wall, listening a moment for any signs of alarm. All was silent. Taking a few breaths to calm her nerves, Trinia launched herself from the wall and tore through the gates past the lit braziers toward the outer stables where they kept livestock and horses housed for the night. Upon reaching it, she glanced over her shoulder to see if anyone had noticed her. She saw no one. She breathed a sigh of relief.

Carefully, she opened the doors and made her way down the rows of stalls, using the light of the braziers outside the gate, until she found a horse staring at her from behind its gate. It was a beautiful russet brown and had a keen look in its eyes. Trinia held out her hand, letting the animal get familiar with her scent before stepping closer. She smiled, petting the side of its face. "Will you be the one to help me? Hmm?"

A horn sounded in a long, mourning wail that made her heart skip a beat. Not wasting a second, she flipped open the latch to the gate, grabbed the horse's mane, and launched herself onto its back, giving it a swift kick to the ribs. She held on as the horse reared and took off toward the open door. Another horn blasted, closer now. "Show me your speed!" she yelled to the horse.

Bursting through the door, she caught sight of men pouring from the gate a dozen yards away, all pointing and shouting at her to stop while launching a volley of arrows. All missed but one, sinking into her pack under her cloak. Trinia glanced back, seeing the fletching. *Hells, that was close!*

The horse stumbled a moment over the rough terrain, almost throwing her off. She squeezed with her knees to steady herself and grabbed the mane a little tighter. "Watch where you're going!"

Trinia counted off the distance between her and the Forest of Nex. She would try to cut through it and circle back around to the Old Road, which would take her to her goal. If she didn't stray into the heart of the forest, she shouldn't have any issues with the creatures rumored to lurk there.

Behind her, she could hear a low rumbling in the distance, which she suspected were the guards she had seen at the gate. With only a few miles to the edge of the forest, she would easily make it with enough time to disappear into the dense brush and escape.

She stole another glance at the star-studded sky as the moon peeked over the eastern mountains, and a small smile parted her lips. It never failed to take her breath away. By the milky light, she could see the dark outline of the forest ahead.

An arrow flew past her head, burying itself in the ground while another flew over her and landed a dozen feet away. Casting a look over her shoulder, she could see ten riders gaining on her. *Figures, I picked the slowest horse!* she thought, giving the animal another kick in the ribs.

She closed the distance between her and the tree line, preparing to dodge between them when the horse came to a dead stop, throwing her over its head. She landed on her back, knocking the wind out of her, and she gasped for breath as she rolled over to let the air fill them again. "Stupid horse," she growled, slowly getting to her feet. She tried to grab it, but it bolted, running parallel to the trees and leaving her on her own.

The thundering grew louder and Trinia saw one rider ahead of the rest, sitting tall and lacking the long silver hair of their people. Her heart froze. *Sweet Vyrni! He came for me himself!*

Bounding into the forest, she ran blindly through the underbrush. Her lungs burned, and her legs ached as she raced away from the one thing she feared most—her father. Even the surrounding trees seemed to claw at her and slow her down, catching her clothes, scratching her skin, and tangling her hair. Everything seemed to be against her. It was as if the forest wanted him to catch her, beat her, torture her.

Panic rose and her palms itched as she ran, her heart racing and cold sweat dripping down her neck. One option was still left to her—one horrible option. As low branches whipped past her in in the dark, Trinia flicked her left hand out, feeling the flow of energy as her flesh separated from her in the blink of an eye and sent a perfect duplicate running the opposite direction into the woods.

Ducking behind a tree, Trinia doubled over as guilt and shame pierced through her. She ran her hands over her hair while tears streamed down her face, her breath coming in shallow gasps. *Gods above, I sent it to its death!*

The woods rang with shouts, one she could recognize as her father; it was so much colder, so much crueler. They grew until a scream pierced the night, one that sounded so much like her own. Trinia bit her fist as the screams echoed around her, paralyzing her and taking her back to her most recent beating a fortnight ago. She screamed in her mind and covered her eyes, praying to each of ten gods of her people to end it.

Then it did end. Silence stretched out, muting all other sounds around her. She held her breath, afraid that the slightest movement would bring him down upon her.

"You die when I say you die!" roared a voice. Her father.

Trinia jumped up and rushed headlong into the forest on shaking legs as her father raged behind her. She had to get away. She had to find help. Only then would she be able to repay him for the wounds he'd given her, both seen and unseen.

CHAPTER 2

———

"You die when I say you die!" Caderyn roared. Grabbing his daughter by the tunic, he brought her face close to his. "And not a moment sooner, do you understand?"

Letting her go, he stood upright, wiping his hands with a linen cloth. He hated making such a mess of things, but how else would his miserable daughter know her place? Had she really thought she could escape him that easily?

Turning to one of his men, he tossed them the now-blood-soaked rag as he remounted his horse. "Bring her back to the city and see if you can stop the bleeding. I shall be terribly upset if she dies before she arrives." The guards gave a stiff bow and began preparing to move her while he made his way back.

Riding back over the mossy tundra, he wondered where he'd gone wrong in raising her. Everything he did was for her benefit, for when she was old enough to unite their people and restore the glory of the Old Empire. The Voice had foretold it before she was born.

Your child will bring about the destruction of their enemies and restore the land of their birth through fire and blood.

Such a thought was enough to bring a tear to his eye. With the moon now high overhead, its light shone fully on the once great city of Rionnagan, illuminating the three-tiered walls and their gates. The Grand Stair led into the Hall of Echoes where the seat of power for their people stood as it had in the days of old. "One day you shall be restored," he whispered.

Arriving back at the main gate, he wondered if he should kill the guard responsible or merely beat him within an inch of his life as a reminder of what happened when people failed him. He sighed. It was so difficult to find people to serve with loyalty these days. *It wasn't like that during the time of the Empire. They kept their servants in line,* he thought. Oh, to have lived during those times!

Dismounting, Caderyn began making his way back toward the palace, going over the plans in his head. *Once my ungrateful daughter understands her place in all this, she will comply with my demands. I am her father, and despite this petty act of rebellion, she will learn to obey. Only then will she ever really control her powers. Then, we will rid our lands of the feeble-minded fools who would prefer to sit in their own waste rather than reclaim what is rightfully ours!*

Taking the steps of the Grand Stair two at a time, he arrived at the top to find the Voice waiting for him, which immediately put him into a foul mood. "What do you want, Tyarch? And if you say you have a message from the gods, it will have to wait until morning."

The grotesque little man bowed his head, smiling in that knowing way that always got under Caderyn's skin. "Not quite. There have been whisperings—"

"Do you think I care about your cursed oracles?" Caderyn interrupted.

"My lord has many more important things to do, which is why I serve you as the Voice of the Gods," replied Tyarch smoothly.

Sometimes Caderyn wondered who, exactly, the "voice of the gods" served. Rubbing his temples, he said, "Get on with it before I lose my patience."

The older Airgíd hobbled closer, dropping his voice to a whisper. "The Baobhan Sith are awakening."

A shiver ran down Caderyn's spine. He feared few things in the world since no one had yet to rival his power in battle, but the Baobhan Sith were another matter entirely. "How can you be sure?" he asked, working to keep any hint of dread from his voice.

Tyarch shrugged. "My cursed oracles have revealed it to me. Something has loosed the shackles of their imprisonment."

Caderyn pushed past the priest, stalking into the Hall of Echoes and cutting to his right toward his private study. He needed a drink. A strong one. Throwing the door open, he walked straight to the bottle of brúan and poured himself a glass, quickly downing it. *This complicates things,* he thought.

The Voice appeared in the doorway like a wraith, silver hair hanging in stringy clumps over his disfigured face. "We should find a way to gain their favor, my lord. An allegiance to them could bring with it many benefits."

Downing another glass, Caderyn shot him a withering glare. "Benefits for whom? Hmm? Do you think I wish to be within reach of rebuilding the Empire of my forefathers, only to hand it over to those... things!" He threw the glass at the door beside the priest. "I will not share my power with anyone!"

"Of course, my lord, I did not mean—"

"Get out!"

The priest slowly backed out as Caderyn crossed the room and slammed the door. Stalking over to the oak bookcases, he rummaged around until he found the books and scrolls with the information he was looking for. He set the pile on his overlarge desk and browsed through the pages of a leather-bound manuscript, finally landing on the title *The Imprisoning of Ulscia*. Most of the first few paragraphs spoke of the kingdoms fighting her and her "daughters."

Further down, Caderyn came across a paragraph talking about the enchantment that had been used.

Year 8853 AE

Many had died over the years striving against the Queen of the Banshees, and many more would have if not for Green Cloak and the power of his god, Elohai. With the White Fire, he, along with representatives from every kingdom, used their power to trap Ulscia within the confines of Mugros Lake where she is to this day.

Caderyn snorted. The author was far too superstitious if they believed in the White Flame, or Elohai for that matter. Setting the book aside, he riffled through the scrolls, finding only bits and pieces regarding the creatures that roamed all the lands of Wintenaeth.

Year 8130 AE

Reports from our scouts have added to the validity of the claims we are hearing from our spies in the other kingdoms of monstrous creatures. Giant lumbering beasts called helwrecks, terrifyingly beautiful spirits known as telgosts with flaming eyes, and a Trifell, something our scouts have not seen yet. More reports are coming in daily. I will report when I have more.

L.

Shaking his head, Caderyn tossed the paper onto the pile of other useless information. It was well into the night now and the sun would rise in a few hours, but his mind would not rest. He needed to keep a tighter leash on his daughter if he hoped to rebuild anything while somehow keeping the Baobhan Sith at bay until he was ready to subdue them too. *So much to do*, he thought, *and so little time to do it in.*

-II-

Trinia finally slowed her pace to give herself time to recover when she regained her senses. The stiffness was settling in from her tumble off the horse, and she hoped it would not be worse come the dawn. Her hands still had a slight tremble to them she could not seem to stop.

She didn't know where she was and the forest cover blocked out all light from the moon, if it was still out. Finally, she forced herself to stop walking and take a breather. *Think, Trinia, think! How are we going to get out of this and figure out where we are?*

The hairs on the back of her neck suddenly rose and she felt like she was being watched. She turned in every direction, but it was too dark to see anything, which only made the feeling worse. Taking two steps back, she ran into a tree. If something was down here, she should be safe in a tree... hopefully. Reaching up, Trinia grabbed at one limb and, with some difficulty and a fall or two, managed to get onto the first branch. Going was slow with her pack getting caught on seemingly every other branch, but she finally it made onto the sturdy limb and settled in.

Try as she might, though, sleep did not come. Several times throughout the night she heard a sniffing and growling at the bottom of the tree. *Vyrni, if you are listening, please keep me safe tonight from whatever is out there.*

When the dim light of morning finally crept through the dense trees, nothing was scattered about but unusually large paw prints. "Note to self, don't sleep on the ground *ever*," she mused as she placed her hand beside the print, which was easily four times bigger. *I need to get out of this forest.*

Staring out into the murky light, she brushed off her hands. "Okay, just need to head east to reach the Old Road, and then it should be straight on to Canämor." She looked up, dismayed at the dense canopy blocking her view of the sun. Not wanting to waste time and spend another night in the forest, she took her best guess at the direction and started back the way she came.

The minutes slowly turned into hours as she trudged on, the only change being the trees, which seemed to grow taller and more menacing if such a thing were possible. The shadows became deeper the farther she walked, and she feared she had strayed from her course toward the heart of the forest. How far had she run last night? She had little memory after she heard her father's voice ring out as she fled in a panic.

Trinia felt the familiar sense of eyes watching her. She had grown sensitive to the feeling back at the palace. The Voice seemed to lurk in every shadow, around every corner, ever watching her until she was alone. Then he would take her. Now it was as though the forest was doing the same.

A twig snapped somewhere off in the trees and she thought she caught glimpses of movement in the dismal light that forced itself through the canopy of leaves and pine.

Another twig snapped, closer this time.

Shadows moved in the distance, sending waves of goose-flesh up her arms as she turned and ran. She only made it a dozen yards when her boot caught on a root hidden under the layers of pine needles. Landing hard, her head collided with a half-buried rock, sending stars bursting in her vision. Her head spun as she listened to whatever it was slowly coming up behind her. *Maybe if I don't move, it won't see me...*

Something gripped her shoulder and she cried out, "Please! Don't kill me!"

It rolled Trinia onto her back, and she stared up into the grizzled face of an old man with one good eye, the other milky white and bearing long scar from brow to cheek. He had a graying beard that once may have been black in his youth, and his hair was wild and unkempt. "Please...please don't kill me," she begged. Her head hurt and the world seemed to move on its own, twisting this way and that.

She was in her room trying to sleep when she heard the footsteps from her doorway. The icy hand of the Voice on her arm had started the flow of tears and the silent pleas.

Trinia was back in the forest, staring up into the face of a Wildman. He was pulling something from his belt, a flask, and he tipped it into her mouth. The cool liquid soothed her pounding head, but she felt her body go limp. She tried to struggle, to punch, to kick, yet her body would not respond. *Gods, no! Help me, Vyrni!*

The Wildman put his arms under her, lifted her up, and began walking, his long legs pumping as he carried her over the rough terrain. Trinia tried to fight the effects of the drink, to reach for her daggers at her waist, but it was no use. Her skin crawled at his touch and she wanted nothing more than to get away from him.

On and on he walked, ever in a singular direction, turning neither to the left nor to the right, and he never seemed to get tired. *He's taking me back to whatever hole he calls home,* she thought.

After a few hours, Trinia finally regained some feeling in her lips and tried to speak to the man. He grunted, looking at her with his good eye, and placed a calloused finger on her lips while shaking his head.

Odd, strangled cries erupted from behind that sent a chill to her heart. *Merciful gods! What is that?*

The Wildman took off running as if Madol's hounds were nipping at his heels.

The sounds seemed to surround them, and Trinia wasn't sure if they would make it to wherever the man was taking her, which at this point seemed much safer than being left in the forest.

Trinia felt a prickling in her fingers and toes, and she thanked Vyrni for letting her regain feeling in her limbs. She wondered a moment if the feeling of weightlessness was a side effect of whatever the man had given her, realizing just before she hit the ground that the man had tossed her.

She landed on her pack and rolled, her face buried in the grass, and let out a string of curses directed at the gods and the Wildman. Despite the slow return of feeling in her limbs, she still couldn't move her head to see what was happening, and judging from the horrible cries, she wasn't sure she wanted to. A low menacing growl came from her right, follow by screeches and snarling.

As quickly as the cries came, they were gone, and the forest was silent once more save for the low growl somewhere behind her, out of sight. Trinia closed her eyes and prayed. *Please! Vyrni! Don't abandon me here!*

Something wet touched her hand and she screamed, tears rolling down her cheeks as she tried to come to terms with what would happen. *I'm going to die.*

Floating on the edge of consciousness, she opened her eyes, blinking several times. She turned her head slowly toward where hot breath fell on her hand, seeing a wolf the size of a horse. A soft whimper escaped her, and she tried to move her hand to cover her neck, managing to only move it an inch or two. Had the wolf killed the Wildman? Had it made those horrible sounds?

Minutes passed, and the beast didn't move. It sat, turning its head and glancing around as if it were keeping watch over her. Maybe Vyrni had sent the wolf as her protector? To watch over her and save her from the Wildman and whatever lurked in the forest.

Between hitting her head and the potion, she slipped in and out of awareness, everything weighing her down. Though she could feel her arms again, they felt leaden. The more the potion wore off, the more tired she became, and Trinia began to drift off under the watchful golden eye of the wolf, finding a strange comfort in its presence.

CHAPTER 3

It was difficult being the Crown Prince of Ungäar. Everyone always looking to you for advice, telling you what they expected from you, going on and on about your "potential." It was all rather draining. Day in and day out, people treated you like you were ignorant of the world when, most times, you were aware because you hadn't buried your head so far up your own backside that you could no longer see.

Jayden sighed, splashing the cold water over his face and drying it with his tunic. "Better off alone, eh?" he asked his reflection. In the three years since he had faked his death at the Academy of Mages and set out on his own, he'd made a living for himself. Granted, stealing wasn't exactly an honorable occupation, but it kept his belly full.

Staring out over the landscape across the border into Thydu, he could almost see making a name for himself training horses there. Was he a master at it? No. Would he learn from the best? Yes. He would have crossed days ago, but something held him back, beckoning him to stay, and he couldn't place it. There was nothing for him back home.

Picking up a rock, he tossed it off the edge of the cliff where he had set up camp at the outskirts of a small wood. *I didn't think it would be this hard.* He hated it when he started having all these…feelings.

"Jayden!"

He startled, turning toward the voice to see a familiar, and rather ugly, face. *Hells below,* he thought. Quickly putting on a smile, Jayden greeted his unwelcome guest. "Gurig! Long time no see! You're looking rather chipper this morning."

Gurig's pudgy face morphed into a scowl. "I've come for my portion of the job," he said, shaking a finger at Jayden. "And I better get it with ten percent of yours since you left me for dead!"

"Well, how was I to know you survived the fall?" Jayden asked, trying to bide his time. Gurig was not a smart man, but he made up for it in brawn, hence why he was so useful when shaking people down. "Don't you think you're overreacting just a little?"

The man took a few steps closer, forcing Jayden nearer the cliff's edge. "I could have pushed you off when you were daydreaming and taken all of it," he replied, a dark gleam in his eyes.

Jayden raised his hands slowly. "You have a point there, and that is why you're a better man than I am. Alright, ten percent it is. If I may?" He motioned to his pack, waiting for Gurig to give him an okay to move.

"No funny business, Jayden. If you try to cheat me now, I promise you will not survive a tumble off the cliff."

"Duly noted, my friend. Give me a moment." Jayden racked his brain for a way to skirt the situation as he moved purposefully toward his pack. There was no way he could fight the man—he was too strong—and while not the brightest gem in the bunch, he knew how to count. He would know if it wasn't correct. *This is why we can't have nice things. You accidentally leave people for dead without checking to make sure they are, in fact, dead,* he told himself.

He could feel Gurig's eyes on him as he pulled the coin purse from his pack, counting out the man's portion plus a few more and realizing he would be about eight pieces short. Jayden closed eyes and grimaced. *I knew I shouldn't have visited that brothel in Kiäxe.* Turning back to his old partner in crime, he handed him the coin. "It would seem I'm a bit shy on that ten percent."

Gurig glowered at him, snatching the coins out of his hand, and began counting. Sweat gathered at Jayden's temples as he watched the man's expression grow darker. *This will not end well,* he thought. Another thought struck him. How on earth did Gurig find him?

Despite the sinister look, the man began to laugh, low at first and steadily growing in volume. He looked at Jayden and dropped the coins on the ground. "I wonder how much I will get for selling a spoiled princeling to the slavers? Perhaps that will cover your ten percent."

Oh hells.

Hands grabbed him from behind and tied a gag in his mouth. He twisted an arm free and sent a burst of air toward Gurig, sending him off balance and over the cliff. The moment of hesitation from the men behind him was all he needed as he aimed a blast at the ground and launched himself and the man who held him fifteen feet in the air. Jayden let out another blast to break his fall while the other man was not so fortunate, landing on his neck with a *crack.* Turning his attention to the other three men, Jayden formed a *soläs,* its light getting brighter and brighter as it solidified.

When it reached its brightest point, he threw it between the men, causing the ball of light of explode and sending the men flying several feet. It wouldn't kill them, but it would permanently blind them. Death would come from local predators like bears or wolves if they were lucky.

Jayden walked over to his pack and threw it over his shoulders, grabbing his cloak before moving to the cliff's edge. He peered over, seeing Gurig's broken body some three hundred feet below. "Looks like *you* took a little tumble off the cliff, my friend. I don't think you'll come back from that one."

He cleaned up his camp as best as he could before heading off into the woods, ignoring the terrified pleas of the men fumbling around. They had made their cot and now they would sleep in it. He would need to pay a visit to one more person—the only person he had confided in since leaving the Academy—before heading into Thydu.

It was time to go see Cal.

-II-

Trinia woke with a start, sitting up and glancing around for the wolf but seeing no sign of him. She frowned, clutching at the silver pin on her cloak. Everything from the day before seemed like a bad dream, like waking up and knowing it happened, yet the details of it were just out of reach. In any regard, she was glad the wolf had scared the Wildman off.

Standing slowly, Trinia groaned as her body protested the many bumps and bruises she had accumulated in such a short time. She reached to the sky, putting her arm over her head as she stretched the stiffness out of the muscles, and nearly tipped over from a wave of dizziness. The Wildman's brew probably had something to do with that as well. Steadying herself, she noticed she was no longer under the boughs of the forest but under a cloudy September sky. *Did the wolf drag me out of there? How did I get out of the forest?*

Taking in her surroundings, she could see a small town off in the distance with high walls about a mile or two from where she stood at the boundary of the forest. Glancing back into the wood, a shiver ran down her spine as she remembered the horrid screeches. *I'm never going back in there*, she thought. She sighed, turning her gaze back to the little town. It would be her best bet for finding out where she was.

Removing her pack, she set it on the grass and rummaged around in it until she found the pieces of bread, now smashed from her landing on it, at the bottom. She took a few bites before she realized her waterskin was gone. *Hells below! Can this get any worse?* she wondered. Swallowing the dry bread, she double-checked to see everything still intact in her bag other than the missing waterskin. A small blessing.

Trinia retied her boots, grabbed her pack and got it back in place before it occurred to her that some of the kingdoms were not friendly with the Airgíd since the end of the Empire. *Probably best not to risk it*, she thought. Slowing her breathing, she brought her palms together until they heated up and then spread them apart and moved them over the length of her hair. Once finished, she checked the layers of her silver hair, making sure the inky black color of the illusion had taken effect. *That should help me blend in.*

Setting off toward the town, she tried to gauge her location based on the surrounding landscape, which proved difficult since she had never seen the lands beyond her own. Behind her stood the Forest of Nex and a tall mountain range on the right rose to the clouds. Before her, craggy hills riddled the land as it sloped down toward gray plains. Pausing a moment to look at the sun's position, Trinia felt a sinking feeling in her stomach. It was headed the wrong way.

"Hells below, I'm in Thydu!" she exclaimed. She would need to travel hundreds of miles south before reaching the southern tip of the Olen Mountains! It would take months to reach her goal now.

Her palms started itching and the tremble returned in her left hand. She flexed it a few times, trying to shake it out as she continued toward the town. There was nothing left to do but move forward and hope for the best.

Hours later, she was still no closer to her goal. Picking her way through the hills was harder than she expected due to the loose rocks and steep inclines. Upon reaching the top of her current rocky nemesis, Trinia noted the sun was past its midpoint. "One more mile," she mumbled to herself, "just one more mile."

Sliding down the other side of the hill as safely as she could, she spotted what looked like a worn path that seemed to lead toward the town. Several smaller hills stood between her and what she hoped would be her guide out of the hills, and she climbed each with a renewed vigor.

After losing sight of it for several minutes, Trinia stumbled on it as she rounded a corner and let out a squeal of joy. Now she could make double the time and reach the town before the mountains blocked the sunlight, which could make it harder to see. Taking off at a sprint, she couldn't help but smile at the little victory after everything had gone so wrong in the forest.

Up ahead she could see a mysterious form lying in the middle of a bend in the path. Skidding to a stop, she ducked behind a boulder, peeking through a crack in it. Nothing moved, but a strange clicking sound emanated from its direction.

Suddenly, the form moved, and raised itself up, and let out a hiss at something she could not see. A gasp escaped her. It was a skaäsa! The insect reared up its segmented body and snapped the pincer-like jaws, lunging forward with the help from its hundreds of spindly legs. There were several shouts and loud hissing from around the bend, and Trinia shivered at the thought of how close she had come to it.

The skaäsa reappeared with two spears dug into its back between the plates of its exoskeleton and a bluish-green goo dripping to the ground from other wounds. Five men followed close behind with bows, spears, and swords at the ready to finish it. One of them, a burly man with a thick brown beard, jumped onto its back and drove the tip of his spear into the base of its plated head. Its legs curled in and twitched as it skidded to a halt a few feet from her hiding place.

Trinia tried to readjust herself behind the boulder to better conceal her position, but the movement caused several loose rocks to tumble onto the path. Within seconds, three men stood over her, spears and swords leveled at her chest as the Skaäsa-Killer walked over. He looked her up and down, his thick brows furrowing. "Who are you?"

"I, uh, I'm Trinia," she replied, eyeing him warily.

"And why are you out here? Hmm? Are you a Thydian spy? He asked.

She shook her head. "No!"

Skaäsa-Killer grunted and motioned to the men. "Bring her back to Salorim. We will deal with her there."

Two of the men grabbed her by the arms while the third took her daggers from her belt. She tried to pull herself free until the man with her daggers placed one under her chin, shaking his head. All the fight left her. *The gods are punishing me for running away,* she thought.

The path did lead to the town like she had hoped it would, and after only an hour, she passed through the small wooden gate on the north side. Skaäsa-Killer led the group through the streets, greeting people from every walk of life—from farmers to what Trinia suspected were nobility. Everyone seemed to admire him. *He must be the leader or some local hero of sorts*, she thought.

They arrived at a large stone building with a short stone wall about ten feet high and reinforced oak doors. While the leader went into the bigger building, the three men took her around the side to a squat structure made from timber with iron bars for windows and a heavy wooden door at the front. The guards ripped off her pack and shoved her through the opening.

Trinia looked around as the door closed behind her and found a corner where she sat and pulled her legs up to her chest. *This is not how I saw things going*, she thought bitterly. The plan had been simple: get out of the city, find a horse, ride to the neighboring kingdom and ask for their help in ending her father's madness before it began. Now, she was hundreds of miles away from her goal!

She scratched her palms, trying to get them to stop itching. As if the feeling of duplicating herself was not horrible enough. *If I don't find a way out of here, I'm going to lose my mind!*

Panic bubbled in her chest and she stood, pacing from one end of her prison to the other for hours as the sun arched through the sky. Six paces, turn. Six paces, turn. *The guard outside probably has my daggers, and with any luck, my pack. If I get him to open the door... then what?* Creating another duplicate was out of the question, so what else could she do?

It was almost night. If she made a noise to get the man's attention, she could get behind the door and use her cloak, a midnight blue, to help her blend in! *Sweet Vyrni, please let this work!* she pleaded. Going to the other end, Trinia screamed, imagining how she would have sounded had she met the skaäsa face to face, before crossing the room and getting behind the door.

"What's going on in there?" the guard called.

Silence. Trinia held her breath.

After several minutes, she doubted he was going to fall for it. *Stupid. Of course he wouldn't fall for something like that!* she chided herself.

When the door opened, she stifled a yelp as his shadow slowly entered the space. Just being in the same place as him brought unwelcome memories she could not afford to deal with at the moment. Quick as a shade, Trinia slipped out, pulling the door closed behind her and throwing the iron lock into place. *By the gods, it worked!*

"Hey! What is this!" cried the man.

Relief flooded her when she saw the familiar handles of her daggers lying on a chair. *He probably claimed them and was admiring them,* she thought. Slamming them into their sheaths, she took a few heartbeats longer, hoping to find her pack, but it wasn't there. The others must have taken it. Going behind the shed while the guard cursed and swore, she found enough space to wedge herself between it and the wall and climbed up.

Within moments, she was up and looking over the stone wall to a ten-foot drop on the other side. Sitting on the side of the wall, she dropped down, her cloak piling on top of her head as she landed and rolled. *Graceful, Trinia, real graceful.* Tossing the cloak back, she flipped up her hood and took off through the deserted streets.

CHAPTER 4

———

Jayden sat in the shadows waiting for Cal to emerge from his home. He had been waiting in the same spot for the last four hours as twilight fell, and his patience was wearing thin. "That lying snake has to come out at some point," he mumbled under his breath. He pulled his cloak tighter about him against the autumn chill.

Townsfolk went about their business, wrapping up last-minute affairs, closing their shops, and walking home either alone or with a loved one. A few gathered in the central square and made for the taverns and brothels on the other side of town. Truth be told, he would much prefer to be in the company of a woman rather than waiting for Cal.

He had played with the idea of walking right up to the man and blasting him with magic, but considering around here the old man was the local healer—if you could call him that—it probably wouldn't end well. Which was why he'd opted for his second idea: wait until dark when Cal was likely to come slinking out of his hole and *then* blast him with magic. No one would be able to tell who had done it.

A smile crept to Jayden's lips at the thought of seeing the scrawny man flying through the air and breaking his neck upon landing. It would serve him right for betraying his trust.

The door to the house opened and Cal stepped out into the night with a small lantern in hand. He glanced up and down the streets before heading toward the north side of town, his partially lame leg giving him an unnatural gait. Jayden frowned. There were more guards in that area and a higher chance someone would see the attack. *Guess I'll give him a little help by launching him to his destination.*

Sneaking out from his hiding spot, Jayden quickened his pace until he was within range. Channeling the magic within him, he threw his hands forward, firing a blast of air at the old man. Only, instead of soaring through the air, Cal turned and squinted at him. With an unnatural speed, Cal closed the distance between them and jumped on top of Jayden, knocking him over.

"Well, look who we have here!" Cal crowed, his cloudy eyes shimmering in the lantern light. "The little jay-bird has come to try and kill the cobra, eh?"

"You betrayed my trust," Jayden growled, trying to wrestle the man off him to no avail. *How in hells is he so strong?*

"The little jay-bird thinks he's stronger than the cobra, does he? Well, he shall find this snake's fangs are still sharp." Cal opened his mouth as fangs appeared, and his pupils became slits.

A scream died in Jayden's throat. All nineteen years of life came rushing back to him in a moment, and he saw how he would do it all differently if given the chance. *Elohai save me.*

As Cal was about to strike, a wooden shovel cracked over his head, and he slumped over Jayden in a heap. Shoving him off, Jayden scrambled to his feet, looking at the dark-haired girl with the shovel. Where had she come from?

"Are you okay?" she asked.

From her accent, he could tell she was not from around here. "Yes, uh…I think so," he replied shakily. He looked at Cal's body. *A mage with magic can't take out an old man, but a girl with a shovel can? Talk about a blow to one's pride.*

The girl dropped the shovel and took off running down the street. "Hey, wait!" he called, following her. He had almost caught up with her when he heard shouts from behind. Risking a glance, he could see a handful of guards as they passed through the light from windows. *Hells!*

Ahead, the girl ducked to her left into an alley and he followed her, getting a swift punch to the gut and a knife to his throat. "Why are you following me?" she asked, her tone low.

"Gods below," he muttered between breaths. "My pride can't take much more of this."

"What?"

He waved his hand. "Nothing. I followed because I wanted to thank you for saving me back there. It would be me lying there if you hadn't stepped in." The thought was a sobering one, even if it was painful.

"Oh." The girl lowered the knife. "You're welcome. I don't really have time to stay and chat, so if you don't mind, I'll be going now."

Jayden straightened up and took a step back when she pointed her dagger at him. "Whoa, whoa, no need for that. You and I are in the same position, I think. While those guards were not after me, they will be now, but they were after you first. Am I right?"

She was silent, which he took to be a yes. "I know a spot near here where we can lie low until morning. Then we can go our separate ways and you'll never see me again. Sound good?"

"Why would you do that?" she whispered.

"I don't like debts."

The shouting was getting closer and Jayden suspected they only had a minute, maybe two tops, before the guards found them both just standing here looking like fools.

"Fine. Lead the way," she said, stepping out of his path.

"Stay close to me." He pushed past her and started down the alleyway toward the old run-down storehouse just a few blocks from where they were. With any luck, the place would still be abandoned, and they could wait out their pursuers. Given the stories he'd spread about it being haunted and how incredibly superstitious folks in Salorim were, he felt good about their chances.

Weaving through the back streets, Jayden tried to remember his way. It had been months since he was here, and moving around in the dark with guards close behind didn't help his memory. *Why must everything be so complicated? Get in, kill Cal before he tells anyone else, and get out. But no, he has to be some demon-snake-man immune to magic!*

"Do you even know where you are going?" the girl asked behind him as they came up to a wide street.

Light poured out of the tavern windows, casting a yellow-orange hue on the ground, and it was one of four. As bright as it was, it would be difficult to get across without being seen. If they made it, it was only a couple more blocks and they would be safe.

"Well?" the girl whispered.

"I'm working on it," he snapped. *Hells below! I should have left her behind.* He wouldn't have, and he knew it; he still had *some* morals.

Jayden turned around, motioning to the alley across the lit street. "That's where we need to go, but the light means someone will see us. Most will be too drunk to care or remember. However, the guards will ask questions. We can pretend to be lovers out for a stroll–"

"No," she replied, holding her dagger between them. "We just run. We don't touch. Got it?"

What is it with this girl? he wondered. "Fine, we do it your way. Ready to go?"

She nodded, and he glanced up and down the street, waiting until a group of men with their ladies walked into one of the taverns. "Go!"

He didn't stop to check and see if people saw them. Their best bet would be to get to the storehouse and then worry about it. Dodging between homes and shops, he finally stopped at the back of a building, panting. Once he caught his breath, he found the left corner and counted sixteen stones up from the bottom and ten over from the left, pushing where the stones intersected. There was a soft grinding sound as they pulled back, revealing an opening about two feet wide and five high.

"Come on," he said, ducking through the hidden door.

When the girl was inside, he pushed it closed, making sure it locked in place properly before guiding her to the rug he had laid out from the last time he was here. Flipping it back, he pressed the small trigger button that unlocked the trapdoor.

"Down there," he said. "It's a four-foot drop and the ceiling is low, so watch your head."

"I'm not going down there," she whispered harshly. "I'll take my chances up here."

Jayden rolled his eyes. "Look, I don't exactly trust you either, but here we are. You already pulled a knife on me, so for all I know, you'll slit my throat and hide my body down there."

"What? Why would I do that?" she asked, her tone rising.

"Shh! Gods below, are you *trying* to get us killed? Just get down there and follow it to the end. I will follow once I reset the door."

The girl crept to the hole in the floor, sitting down and sliding in. "If you try anything, I will stab you and make sure no one finds you," she hissed.

"Likewise," he replied, moving to the boarded-up windows. No signs of the guards. He breathed a sigh of relief. Now, if the girl didn't find a reason to stab him while he slept, he would be back on the road to Thydu and out of Ungäar by morning and off to build his dreams.

Hopping into the hole, Jayden crouched down, relatched the false floor, and pulled on a cord to his right that connected to the carpet and would spread it back over the trapdoor. It had been quite the happy accident when he stumbled across it on his last visit. The stupid thing had rotted out and he'd fallen through, but after a few repairs, you couldn't even tell it was there.

Following the well-worn tunnel, he made it to the hiding place and created a small *soläs* to provide some light, focusing his energy on making it solid and then setting it on a pedestal. By its light, he could see the girl sitting in the corner with ornate daggers in her hands. *She's an edgy one.* The girl's eyes were wide and focused on the light next to him.

"What is that?" she asked.

Jayden snorted. "About the only thing I can create that doesn't end in failure, but I suppose you northerners don't see magic too often. It's called a *soläs*, or 'light orb.'"

"I've not seen anything like that before, my people..." she seemed to catch herself before saying something she had not meant to say. "Like you said, we don't see magic often."

Sitting down as far from her daggers as possible, he nodded, wondering what she was going to say before. "Where do you call home? Vyrbrake?" By the blank look she gave him, he was going to take that as a no.

"I'd rather not talk about it," she said, averting her eyes.

Why is she so anxious? We're in the safest place we could be. Gazing around the room, Jayden guessed it was about ten feet wide and roughly the same in length. He could stand up in it with some room to spare. Being over six feet tall, that left maybe another foot or two above him. *Perfect for hiding things you don't want found,* he thought.

"Well, I'm going to get some sleep. Tomorrow you can head your way once we get out of Salorim," he said, propping himself up in the corner.

The girl looked at him silently, as if waiting for him to do something. When he didn't, she said, "I don't know your name. I would like to properly thank you for helping me."

He smiled. "Call me Jayden. And you're welcome..."

She returned a small smile. "Trinia."

"Trinia, huh? Pretty name."

The girl's cheeks reddened and she turned toward the wall. "Thank you."

Jayden watched her back for a few moments longer. *Trinia... what a strange name.*

CHAPTER 5

The door to her room slowly creaked open and the huddled form of her tormentor glided toward her. She could feel her heart hammering against her ribs and the panic begin to rise as she prayed silently to Vyrni to protect her.

A cold hand touched her shoulder...

Trinia startled awake to find Jayden's concerned face beside her. "Get away!" she screamed, trying to scramble back from him.

He fell backward and moved across the room, holding up his hands. "I was checking to see if you were okay, you seemed like you were having a nightmare."

Clutching at her cloak, she tried to take calming breaths, but her heart was still racing, the terror too raw. Even though she had left the city, the Voice still followed her, haunted her. She closed her eyes, holding back the tears as she worked to calm herself. Flipping back her hood, Trinia ran her fingers through her hair, undoing the braid and starting over.

"You're an Airgíd!"

Trinia's eyes snapped to Jayden's astonished face and then to her hair, which had returned to its natural silver color. *Hells! The illusion wore off!* Her gaze returned to him. "I–I can explain!"

His jaw hung open. "Your kind hasn't been seen in the Four Kingdoms in a thousand years!" he exclaimed.

Well, that is partially true, she thought. Her father had sent plenty of spies over the years.

"How did you get here? Why are you here?"

While she was happy to find something to distract her mind from the memory, Trinia mentally kicked herself for not remembering her illusion. She had no idea what this stranger was going to do.

"This is getting too complicated," he mumbled to himself.

"I don't want any trouble," she said. "I just want to get to Canämor."

Jayden stopped and stared at her, a curious look in his eyes. "Why? They are your enemy."

She nodded. "Yes, I know."

He ran his hands through his reddish-brown hair. "I'm being punished. That's the only explanation for all of this." He buried his face in his hands as he continued to talk to himself.

Trinia racked her brain for a way to keep him on her side, at least for now. Once they were out of the town, he would never have to see her again, but she couldn't risk leaving him as she had no idea where she was. Clearing her throat, she said, "If you help me get out of here, I promise I won't cause you any trouble. Just point me toward Canämor."

Jayden heaved a dramatic sigh. "You'll get killed before you even get there. You're an Airgíd! And let's say you do get there, what next?"

She stood, brushing herself off. "That's my business. The less you know, the better." Crossing her arms, she waited for him to decide.

Groaning, he stood and pointed at her. "Once we're out, I wash my hands of everything you're doing. Deal?"

Trinia nodded. "Deal. Let's go."

"Oh no, not until you make your hair a different color, or whatever you did. It'll be hard enough as it is without you standing out."

He had a point. If his reaction was any indicator of how people would receive her, it did not bode well. "Give me a moment," she said. Closing her eyes, she went through the same ritual she had the previous day. When she was done, she was happy to see her hair was now a dark brown. *That should help them not recognize me.*

Jayden stared wide-eyed at her, and it struck her that she didn't know what it looked like to others when she did this. "Can we go now?"

"That was amazing," he whispered, moving his head like an owl trying to catch a glimpse of a field mouse. "It's a perfect illusion. I can't tell your hair is silver at all!"

She felt her cheeks warm. Very few people had ever given her a compliment for anything, much less her magic. "Time is wasting," she said, moving past him to the entrance of the tunnel and waiting for him to take the lead.

Regaining some measure of composure, Jayden nodded and headed into the tunnel. A few minutes later, they were standing back in the storehouse. He went to the windows and was quiet for several minutes. "Normal patrols, which is good. It means they think we escaped already and they're not looking for us," he said at last.

Trinia raised a brow. "How can you possibly know that?"

He walked over to where she stood. "Look, you're not from here, so I'll indulge you with my knowledge of patrols. Vald doesn't pay his men nearly enough, so they likely spent half the night looking for us before going back to him and saying we slipped out the gates. If they'd known you were an Airgíd, maybe they would have continued, but for a petty thief, you're not worth their time."

The words stung and rang with a strange authority on the subject, which Trinia found odd. "I'm not a thief!" she said, her hands on her hips. "Besides, how do you know this person is such a horrible leader?"

Jayden grunted. "I said he didn't pay his men enough, not that he was a terrible leader." He moved to the secret door, counting up and over until he found the spot and pushed it.

How does he know these things? she wondered. *Who exactly am I escaping with?*

As they slipped out the secret way, they moved from one shadowy alley to another, working ever closer to the south gate. The spaces between the homes and other buildings where full of refuse and filth, along with a plethora of other unsightly things. Clouds hung low in the sky, obscuring the sun, and a soft breeze ruffled the fringe of her cloak as they came to the final set of homes between them and the gate. Trinia peeked out of the alley to see a group of six guards babbling on about one thing or another directly across the road. *Shouldn't they be watching the gate?* she wondered.

"Old Cal got knocked. Did ye hear?" said one of the guards, a tall man with a scraggly beard.

"Aye," replied the other, sitting and focusing on the game board in front of him.

"Some failed mage tried to pick a fight with 'im, and a lass saved him."

"Aye," replied the guard again, seemingly uninterested in the conversation.

Trinia snickered at that, and she saw Jayden mouth the words "failed mage" like he had an unpleasant taste in his mouth.

"Leave the poor man alone," said another who was sharpening his sword. "He's trying to focus."

"Pah!" bellowed the tall one, waving his hand.

Jayden turned and looked at her. "They're distracted. It's twenty yards from here to the gate if memory serves me well, so if we act like every other person and try to blend in, we should make it out. If they notice us and give chase, we make for the forest." He smirked. "They are a superstitious bunch after living so close to it, which benefits us."

Trinia shook her head. "Oh no, I'm not going back there. Skaäsa live in those hills and one night was more than enough for me, thank you."

He gave her a confused look. "What do you mean one night? You spent the night in there?"

The palms of her hands started itching. "Let's just go. I don't like waiting."

Jayden narrowed his eyes at her a moment before motioning for her to follow him. He backtracked a couple of houses, and then they moved into the flow of people roaming the streets, a few of whom were heading toward the gate. Trinia took in the people around her, with their dirty faces and unwashed clothes, wondering why anyone would live like that. She looked behind her and froze. It was the old man!

"What is it?" Jayden asked, following her gaze.

The man narrowed his eyes and Trinia pulled Jayden by the arm. "Run!" She could hear Cal screaming behind her along with the startled voices of the guards to her left.

Jayden pulled ahead with his long legs, and she did her best to keep up with him. Glancing to the guards, she saw one pull out a long knife and throw it. *"No!"* she screamed, flicking her hand out in front of her. The energy flowed through her and a brown-haired duplicate appeared right in the knife's path. She heard the sickening sound of metal slicing into flesh as it dug into the duplicates back.

Out of the corner of her eye, Trinia could see the guard's jaw go slack as the duplicate dropped dead. Jayden spun and she could see the shock and horror written on his face. "Run!" she yelled at him. She grabbed his arm and pulled him, but he tried to look back. "No! *Run!*"

When they were past the gates, Jayden pulled her to the right, back toward the hills and the forest. She tried to pull free of him, yet his grip was iron tight. "Let go of me!"

"They will be after us once their shock wears off," he said between breaths. "Only chance is the forest, so shut up and run."

Trinia wanted to argue, but the angry shouts from behind left her no choice but to follow. *This is insane! We're as good as dead in the forest as we are taking our chances outrunning the guards!*

The sun rose to its midpoint before they reached the carcass of the skaäsa from the previous day. Trinia could finally pull her arm free as Jayden collapsed to the ground, his chest heaving and his eyes squeezed shut.

"Hells below, what happened back there?" he asked, breathless.

Trinia avoided his gaze.

"Explain! Because that," he motioned back the way they had come, "needs an explanation!"

She shifted uncomfortably. "It's complicated."

The image of her duplicate taking a knife in the back flashed in her mind and she winced. It had been an accident that time. A split-second reaction had cost her another little piece of herself... that's how it felt, anyway. If word somehow got back to her father, the previous sacrifice would mean nothing, and she could not stomach that.

"Complicated? Complicated!" Sitting up, Jayden looked like he was going to unleash all his thoughts on her when his eyes shifted to the hills behind her. "Is it just me, or is there a giant wolf up there?"

"What?" Trinia followed his gaze and, sure enough, a gigantic wolf stood at the top of the hill above them. Her eyes widened. "It's the protector Vyrni sent."

"Wait, you mean that's real?" he asked, jumping to his feet.

The wolf looked down at them for a long moment before bounding down the hill toward them. Jayden jumped in front of her, and she watched him blast air at the creature strong enough to send several boulders flying, but the wolf was unfazed. He tried again and the same thing happened.

Trinia stepped out from behind him, glaring. "The goddess Vyrni sent him. Don't make her upset!"

He looked at her. "Don't make *who* upset?"

The creature jumped and landed a few paces away from them, standing at eye level and looking between the two. Its gaze settled on Trinia and she gulped.

"Your pursuers are not far behind you," it said. "Keep making for the forest, and I will hold them off."

"Did–did the... Did it just talk?" Jayden asked, stunned.

She nodded. "Yes."

The wolf looked toward Jayden. "There will be a time for questions later. Right now you need to listen. Understood?"

"Okay," he replied, face white.

"Good, now go!"

Trinia needed no more encouragement and took off along the path with Jayden beside her. *It talks! Vyrni sent a talking wolf to protect me! Thank you, Vyrni!*

"This is crazy," Jayden called beside her. "We are listening to a talking wolf! He's probably going to eat us!"

She rolled her eyes, biting back a retort. It was already taking every bit of energy left within her to not pass out and keep her legs moving. *Keep pushing. You can make it*, she told herself.

Finally, the trees came into view. With a last push, she cleared the tree line and sank to her knees beside a stump with Jayden close behind. Spots clouded her vision, and everything seemed to move with a life of its own. Her chest burned, her legs ached, and her heart beat like a war drum against her ribs. *I hate running. I hate it so much.*

The wolf appeared a short time later. As far as Trinia was concerned, if it ate them like Jayden had suggested, at least she wouldn't have to run again. She couldn't go another step.

It chuckled as it walked up to them, shaking its head. "I see you arrived in one piece. Come, we will head back and get something in your bellies before nightfall. I'm sure you're hungry."

As if in answer, Trinia's stomach rumbled. Her cheeks flushed as she stood on wobbly legs. "I've not eaten since yesterday morning." She looked at the wolf, frowning. "Right after I woke up, and you had abandoned me."

"I didn't abandon you. I was making sure you would be safe when you woke up, and when I returned, you were gone." It sat on its haunches. "I followed you as far as Salorim, so I thought I should wait in case you returned. Turns out I was right."

"Oh." She felt ungrateful now. Here she was thinking her protector had left her and Vyrni had kept him around to keep an eye on her. "Sorry," she said. "It's been a long couple of days."

Jayden sat up and clapped his hands. "Well, thanks for all the excitement and close calls with death." He stood facing her while keeping the wolf in view. "Do me a favor and don't mention my name to anyone in your travels. In fact, please forget all about me, hmm?"

The wolf raised a brow at him. "They are still in pursuit. I merely bought you time. Leave now and they will catch you. Whatever you did back there has them quite riled."

Trinia stepped toward the wolf, getting his attention. "You said something about food? There is nothing but forest here."

"Not quite," replied the wolf. "There is a place not far from here that you can rest for the night. The owner won't mind."

"It's not the Wildman is it?" Trinia asked, a sliver of dread running down her spine.

"Wildman?" Jayden exclaimed. "What in the world is going on here?"

The wolf looked at him again and then back to her. "No, it's not the Wildman. You need not fear him." Standing up, he started walking off into the forest. "Come along. We shouldn't keep Green Cloak waiting."

CHAPTER 6

Údar knelt beside the gravestones, gently pulling the moss off them and sweeping away the leaves. He had followed the same yearly ritual for the last three hundred years.

Sitting down on a boulder, he looked out over the tree-tops, his hands clasped together and his face hidden by the cowl of his green cloak. "I miss you both," he whispered. His eyes drifted over his wife's name carved into the first stone—Nisha. A picture of her dark curls and rich brown eyes filled his mind. He could almost smell her, that scent of pine and lavender.

Beside Nisha's grave was his daughter's, his little Lyniel. She'd had her mother's curls and his stormy gray eyes. Her smile had been his entire world once upon a time.

He squeezed his eyes shut, the ache in his heart growing with each passing minute he stayed here. *I'm sorry I couldn't protect you*, he thought. It wasn't something he could admit out loud. The failure was too painful.

Údar stood and placed a kiss on top of each stone before turning to head back down the mountain, but then he stopped short. Before him a youth, not more than nineteen years, was staring at him. His hair was the color of charcoal and his skin umber. He wore a plain brown tunic and trousers with no boots to cover his feet. "Hello, Údar," said the boy.

Údar rubbed his eyes, yet the boy remained. "Elohai?"

The boy smiled. "I am."

Burning rage replaced shock as he pointed an accusing finger at the boy. "You choose now to show yourself? At the graves of my family?"

The boy walked past him to stand in front of the graves. "Do you really believe I abandoned you, Údar? After all this time?" He turned and looked at him. "Do you forget so easily?"

He knew Elohai would never abandon him, which made his silence over the last three centuries even more painful. It wasn't that Elohai was not there. He *chose* not to answer. Údar began walking down the hill, tears stinging his eyes. "I remember just fine!" he called back. "I remember holding my wife in my arms as she slowly bled to death while she held my daughter who had already passed."

Elohai stepped out from behind a huge rock in front of him, sadness dimming his eyes. "Do you think I don't know?"

Údar paused, emotions long kept buried threatening to surface. "Then why did you let it happen?" he asked, voice breaking. "Tell me why they had to die."

"You make it sound like it was to punish you, but in your heart, you know that isn't true." Elohai leaned against one of the ancient pines along the path. "The world is broken, Údar. And while you may be angry with me over your loss, it stems from you leaving the calling."

"To hell with the calling!" Údar shouted, tears stinging his eyes as he stormed past.

Elohai appeared a little way ahead, sitting next to the path with his arms resting on his knees. "You can't run from it, Údar. You prayed to know every aspect of me as God as a boy, and I granted it. It did not look how you thought it would, and when it got too hard, you ran. But like all the other times, it's come for you again."

Pausing, he glared at the boy. "I was a child! I did not understand what I was asking, nor of the pain that would come of it." He felt the anger die out, leaving him with nothing except the aching loss once more. "I'm so weary. Weary of the pain, of the loss, of the endless striving. Yet I have no choice in the matter."

"You have always had a choice, Údar. That has not changed," replied Elohai evenly.

Údar looked down the path that disappeared into the forest and its murky shadow in silence. What was there to say? Here was Elohai, Creator of the World, sitting before him and waiting for an answer he was not sure he could give.

Elohai nodded and stood, brushing off his pants. "Your journey awaits you, Údar, should you choose to finish it." He turned, walking back up the trail slowly. "When you're ready to tell me your thoughts, I shall meet you again," he said.

"You know my thoughts," Údar said bitterly.

The boy turned, nodding. "Yes, but that does not mean I don't wish to hear them."

Údar blinked, and he was gone. He remained standing there for a few heartbeats before making his way once more down the path. *Why today of all days?*

Reaching the tree line, he found the shelter of the trees a comfort. Perhaps it was because, like his soul, a shadow lay over it.

You will never finish your journey if you keep hiding in the shadows.

He shook his head. It was easier to hide in the shadows than face the truth in the light.

Pushing through the branches, his eyes adjusted to the familiar dim light. *He said I could choose, so what if I choose to never finish it? What then? Shall I be forced to wander forever?* he wondered.

Coming up over a rise, he looked down on the cabin he had called home for the past three centuries. *Why should I leave my home? It makes more sense to live here, close to them.*

Making his way down a low hill, he heard noises that didn't belong coming from the cabin.

"You're late."

Údar spun around to see the outline of a wolf at the top where he had been moments ago. He glared at his friend. "Not now, Mandar. I'm in no mood."

"Clearly," replied the wolf, raising a brow. "Before you go into the cabin, may I have a word?"

His friend's tone held something in it he did not like—something he could not quite place. He studied Mandar sitting patiently before him, sighing. "What is it?"

Mandar gazed at him with his one good eye, which seemed to gleam with a hidden delight, something that always worried him. "Out with it!" Údar said.

"We have company," said the wolf.

"What do you mean company?" he asked, eyes narrowing.

Mandar smiled as he sat and scratched his ear. "They are inside waiting for you."

"For me?" He clenched his fists. "No one knows I am here, Mandar. Why on earth would they be waiting for me?"

His friend became serious and stood, walking over to him. "Elohai sent them."

An icy chill ran down Údar's spine. That is why Elohai had come to him. "You know why I was late then," Údar mumbled.

"I know it is the anniversary of your wife and daughter's death," the wolf replied. "But I didn't know Elohai had planned to bring them here until He spoke to me this morning after you had left."

You will never finish your journey if you keep hiding in the shadows.

Údar's breath quickened. *No, no, no, this cannot be happening!* The woods suddenly seemed gloomier, more claustrophobic and menacing than they had in ages. The air was stuffier and hotter than it should have been in September, and it all pointed to a change he was not ready to face.

"They are young and a little skittish after fleeing for their lives from Salorim. I only convinced them because the girl thought I was some protector sent by Vyrni," said the wolf after a moment. "So, when you go in, try not to scare them."

Vyrni... "She's the goddess of protection to the Airgíd, Mandar. The same race that took my family from me."

Mandar's brows rose slightly. "Her hair is not the right color. The Airgíd ruled for a long time, Údar. Is it not possible that others adopted their gods as well?"

He shook his head, and his hands trembled. "Elohai brought her here to allow me my revenge. And I shall take it happily!" Spinning on his heel, Údar tore the rest of the way down the hill before Mandar could stop him. Coming up to the door, he threw it open.

Standing in the center of the cabin was the spitting image of his Lyniel. The dark curls, the gray eyes...only she was too old to be his daughter. Pain lanced his heart and stole his breath. *Elohai! Why would you do this?*

CHAPTER 7

The walk through the woods behind the wolf had not been as unpleasant as Trinia had expected. Wherever they were now was far lighter than where she had been the previous day, which only confirmed in her mind she'd wandered into the heart of the forest. And while she was nervous about following a giant talking wolf to meet with someone named Green Cloak, it was clear Vyrni had sent him, so she would trust in that for now.

Now, she and Jayden sat at a small oak table inside the cabin where the wolf had left them over an hour ago. *Did I make the right choice? What if this is the home of the Wildman?* The same thought had repeated in her mind every couple of minutes.

Jayden sat opposite her, his eyes distant, and she wondered what was running through his mind. Was he thinking about the duplicate? Did he think she was a freak? As far as she knew, no one in the history of her people had ever had a Gift like this, though calling it a "gift" seemed a stretch. *More like a curse*, she thought sourly.

"Thank you."

The sudden end to the silence startled her and she looked at him. "What?"

He ran a hand through his hair as he spoke. "Thank you...
you know, for saving my life back there. I, uh... I owe you."

From the strain in his voice, Trinia could tell he *really*
did not like the thought of owing her anything. "Oh. You're
welcome." She rubbed the back of her neck. "Truth be told,
it was an accident. I didn't mean to do that. So, if that helps
you not feel—"

"Accident or not, you still saved me," he replied stiffly.

Silence fell between them again, far more awkward than
previously, but only a few heartbeats later, he leaned on the
table, his brown eyes staring at her intensely. "Does it hurt?
When you create a duplicate, I mean."

Trinia sat back in the chair, folding her arms and looking
away. "A little."

"Did you feel it when the knife... you know."

She shook her head. "No, I'm not connected to them. Not
that I know of anyway." Taking a steadying breath, she added,
"It feels like I lose a little piece of myself when it happens."

Jayden frowned. "What do you mean?"

Gods above, do we have to do this now? she wondered. "It
just feels like a piece of me goes with them, that's all. I don't
know how to explain it."

He sat up, seeming to sense her discomfort with the
topic. "Fair enough. I can imagine a Gifting like that would
be difficult."

"You could say that."

Voices from outside caught her attention. They were too
far away for her to make out, though she suspected it was the
wolf—what did he say his name was? Mandar?—and another
whom she suspected must be Green Cloak. The name was
strangely familiar, yet she could not quite place it. *I know I've
heard that name before.*

The voices rose along with her unease. What if Green Cloak was not as friendly as the wolf? Did he serve Vyrni and the other Old Gods? She could hear footsteps coming quickly. Both she and Jayden stood up as the door burst open and a man rushed in, halting abruptly.

He looked stricken, like he'd seen the ghostly shade of a telgost, and he backed into the doorpost. "No," he breathed. The man's surprise melted away into something Trinia had seen so many times in her father's eyes—burning rage.

She pulled her daggers from her belt as the man recovered himself and strode toward her, pulling out a knife of his own, the sharp look of death in his eyes. "You will not mock my grief," he snarled.

Jayden appeared by her side, throwing up his hands and creating a glowing orange barrier around them. "Some welcome," he said as the crazed man smashed his knife against it.

Another man, slightly taller than the first, entered through the door and Trinia immediately recognized him as the Wildman. *He and the wolf are working together! It was a trick!* she thought.

The Wildman came up and grabbed the enraged one from behind, lifting him off the ground. "Údar, that is enough! Enough I say!"

Trinia's eyes went wide. His voice was that of the wolf!

The one called Údar thrashed and tried to get free. "Put me down, Mandar!" he raged.

Jayden cast a glance her way. "Mandar? Isn't that the wolf?"

She nodded slowly, trying to reconcile this new information. He was one of the Shifters? Why had he appeared in wolf form? Trinia squeezed her eyes shut. This was all too much.

"She's not responsible, Údar," said Mandar, now having pinned one of Údar's arms behind his back. "Come to your senses!"

After several more minutes, Mandar let the man go and Údar stormed outside, muttering a long string of curses as he went. Turning his attention to them, Mandar said, "I shall get a meal ready for us. He will be gone for a while so you don't have to worry about him."

He walked toward the door, pausing a moment before looking at her. "I would recommend removing the illusion, young one. For both of your sakes."

Trinia nodded and slid the daggers back in their sheaths. When the door closed, she looked at Jayden. "We need to leave."

Dispersing the barrier, Jayden rubbed his face. "Do you know who that was? The man who attacked you?" He didn't wait and continued, "*He* is Green Cloak, the Watcher of the Forest, the Banisher of Shadows."

Glancing toward the windows, she said, "Banisher of Shadows… you mean he's the one who defeated the Baobhan Sith? *That* Green Cloak?"

Jayden nodded. "The very same."

"But that was four hundred years ago!" she exclaimed, throwing her arms in the air. Based on what she knew, only an Airgíd could live so long. "How is that even possible?"

He shrugged. "No idea, but considering I've seen someone duplicate themselves and met a giant talking wolf who can apparently shape-shift, I'm not ruling it out."

Ugh, he's got a point, she thought. Trinia rubbed her forehead. "So, what are you saying? We go have dinner with them?"

"Do you have any better ideas?" he asked, raising a brow.

She did not, which annoyed her. While she wasn't starving, the hunger pangs she had been ignoring since this morning were coming back with a vengeance. Not to mention, with all that running, her mouth was feeling parched. *I suppose we should play nice, just until I know what the wolf-man wants. After that, I need to keep moving.*

Closing her eyes, Trinia focused on the illusion, imagining it dissipating like a morning fog. When she opened her eyes again, she could tell it had worked by the look on Jayden's face. Didn't he use magic? Why was he so enthralled with a simple illusion?

"Shall we?" she asked, motioning to the door.

"Uh, yes, let's."

Stepping out into the afternoon light filtering through the trees, Trinia saw Mandar sitting beside a roaring fire turning what looked to be the remains of a deer on a spit. He waved them over.

"Please, please, take a seat. Food will be ready in a few hours, but until then, here are some jerky strips to hold you over." He tossed a few to Jayden and then to her.

Sitting on an old stump, she bit into the meat, ripping off a large chunk and chewing it until her jaw hurt. She looked at Jayden and saw he had taken a much smaller bite out of his. She glanced back at hers, frowning. She had stuffed half of hers into her mouth. *This is going to take a while.*

"I'm sure you both have some questions," said Mandar, slowly turning the spit. "Where would you like to start?"

"Are we your prisoners?" Jayden asked, ripping off another chunk of jerky.

Mandar threw his head back and laughed. "No, you are not. You are guests."

Jayden shifted on the boulder he was sitting on. "Is your friend in the habit of attacking guests?"

Trinia watched the man's brows furrow together as he answered, "No."

Moving the piece she was still chewing to the side of her mouth, she asked, "Why should we trust you?"

He leaned back, pausing the spit mid-turn, and scratched his beard thoughtfully. "All good questions."

In the light, Trinia saw that maybe she had conjured up the thought of him being a Wildman. Mandar's brownish-gray hair was thick, hanging to his shoulders, while his beard was neatly combed if not a little bushy. One of his golden eyes was slightly clouded over with a jagged scar running from above his left brow, down and over his right eye. His tunic was a dark gray and his breeches were an earthy brown.

If she hadn't seen him in wolf form, she doubted she would have noticed anything strange about him at all.

"I suppose you shouldn't trust me," he said after a few minutes. "You don't know me or my friend. However, I hope that will change in time."

Trinia finally managed to swallow the jerky. "In time? Do you mean to keep us here?" She couldn't afford to stay, she needed to reach Canämor so they could stop her father.

Mandar shook his head. "No, no, you are free to leave any time you choose. I have but a simple ask of you."

She exchanged a glance with Jayden before answering. "Which is?"

The man leaned forward. "Elohai, not Vyrni, sent me to protect you. I do not know why, though I suspect it involves Green Cloak, or Údar as he prefers to be called." Mandar turned the spit again. "And if I am right, you will need his help as much as he will need yours."

Trinia shook her head, her gaze sweeping the forest around them. The thought of a man needing her help with anything was beyond unbelievable, let alone one who had wanted to kill her not half an hour ago. It was like summer and winter—two opposing forces.

And to add to that, Mandar served Elohai, the god that had brought about the destruction of the Airgíd Empire in the first place! Why would he want to save her when he had destroyed her people? It made no sense.

"Well, I for one would prefer to stay out of all of it," said Jayden. "I have plans of my own, thank you very much, and it doesn't involve people who duplicate themselves talking wolves, or murderous men of legend."

Trinia shot a look at him and could see Mandar turn her way from the corner of her eye. The last thing she needed was a servant of Elohai needing a reason to end her life, though now that she thought about it, it made sense for why the other one had attacked her. He served the same god.

She met Mandar's gaze, hoping to change subjects. "How is it you can change form? Are you one of the Shifters, the Iomlíad?"

He gave her a knowing smile, shaking his head. "Elohai Gifted me with the ability to change when needed and to speak while in my true form. I have met many Iomlíad, however, and they are wonderful people."

"Wait a minute," said Jayden, pointing the last bit of jerky at the man. "You're really a wolf? Not a man who can turn into a wolf?"

Mandar nodded. "That's right."

Jayden shook his head. "They did not teach about that at the Academy."

"I suspect not," replied the man, his golden eye twinkling in the light.

That brought to mind several questions Trinia had about the Academy since she was curious how Jayden learned magic.

As far as she knew, the kingdoms had restricted or outright banned the use of Gifts after the fall of the Empire. She was about to ask when Green Cloak emerged from the brush opposite them, heading straight for the cabin and slamming the door once inside.

Mandar sighed, frowning at the door. "Stubborn as ever," he mumbled.

Unhinged would be more like it, she thought. "Is he going to attack me again?"

Standing, Mandar cut the meat in a few places before returning to slowly rotating it, eye on the fire. "He wasn't angry with you, young one," he said softly. "Today is a painful day for him, and your illusion made it even more unbearable."

"What did I do?" Trinia asked, frustrated at the thought of being blamed.

"You look like his murdered daughter," he replied. "That is why I asked you to remove the illusion."

"Oh," was all the reply she could muster. Even Jayden didn't seem to know what to say. After a moment, she ventured another question. "You said he wasn't angry at me. If not me, then who?"

Mandar sighed again, folding his hands in front of him before looking at her. "Elohai."

CHAPTER 8

It had been a long while since Jayden had eaten so much food in one sitting, and he was feeling it. *I should have stopped after the sixth helping,* he thought. If it wasn't for the talking wolf who could randomly turn into a human and an Airgíd with the power to duplicate herself, it would have been perfect. *How is it I always find myself in strange situations?*

There had been a time when he was ten that he'd thought it would be a great idea to hide in the cooking cauldron when playing hide and seek with the servants. It had been, at least, until the cook had thrown half a pig on top of him and he screamed. Poor cook had taken off, never to be seen after that.

Then there was the time at the Academy when he had fooled around with the Head Mage's daughter. That hadn't ended well, and if not for his royal lineage, he suspected the Head Mage would have turned him into something quite unnatural as punishment.

Memory after memory played in his mind until he was convinced his troubles boiled down to one thing. He loved the danger. Which explained a lot regarding many of his poor life choices as of late.

Closing his eyes, Jayden wondered if that was what constituted a character flaw. How did one go about fixing something like that, anyway? Sheer force of will? *Trying to not kill old snake-men and then running after strangers might be a good place to start,* he thought.

"Did you get your fill?"

Jayden opened his eyes and focused on Mandar. "More than my fill, thank you."

Mandar smiled, nodding. "Excellent. And how about you?" he asked, looking to Trinia.

She took another huge bite. "Mmhmm."

He cracked his neck and relaxed with his back against the boulder he'd been sitting on earlier. Admittedly, the girl was not what he expected of the infamous Airgíd. For one, she didn't have pointy ears, sharp fangs, or clawed hands like the stories had portrayed them. She looked, well, normal, save for the silver hair and eyes. Her face was slightly oval, her nose straight and her eyes deep set with a high brow and cheeks.

Or maybe it was all an illusion to fool them and she would kill them all in their sleep and laugh about it as she sacrificed them to her bloodthirsty gods. But he doubted it. While she certainly knew how to handle a dagger, he wasn't convinced she knew how to use it.

Mandar carved a piece of meat off the spit and stood. "I'm going to speak with Údar and get him to calm down. You two stay out here until I return and don't go running off into the woods. Dark things have been lurking about the past few weeks."

Jayden watched him go, casting a wary eye out into the woods afterward. He didn't like the dark on a good night and doubly so in a forest whose name meant "shadow." It was rather unsettling how quickly the light seemed to fade and how the forest swallowed it up.

Trinia finished chewing and set the wooden plate Mandar had given her on the ground. By the way she was nervously rubbing her hands, he had a feeling he would not like whatever she was going to say. "So, I was wondering, what is the Academy like?"

Yep. Didn't like it. "It's old, dusty, and filled with pompous old airbags who think they are smarter than everyone else," he replied, doing his best to make it sound boring.

"How long did it take you to learn your magic? What is your Gifting?" She stared at him, waiting expectantly.

Okay, boring didn't work. I'm going to need to give her a little something to get her to drop it, he thought. He sat up and wrapped his arms around his knees. "Honestly, I still haven't figured out what my Gift is. My family shipped me off to the Academy when I was sixteen." That much was true. "I learned about Elohai there and all the things I'm supposed to do and not do to follow him and such."

She leaned back, grimacing. "You follow him too?"

"Eh, when it suits me," he replied, pulling at the sleeve of his tunic. "A lot of the teachings never made much sense, so I picked which ones fit best."

"And he doesn't get mad at you for that?" she asked confused.

Jayden had never really thought of that before. Since he hadn't been smote or whatever the gods did, he supposed he must be doing an okay job. "I guess not."

Trinia shook her head. "My gods wouldn't take kindly to such an affront. They demand offerings, which vary depending on the season and the god." She looked down at the silver broach on her cloak and then back to him. "This is the symbol of Vyrni, the goddess of protection. Between you and me, she's my favorite."

"Why is that?"

Her mood changed suddenly, and she turned away from him. "Because."

What did I say? It's okay to ask me personal questions, but when I ask one, oh no, can't talk about that. He rolled his eyes. *Girls.*

-II-

Údar sat in the cabin, pipe in hand, blowing smoke circles at the ceiling and scowling as they vanished. He rested his long legs on the oak table and leaned back in his chair. It was a slap in the face that an Airgíd was even allowed to breathe in his presence after everything they took from him, and now Mandar was cooking one dinner. It was cruel.

The door opened and Mandar's tall human form walked in, carrying a steaming pile of meat. Closing the door behind him softly he said, "We need to talk, Údar."

Taking a long drag from the pipe, Údar blew out another smoke ring. "I don't want to speak of it."

His friend walked over, setting the food down next to him on the table, and took a seat. "The girl thinks you're going to kill her."

"She's not wrong. I swore to kill any Airgíd I came across. Remember?" He blew another ring.

Mandar sighed. "That was three hundred years ago. Killing won't bring them back."

Lowering his gaze, Údar glared at him. "But it will make me feel better." Another ring. His gaze drifted across the cabin. Two small birch chairs sat unused by an ash end-table and another two oak rocking chairs were situated in front of the stone hearth. The floors were a polished hardwood from a distant land he no longer recalled the name of and beautifully woven rugs were spread about.

He had made the rocking chairs for Nisha when she was pregnant with Lyniel and the birch ones for his daughter to play with. The few precious relics of a past he couldn't forget or move past were all he had salvaged from their home in Canämor. It was his way of keeping them alive.

"Údar."

He looked back to Mandar's concerned face. "What?"

"I know you wish it were different, but Elohai brought them here for a reason." Mandar spread his hands out in a pleading gesture. "Let them stay tonight, and in the morning we shall find out more. Hmm?"

Setting down his pipe, Údar grabbed a piece of meat. "You seem to be the only one interested in them staying. Whatever Elohai has planned, I want no part of it, not this time."

"Very well," said Mandar, standing and heading for the door where he paused. "We've known each other for a long time, Údar, and you've been running for as long as I have known you. Why? Did you not ask for this?"

Scowling at him, Údar picked his pipe back up. "Do not lecture me on this, Mandar. There are things you do not know–"

"Because you do not share them!" Mandar shot back. "You hide behind your walls, refusing to let people in because you have been hurt in the past, and yet, you wonder why you are alone."

Údar set the pipe in his mouth and looked back at the rocking chairs. "Get out."

Mandar sighed and opened the door. "There will come a day when you cannot run anymore, and you will face the same choice He has presented you time and time again. There will be no way out, and you will have to choose. I hope you make the right one."

Watching the door close, Údar was thankful to once again have some peace and quiet in the cabin. *He doesn't understand*, he told himself.

Getting up, he wandered down the hall toward his room. It had taken months to rebuild the cabin like it had been in Canämor, and while it lacked the memories, he could still hear the echoes of Lyniel's laughter.

His mind turned backward, spiraling through the years to that night as he stood in the doorway to his room.

The door hung ajar, and his stomach fell. There had been rumors of Airgíd scouts in the area, but he had discounted it.

Rushing through the door, he could see blood stains everywhere on the floor and rugs. Moving through the cabin he called their names, hearing a faint sound from their room.

A strangled cry came out as he saw his wife's bloody frame holding their daughter. Dropping beside her, he gathered her up into his arms. "Shhh, shhh, it's okay. I'm here now. It will be okay."

Nisha gazed at him with distant eyes, a small smile tugging at her lips. She placed a cold hand on his cheek, wiping the tears away as they streamed down. "I prayed you would come back. I wanted to say good...goodbye."

He ran his fingers through her hair and kissed her forehead. "It's not goodbye. You're going to be alright."

A single tear trickled from the corner of her eye. "Údar, I... I love..."

The life faded from her eyes, and she looked almost serene despite the blood covering her. He held her to his chest, a primal cry shattering the surrounding stillness.

Údar leaned against the frame, holding his chest. All the pain boiled up to the surface again. As he dropped to his knees, the pipe clattered on the floor, forgotten beside him, and he wept.

CHAPTER 9

Údar woke with a start on the floor of his room. The small room was dark, and no light filtered in through the windows. He groaned as he got up, stretching his back and hearing little cracks and pops. *Plagues, I'm getting old*, he thought, rubbing the sleep from his eyes.

Try as he might, he could not remember when he had fallen asleep, nor did he remember dreaming. Walking over to the bed, he found his cloak lying there. Odd. Mandar must have checked on him at some point and put it there. Picking it up, he threw it around his shoulders and pinned it in place with a golden broach—a gift he had received from the king of Ungäar for his help in imprisoning Ulscia four hundred years ago.

Pulling his sword from its mount on the wall, Údar checked the blade for sharpness before sliding it into the scabbard and fastening the belt around his waist. Through the many centuries, it had been his only consistent companion aside from Mandar, and thankfully, talked far less.

He opened the door, stepping quietly through the hall and pausing when he saw the girl lying on the floor in front of the hearth, which showed signs of use. His hand slid to the hilt of the sword. Stepping closer, he noticed a faint shimmering around her. The young mage had put a barrier up. *How interesting. I wonder why that is.*

Glancing over the sleeping figure of the boy, Údar saw him propped up against the ash end table, snoring softly. Something was familiar about him that he couldn't place. Not that it mattered since they would be gone in the morning.

Once he stepped outside, he felt like he could breathe again. The early September weather was crisp, but not unpleasantly cold, and the smell of rain filled the air. It was his favorite time of year, with the leaves turning a myriad of colors and the smell of the forest after a heavy shower.

Crack.

Twigs snapping in the distance caught his attention, and he turned to his right, his eyes igniting in white fire. The surrounding darkness became clear as day, and he could barely make out a figure moving through the trees a short distance away. It looked too small to be Mandar and too fast to be a helwreck. Their bulk slowed them down.

Údar sprinted after the fleeting figure, trying to keep up as he dodged ancient trees and gnarled branches. On and on he chased it until at last his feet hit the familiar path leading up the mountain to the gravestones. Drawing his sword, he approached slowly, one foot in front of the other as the figure, who seemed to be cloaked in shadow, stopped at the foot of Nisha's grave.

"Who are you?" Údar asked, every muscle tensed and ready for a fight.

The shadows melted off, like wax on a candle, revealing a lithe woman clothed in an emerald and cream-colored robe that was almost sheer. Her hair, red like fire, fell about her shoulders and had a wild look to it. Her features were pale, bearing an ethereal beauty that stood out in contrast to her eyes—one red, one violet.

He nearly dropped the sword, his eyes wide as he took several steps back. "No!"

The woman grinned at him, revealing pointed teeth. "Hello, Údar. It's been such a long time."

It couldn't be. It was not possible. "Ulscia…" was all he could manage.

The Queen of the Baobhan Sith folded her arms, hips swaying as she walked toward him. "And here I thought you had forgotten all about me," she replied. She looked him up and down with a hungry eye that sent a cold chill down his spine. "You've not aged well."

Recovering a little, he held the sword out between them, the tip resting against her collarbone. "How did you get out? You are bound by Elohai!"

She shook her head and stepped back, returning to her place beside the grave and sitting on small boulder. Leaning back a little, she crossed her legs, exposing a thigh. "Always so predictable. Did you really think the belief in your God would last forever? Tsk tsk. No one follows him anymore. The world is changing, Údar, and as far as you are concerned, it's not for the better."

Watch yourself. She's baiting you, he reminded himself. "What are you doing here, Ulscia?"

Ulscia laughed. "Why do you think? A little bird told me you lost your loved ones." The hungry look in her discolored eyes returned when her gaze fell back on him. "I thought you might need company. Like old times."

He grimaced at the thought and spat. "I may have fallen for your temptations once, but I know better now." In one fluid motion, he rushed her and went to drive his sword straight through her heart. Only his blade stopped, hovering just above her skin, his body tense.

Smirking, she rose. "Oh, Údar, did you really think it would be that easy?"

"What sorcery is this?" he growled. *Elohai, how is this possible? Are you not stronger than she?*

Coming up next to his ear, she whispered, "You bedded me, remember? A part of you is forever bound to me, and just as you cannot kill me, I cannot kill you." She placed a soft, seductive kiss on his cheek, making his skin crawl. "But I can be a thorn in your side."

Údar felt his body regain its control, and he tried again to strike her with the same effect. He yelled in rage, trying several more times to wipe the victorious grin off her face. Each time left him feeling weaker. Glaring at her, he said, "I swear to you. I will kill you."

The banshee prowled around him, her every movement a promise of unspeakable pleasure, one he knew all too well was anything but. Returning to her boulder, she sat, leaning forward. "My children in the forest have brought me some very interesting news, something I think even you may be interested to hear."

"Doubtful," Údar replied, wiping the sweat from his brow. "Nor would I trust anything you or your abominations have to say." He turned and started walking away. *If she cannot kill me, I have nothing to fear from her. Should buy me some time to figure out a way of destroying her.*

She snickered behind him. "My children told me you sought the ones responsible for killing your wife and daughter."

He paused mid-step, images of riding through the forest hellbent on finding the killer flashing through his mind.

"They said you found them and one was bragging about killing a young woman and a girl. It was a group of Airgíd scouts."

He had found them in a clearing not far off the path deep within the forest, drinking and celebrating. The one bragging was younger than his comrades and boasting about rebuilding the empire through the spilled blood of "the lesser peoples."

"Well done, Caderyn! Masterfully done!" said one of the scouts.

"Women and children are hardly worthy opponents, Macsen."

Ulscia's voice drew closer from behind him. "You killed all of them, save for the one who had bragged about murdering your family. Why?"

Spinning to face her, he found her only feet from him. The burning anger welled in his chest again like it had that night. "Because I promised him I would make him suffer as I had suffered."

She smiled knowingly, and he realized he was falling into her trap. "And did you make him suffer?" she asked.

I should run, he thought, yet his feet remained rooted to the ground. "No."

Drawing close to him until he could smell the faintest hint of cherry blossoms, Ulscia stopped just shy of kissing him. "Do you want the chance to do so?" she breathed.

The young Airgíd stared up at him with prideful eyes, face twisted in disgust. "Go ahead, kill me! But the Airgíd will rise again."

"Do you think I give a damn about your kind?" Údar asked. He brought the youth to his face. "I don't care whether you rebuild your pathetic empire. Just know that I will haunt your steps all your long life and make sure you regret every waking moment. I will burn everything you love to the ground and strip every good thing away from you until you are left hollow and alone."

Údar threw him to the ground and grabbed his knife as he pinned the young Airgíd on his back exposing his chest. Using the knife, he cut through the clothing. He leaned in close. "Heed my words, Caderyn. And should you forget, I shall give you a reminder that Green Cloak will ever be near."

With that, he carved a bloody U into the Airgíd's chest.

The memory was one Údar had avoided for many years because it brought with it the terrible pain of his loss. Now, it felt like it was time to make good on that promise. "What do you know, Ulscia?" he whispered.

She leaned back, a light flickering in her eyes. "He has a daughter. My children have seen her and know she means the world to him."

The thought of a monster such as Caderyn having a child brought Údar's rage back with a vengeance, and it provided him with the perfect way of fulfilling his oath. "Where is she?"

Ulscia shook a finger. "Not until you promise *me* something."

He narrowed his eyes. "What is it?"

"It's been a long time since I've tasted Airgíd," she replied, licking her lips. "I want a vial of her blood. After that, I don't care what you do to her."

"Done. Where is she?" he asked impatiently. Whatever Ulscia wanted the blood for, he would figure out how to stop her later after he was done destroying Caderyn's life.

"I thought you would know," she replied in mock innocence. "After all, she is staying with you, is she not?"

Reality slammed into him. *The girl!* Turning, he took off back down the path, the Baobhan Sith's maniacal cackling echoing behind him.

-II-

Caderyn stood in front of the mirror, running a finger down the jagged scar on his chest. *Where are you now, Green Cloak? Have I outlived your empty threats?* The likelihood he was still alive was not something he could discount given the man's reputation.

"My lord?"

He turned to the Airgíd woman in his bed, dismissing her. "You may go." He needed to be alone to think of his next moves.

The woman gathered her things and slipped out the door, leaving him to his thoughts. Sitting down by the fire, he poured himself a glass of brúan. With his daughter locked in the dungeons, there would be no second attempts at escaping his plans for her. She would comply in the end.

Taking a sip and savoring the burning liquid, he wondered how best to persuade her to see his side of things. The beatings had not been effective as she was too strong willed, much like himself. While an excellent trait to have as a ruler, if left alone without proper care, it could grow into something rather frustrating. Her mother had been the same way.

Caderyn refilled his glass, swirling it in front of him. *How to get her to cooperate?* Tyarch could call upon the gods to curse her unless she helped, but would that be enough? Setting the drink aside, he stood, grabbing his shirt and pulling it on before stepping out into the halls as he made his way toward the dungeon.

Why does she resist? Why can she not grasp the importance of what I'm teaching her? What I am building for her? It was a mystery.

Descending the steps, he approached the iron door, knocking on it three times. It squeaked and protested as it was pulled inward, revealing a guard who bowed low. "My lord, welcome."

Caderyn ignored the greeting, making straight for the cell where his daughter was being kept. Looking through the bars, she huddled in the far corner. Her face was still badly bruised. Even he had to admit he had gone a little far in his just punishment, but a lesson had to be taught. "Hello, daughter." His voice echoed off the stone walls around them, giving it a more ominous tone he quite liked.

"I'm not going to do it, Father," she mumbled.

He sighed. "The glory of the Old Empire depends on you. Why do you refuse to see it? The prophecy foretells it. Therefore it *will* be so." Caderyn stepped closer to the bars, leaning against them. "How far do you think you can run to escape your future, daughter? You tried once, and yet here you are. Why not just accept it?"

She turned, glaring at him through swollen eyes. "Because you would murder our people to bring it about."

"A few stubborn men here and there can hardly be counted as 'our people,' now can they? Besides, once they see your powers, they will submit to my authority as is right." He smiled. "It is so very simple."

She looked away, silver hair falling over her face. "I won't do it. Never."

Caderyn chuckled, stepping back from the bars. "Never say never, daughter. For never has a way of finding its way to fruition."

Walking out of the dungeons, he stopped by the guard. "Give her no food or water for three days, and do not allow her to sleep. If I cannot break her will through force, I shall break her mind first. Is that understood?"

The guard saluted. "Yes, my lord!"

Heading back to his study, Caderyn smiled. He would give her a week, max, before her mind broke and things began to move into place.

CHAPTER 10

———

For the first time in several days, Trinia woke up feeling happy. She was warm, fed, and relatively safe. *Well, as safe as I can be,* she thought, rubbing her eyes. It was also one of the few nights when she had not had a nightmare.

Since leaving Rionnagan, nothing had gone according to plan, which meant each passing day gave her father more time to figure out how to fulfill his dream. If he didn't have her power, that would delay him, but for how long, she didn't know. The thought soured her mood. She needed to get moving again.

Getting up, she folded the blanket and set it on one of the two wooden rocking chairs, admiring the craftsmanship of each. They were stained a dark brown with little silver etchings, which stood out against the grain. Trinia ran her fingers over the smooth surface.

Did his daughter ever sit on his lap while in this chair? she wondered.

Looking around the room, everything seemed to have a place. *I wonder if this is what it's like to have a home? To belong?* The thought cut through her and she decided to not dwell on it. It was far too painful.

Walking out into the morning light, Trinia saw Jayden lounging against his rock about ten yards away and Mandar once again before a fire, warming what was left of the deer from the previous night. Peering up, she thought she could almost see the sun through the branches, which were far thinner here. Only a tree or two stood in the midst of the clearing, which spanned a couple hundred feet in front of the cabin, allowing for *some* light to filter through.

"Ah, there you are. I was wondering when you would wake up," Mandar said smiling, still in his human form. "Sleep well?"

She nodded. "I did. Thank you. Did, uh… did Green Cloak leave?"

"I have not seen him yet. It's not unusual for him to walk the woods alone," Mandar replied.

Trinia sat down on the stump by Jayden, gazing off into the forest. "Will he be back?"

"I don't suspect he will. He was in a rather foul mood last night, as you may remember."

Jayden snorted. "An understatement."

"Indeed," she murmured.

The morning sun felt cooler, and Trinia regretted not choosing a warmer cloak. While she hadn't planned on more than a week or two of traveling, it would have been wise to think farther ahead. Autumn was here and she only had her breeches, undergarments, tunic, a light leather jerkin, and a wool cloak to keep her warm. If winter came early, she'd probably freeze to death.

Mandar cleared his throat and she looked over at him. "Yes?"

He settled an elbow on his knee, his golden eye gleaming. "I know Elohai has brought you here for a reason, but he didn't tell me why. In order to help you, I need to know what you were doing in the forest and why you were running."

Trinia's breath hitched, and her stomach curled up into a knot. Her palms itched. "Uh."

Jayden sat up, folding his arms around his legs. "I've been wondering that as well."

She looked to him and back to Mandar. *Should I just tell them? The wolf says he serves the enemy god of my people, so maybe his god will want to stop my father? But what if it's like last time and the god curses them all for the sins of one?*

Her gaze flicked between them, both wearing looks of keen interest, which only made the rising panic worse.

Rustling to her right drew her attention and she saw Green Cloak burst through the brush, his stormy gaze catching hers. He ran over before either Jayden or Mandar could react and lifted her by her jerkin. She screamed in surprise as her feet left the ground and he carried her toward the cabin, slamming her back against the wall.

"Is it true?" he yelled.

"Údar!" Mandar called, jumping to his feet and swiftly becoming a wolf once more.

A knife appeared at her throat and Trinia tried not to move less it slice into her. He pinned her to the wall with his knee to her stomach and his left hand holding the jerkin.

"Stay back, Mandar!" he shouted. "The boy too. I need answers."

"I don't know what you're talking about," she whispered. "Tell... tell me what you want to know."

Údar's gray eyes flashed and his brows came together. He eased the knife back a hair's breadth. "Are you Caderyn's daughter?" he growled.

All hope of making it out of this alive left her. Tears welled in her eyes and she took a shaky breath. "Yes."

His eyes grew wide for a moment before he pressed the blade against her throat again, harder this time. "And do you mean the world to him? Does he love you like I loved my daughter? Would he give up his very life for you?"

"Enough, Údar! This is madness!" cried Mandar, circling to the left.

The absurdity of the question hit something in her, and she broke into a fit of panicked laughter. Green Cloak stared at her, confused. "The only thing I am to that monster is a means to an end," she said after the fit had passed.

Some of his wrath dimmed in his eyes and she could see the tension in his shoulders ease ever so slightly. "Meaning?"

"She can duplicate herself."

Trinia glanced over Green Cloak's shoulder to Jayden, who stood there, his hands glowing. "I've seen it myself, as did several guards in Salorim. That's why we were running." He looked at her apologetically.

Green Cloak lowered her so they were eye to eye, his gaze searching. "Is this true?"

She nodded.

"Plagues!" he swore, dropping her to the ground and pacing back and forth in front of her like a caged animal.

Trinia backed up against the wall, trying to the calm herself down. Her hands felt like they were on fire and it took every bit of willpower she had not to create a duplicate. It would sign her death warrant.

Green Cloak yelled, falling to his knees and driving the knife into the ground a few feet from her. Mandar quickly put himself between her and the crazed man who was now weeping.

"He killed them," he cried. "He killed them!"

"Who?" Mandar asked.

"Her father, Caderyn," said Údar, grinding out every word through clenched teeth.

Suddenly, the missing piece fell into place for Trinia. *By the gods! He killed Green Cloak's family!*

Mandar seemed to have reached the same conclusion and answered his own question. "Caderyn was the one you let live the night your family was murdered."

Jayden came and stood beside her, his hands still glowing with an orange light, and she saw the barrier go up around them. She looked up at him, but he didn't meet her eyes.

Green Cloak stood unsteadily. He wobbled over to a tree a couple of feet away and sagged back to the earth, looking like he had aged ten years. Trinia had never known the loss of loved ones before, not in a way that drove a person mad, and she wasn't sure she ever wanted to.

The man looked at her. "Your father butchered my family, and I swore to him I would make him suffer in the same way I have suffered." He wiped his eyes with a sleeve and sniffed. "I thought the time had come to make good on that oath."

Was that why Father was always so overprotective of me? Why he restricted everything I did? she wondered.

He gave a mirthless laugh. "And now, it seems he does not care for you in a way which would satisfy me in killing you. To add to it, now the Baobhan Sith are after you as well."

Trinia leaned forward, all thoughts of her father pushed to the side. "The Baobhan Sith?"

The man nodded, staring at the ground. "Ulscia herself, to be exact."

"Wait, *the* Ulscia?" Jayden asked, running his hand through his hair. "I thought she was locked away in Lúinor Keep in the middle of Mugros Lake?"

Mandar walked over to Údar, his tone low. "How do you know this?"

"Because I spoke with her," he replied, still staring at the ground. "I made a deal with her."

"What?" Mandar exclaimed.

I need to get out of here! I need to leave right now! Trinia stood and pressed against the barrier, shouting to Jayden. "Let me out!"

"You can't leave," said Údar.

Trinia looked at him, heart racing. "Watch me!"

He shook his head, slowly getting to his feet. "She wants your blood. I didn't know why she would want something like that, and I was too stupid to ask why."

"You were stupid for talking to her in the first place," growled Mandar, his eyes narrow.

"I'm going to second that," said Jayden, looking a little pale.

Trinia grabbed his arm. "Let me out, Jayden. Now!"

"The means to the end," said Údar. "Was that creating duplicates for Caderyn?"

She glared at him. "Yes, why?"

His shoulders sagged and he sighed. "Because I believe Ulscia wants to do the same thing."

CHAPTER 11

———

Trinia sat at the oak table nursing a foul-tasting herbal tea Mandar had given her to help ease the pain in her back and sides. Sipping it again, she grimaced as she swallowed. *Hells, this is awful!*

While she could not place the taste, the only word that came to mind was "mud." Her reaction elicited a soft chuckle from Jayden, and she glowered at him.

Mandar laid down on the floor, having changed back to his true form. He kept a wary eye on Green Cloak as he paced back and forth in front of the hearth. The wolf sent her a concerned look, and something in it worried her. She was not sure she wanted to find out what it was.

Mandar had convinced her to not go running off. If not for Green Cloak knowing, or suspecting, why the Queen of the Baobhan Sith was suddenly after her, she would have.

Trinia watched Údar pace back and forth. He was volatile, unpredictable, and now had tried to kill her twice—first for simply being an Airgíd and the second because she was Caderyn's daughter. *If father had loved me, would I now be buried in the forest?* she wondered. It wasn't a pleasant thought.

"If you're going to say something, I suggest we get on with it," said Mandar testily.

She got the sense that speaking with the Baobhan Sith was something Údar knew better than to do, yet he had gone and made a bargain with one for her blood. From what she remembered from her people's lore, the creatures were not to be trusted. Ever.

Údar sat down in one of the rockers, leaning his elbows on his knees, head down. "What do you know about Gifts?" he asked.

Is he asking me? She looked at Jayden and then to Mandar, who nodded. "It's something everyone has. The gods bestow them to us when we are of age at sixteen."

"*God,*" Údar said, glancing at her. "Singular. The Gifts come from Elohai, going back to the foundations of the world and long before Caluvan arrived and brought with him The Deception."

"That's not what our histories tell us," she replied.

He snorted and shook his head. "They are wrong, but that is for another time, perhaps."

Trinia bit back a reply, instead taking another sip of tea. *No wonder he is so bitter. He only has this stuff to drink.*

"But is Elohai actually real?" asked Jayden, chiming in from the end of the table. "No one has ever seen him."

"Perhaps they were not looking hard enough," Údar replied sharply, looking his way.

"The Gifts, Údar," said Mandar.

The man looked at the wolf and then again at her. "I've been alive a long time, and I've studied the histories and know the Gifts. Yours is new. All Gifts serve a purpose, but this… I do not know what that might be."

Not exactly comforting, she thought. "And how does this Gift play into a demon woman wanting my blood?"

Údar stood and began pacing again. "Caluvan took a wife long ago and bore two children, raising them in secret. The male was Iudran, and the girl was Ulscia."

Trinia knew a lot about her people's history, but never had she heard such a story about Caluvan, king of the Old Gods. *He's just making it up.*

"Iudran killed his father when he was older and sailed east through the Straights of Fire and disappeared," Údar continued. "Ulscia mourned for her father and chased after her brother. When she didn't find him, she returned to find the Airgíd Empire crumbling."

Jayden leaned back in his chair, putting his booted feet up on the table. "Then all manner of terrible creatures started showing up and the Order of the White Flame launched an attack, sealed her up forever, and left. But what about the blood?"

Trinia saw Údar pause to give Jayden an ominous look, and the young mage took his feet off the table. "The reason I believe Ulscia wants the girl's blood—"

"My name is *Trinia*, not *girl*," she said, frowning.

Údar raised a brow, continuing on like he hadn't heard her. "Like I was saying, the reason I think Ulscia wants the blood is to perform a blood ritual that would let her absorb *Trinia's* Gift."

Trinia sat back in her chair. "Why would she want to do that?" she asked, bewildered.

The man's face grew serious as he turned to her. "Because she could create a thousand Baobhan Sith, all duplicated from herself, posing a threat to all life."

She felt the blood drain from her face. *Vyrni, no!*

Mandar put a paw over his eyes. "And you promised to give her the blood?"

"I was not in a good place, Mandar, and I'm still not." He pointed at her, voice rising. "The daughter of my family's murderer sits at my table and an evil has escaped that should not have. So, forgive me if I am a little outside of my mind at the moment."

Silence filled the room. Trinia found herself surprised by the odd feeling of understanding she felt for the man. For as long as she could remember, the Voice had tormented and taken advantage of her while her father beat her whenever things did not go his way. It had driven her to a point where the thought of going to her enemies to seek their help in destroying her father and his priest seemed like her only option. Had she told Niren, he would have said she was out of her mind, too. *Maybe he and I are just two different kinds of crazy?*

That aside, it looked as if she was in a worse place than before with her father. Now she had the supposed daughter of Caluvan after her. If Elohai had given the Gifts, he seemed hell-bent on punishing her with hers.

"—can't stay here," Mandar was saying.

Údar gestured toward her. "And I didn't want her here to begin with, yet here we are." He pinched the bridge of his nose. "Why are you here, Trinia?"

She leaned back in the chair and folded her arms. "Why does it matter to you?"

He walked over slowly, placing his hands on the table and leaning toward her, brows furrowed. "Because your Gift will bring about destruction in the hands of Ulscia. Now talk."

The words of the prophecy flitted through her mind, speaking of her power destroying the world. *Your child will bring about the destruction of their enemies and restore the land of their birth through fire and blood.*

There wasn't another option. Her shoulders sagged. "I was trying to get to Canämor to see the king there. I thought if he knew my father was trying to rebuild the Old Empire, they would go there to destroy him."

Údar looked at her with genuine surprise. "You wish to see him dead?"

Trinia could feel the emotions rise, and she swallowed past the lump in her throat. "More than anything," she whispered.

He stood and walked over to the fire, bracing himself against the mantel. After a moment, he turned around, looking straight at her. "We both have reasons for wanting revenge, so I propose a deal. I will help you raise the army you are looking for, but in return, I get your vow to let my blade be the one that ends Caderyn's life." He moved back to the table, extending a hand. "Agreed?"

She cast a glance at Jayden who shrugged and then to Mandar who looked discouraged. Coming back to the hand in front of her, she met Údar's gaze. Could she really trust a man who had not an hour ago tried to kill her for the second time? *Am I really so desperate?* She wondered. "Under one condition," she said cautiously.

He frowned slightly, lowering his hand. "And that is?"

"You swear not to kill me, and you don't let the Baobhan Sith get my blood." She extended her hand. "What do you say?"

"I think that's fair," said Jayden, smirking. "All things considered."

Údar's lips twisted into a rueful smile. "Agreed, on both counts. You wouldn't be of any use if you were dead."

Trinia flinched inwardly. She may have found someone to help her meet her desired goal, but it came with strings attached. *I'm still a means to someone else's end.*

-II-

Jayden sat in front of the fire in the rocking chair as the afternoon wore on. He had seen a lot of things over the past few years, but this was by far the strangest. *How on earth did I end up here? Oh, that's right, I tried to get my revenge on an old demon-snake-man and then followed a stranger who turned out to be an Airgíd with a Gift allowing her to duplicate herself. Who, turns out, is the daughter of Caderyn, the arch-nemesis of Green Cloak.*

He took a sip of tea, gagging it down. *Gods, Mandar needs to learn how to make tea! Now, where was I? Ah, turns out Green Cloak, who apparently existed over four hundred years ago, is still alive and knows Ulscia, Queen of the Baobhan Sith, whom he has previously helped imprison. Ugh, it's making my head spin.*

Rubbing his eyes, Jayden made a mental note to never follow strangers into dark alleys ever again. Too many complications—something he had tried hard to escape from back home. To make matters worse, he was under a life-debt to Trinia.

He stared into the fire, massaging his temple. She had saved his life by sacrificing herself, or part of herself, or however the hells it worked, and now he was bound by it. His morals might be hazy at times, but breaking that was not something he could bring himself to do. Only the worst of the worst broke such a thing.

I'm not a bad guy, he told himself.

Trinia appeared beside him, sinking down into the rocking chair to his left. Something about her struck him, something just beneath the surface he could not quite put his finger on. It was as if she wore a mask and the Trinia next to him was not there. Just a shadow.

What is your story? he wondered.

She shifted, folding her arms around herself. "Údar says he knows someone who may be able to help me," she said, breaking the silence.

Jayden raised a brow. "Oh?"

Trinia nodded, eyes intent on the fire. "In Ungäar. Said his name was Arthfael."

Jayden's stomach twisted in a painful knot and he gritted his teeth. *King* Arthfael. His father. *Hells below!*

She looked at him, seeming to pick on his unease at the thought of returning home. "Are you alright? You look like you've seen a telgost."

He tried to smile but suspected it looked more like a grimace. "I have a... reputation in Ungäar."

"Tried to kill other old men there, too?" she asked, giving a small smile.

Jayden couldn't help but laugh. "Not exactly, no."

She grinned, and it hit him it was the first time he had really seen her smile. "You strike me as the kind of person to cause trouble," she remarked.

Raising his hands, he said, "Guilty."

Trinia chuckled and turned her attention back to the flames dancing in the hearth. *This is the most relaxed I've seen her. It's like she's a different person,* he thought.

The door opened behind them, and Jayden turned to see Údar standing there. "Come on, we'll discuss our plans while we eat."

"Mandar didn't make more of the tea, did he?" asked Jayden worriedly.

"I heard that," Mandar called.

Hells!

Údar huffed. "I gathered some rabbits from traps I have in the forest and we'll be having those. To your point, no, Mandar did not make more tea." He turned and strode back outside, saying something to the wolf about needing a side dish.

Back home, the cook would typically use sprouted greens or potatoes for such a dish, but Jayden doubted today's meal would be so sophisticated. He stood, offering a hand to Trinia, who ignored it and took the long way around him and out the door. *This is why I stopped being a gentleman*, he thought.

Jayden took a moment to gather himself, knowing the planning would revolve around going back to his home city of Tranâes. Back to his father. Back to everything he had tried to escape. He sighed. *I have got to figure a way out of this.*

CHAPTER 12

———

To think he was going to get revenge on Caderyn through his own daughter after all these years put Údar in a far better mood than he had been in prior. It looked a little different from what he had expected, but it was going to happen. All there was left to do was take her to Arthfael in Tranâes.

Night was quickly settling about them as they ate, and the chill in the air would get harder to ignore when they were on the road. *I'll need to pack some additional blankets*, he thought.

Trinia set her meal down, wiped her fingers on the moss beside her, and then looked his way. "So how long will it take to reach Tranâes?"

He finished chewing before replying. "It's over eight hundred miles from here to Tranâes, if I remember correctly. With horses, it should take us a little over a month."

Her shoulders sagged. "Is there no faster way?"

"Not unless your mage friend knows how to give horses unlimited endurance," he replied, taking another bite of meat.

Trinia looked at Jayden who shook his head. "Oh no, don't look at me! First, pretty sure that is impossible to do because of the energy required to maintain something like that," said

Jayden. "Second, it wouldn't do you any good because you would fall asleep in the saddle and be unable to ride."

"Are Gifts always limited to energy?" Trinia asked.

"Depends," said Údar, swallowing. "It's possible for a blacksmith to imbue a sword with magic from his Gift, but to make it last requires the help of Elohai."

"But they outlawed such use," Jayden quipped, leaning forward. "Something about not wanting people using it for the wrong reasons."

Údar set his plate aside, pulling at his beard. *They do not even know the history. Why am I not surprised?* "The kingdoms thought it would be a good way to protect each other, yet they then founded the Academy of Mages and twisted the Gifts to fit their own purposes."

Trinia shook her head. "How will anyone stand up to my father if they do not even use their magic?"

"That will be up to Elohai," said Mandar, finally speaking up.

The wolf was lying just a few feet away from Údar and had been strangely silent up to this point. Údar doubted his friend approved of the current course of action, but surely he would understand in time.

Mandar looked at him. "Not to change topic, just where do you plan on getting the horses?"

"Salorim. Since our guests have likely frightened the people there, I think it would be wise to leave them outside the town while I get what we need," Údar replied, pulling out his pipe and cleaning it.

"Fine by me," said Jayden, shivering. "If I see Cal again, it would be too soon."

"No argument there," Trinia added.

"Excellent," said Údar, knocking the old pipeweed out. "We'll leave at first—"

A long wail erupted off in the distance, sending a wave of goosebumps up his arms. There came a second and then a third, growing ever closer to where they sat. He jumped to his feet, drawing his sword. *Ulscia is more impatient than I thought.*

"What was that?" asked Trinia, edging toward the cabin.

Údar grabbed more wood, throwing it on the fire to get it blazing. They would need all the light they could get. He turned to her. "Don't leave the firelight."

She stopped, casting a wary glance behind her before moving toward the fire and taking her daggers out of their sheaths.

Mandar sniffed the air and let out a low growl as Jayden placed himself near the fire, adding a little wind to stoke the flames higher. Údar gave a slight nod. *Maybe the mage is useful after all,* he thought.

There came a sickly gurgling noise from the just beyond the firelight, and Údar closed his eyes, summoning the power of Elohai within him. He could feel the light and warmth radiate through him until white flames kindled to life in his hands, traveling down the sword to the tip. When he opened his eyes, he could see everything around them as though it were day.

He watched as the shadows rose from the ground in a seething mass of bulbous black forms. Celnísh—spawn of Ulscia.

Each one was uglier and more hideous than the last, with their deformed bodies, contorted limbs, and swollen tongues dangling from their misshapen mouths. Creatures of darkness and shadow, they lived beneath the shelter of the forests' thick boughs. He had not seen them in years as they had retreated to the heart of the forest, but now, it seemed, their mother had called them forth and that made them braver. Not that the maggoty carcasses could feel anything but hunger.

There were dozens of them now, and all at once they charged, hoping to crush their prey by the weight of sheer numbers.

Údar let out a furious battle cry, tearing into them by wielding his flaming sword and slicing through their ranks like a scythe through wheat stalks.

Somewhere behind him he heard a scream and shouting, but he kept his focus on what was in front of him. Beheading one creature after another, he watched them vaporize into nothing more than a black smudge on the ground. Unfortunately, the same odious goo covered him as well.

Mandar appeared beside him, ripping the head off a creature with his bare teeth. His fur was slick with sweat and black blood. After taking out several celnísh, the wolf leapt back toward the fire and out of sight as Údar continued dispatching the spawns to the abyss.

A form appeared from behind a tree, and he could make out Ulscia's lithe body as she threw her head back and laughed. Everything in him wanted to silence her with one well-placed knife throw, but she was too far out of range.

Glass shattered, and he glanced over his shoulder to see celnísh climbing through the windows. Two things hit him in that moment—the first being the creatures were bypassing him and making for his home.

The second was that Trinia was nowhere to be seen.

-II-

Trinia watched in horror as creatures began to pour through the windows of the cabin, their noxious breath filling the space and making her want to vomit. She wished she had listened to Údar when he told her to stay by the fire.

Jayden sent a blast of air, throwing the creatures against the walls while she cut and stabbed with her daggers at any that slipped past. Her palms burned with the desire to make a duplicate, to distract the monsters from getting her, but she could not bring herself to do it.

A celnísh jumped at her and knocked her into the mantel of the hearth. She quickly rammed her daggers into its multiple eyes and it screeched in agony. A split second later it was blown across the room by a gust from Jayden.

"You okay?" he called, sending several more flying.

She stood, trying to get her bearings again. "Yes, I think so."

The words were no sooner out of her mouth than her feet were taken out from under her, causing her to drop her daggers as she was dragged away down the hall. "Jayden!" she screamed. "Help me!"

Trinia twisted and tried to get her leg free, but the grip was too strong, and the monster was moving too fast. Her heart raced, and the fear was overwhelming. She couldn't think, couldn't breathe.

The deformed body broke the window in the bedroom it had dragged her into and threw her through it. Rolling to a stop, the thing was on her before she could recover and continued dragging her into the forest. "Help!" she screamed.

A wall of fur smashed into the monster and she curled up, hands over her head as if that would protect her.

"Trinia, get up, quickly."

She opened her eyes to see Mandar standing over her, golden eye reflecting the light of the fire on the other side of the cabin. Getting up, she hugged his neck, tears spilling down her cheeks.

"We cannot stay in the dark for long, hurry now, back to the fire," he said, his tone gentle yet firm.

She followed his lead, sticking close to him until they reached the fire where Jayden was sitting. He looked exhausted, covered head to toe in black. She couldn't see Údar.

"Mandar, toss me a log from the fire!"

Trinia turned to see Údar standing in the door of the cabin, hand outstretched. *What is he doing?*

Without hesitating, Mandar grabbed a burning log with his mouth and tossed it toward the man to land at his feet. Spearing it with his sword, Údar disappeared into the home.

Trinia noticed she was trembling as more cries erupted around them. *We're going to die.*

-II-

Údar took one last pass through the cabin, grabbing the money purse he'd hidden behind the cupboard in the kitchen and the two swords he had tucked under a floorboard. Arms full, he paused, taking in the ruined insides of his home. Black stains coated almost every surface, ruining any shred of the past he held dear. The chairs lay broken on the floor, and the table was splintered and cracked in numerous places. Now it would all burn to save the daughter of his enemy. It wasn't fair.

He took the burning log, set it against the wooden table, and blew on it until it lit, watching it to make sure it would take. When it did, he ran to the door and took one look back. *Goodbye.*

"What on earth are you doing?" Jayden asked as he returned to the fire.

"Saving us," Údar replied. He laid the weapons down, taking more time and care to wrap them in cloth bundles.

"Celnísh hate light, and we should now have enough to last through the night."

"But where are we going to sleep?" the boy asked, the glow of the cabin lighting his face.

Údar stood and spat, frowning down at him. "Who said anything about sleeping?" He glanced at the girl. "I told you to stay by the fire."

Mandar must have suspected where he was going with that line of thought because he spoke up. "Let he who has never made an error cast the first stone."

"Hmph." Údar took out a cloth and wiped his blade clean. "We will do a cleanse in the morning and then head for Salorim for the horses. After that, we pray we can outrun Ulscia."

Here and there throughout the night, he heard Ulscia laughing in the distance, followed by long wailing cries. She was toying with them, trying to get them to run headlong into the forest and into her grasp, but he would not allow it. When dawn finally broke, a small sense of relief flooded him, and a deep weariness settled into his bones. *I'm getting too old for this,* he thought.

He walked over to Trinia and Jayden and nudged them to wake them up. Both startled awake and Údar smiled grimly. "Have a good nap?"

Jayden groaned and muttered something Údar couldn't make out.

"We need to get moving, and we need to do a cleanse first before anything else. Get on your feet," he said, turning to Mandar. "Will you scout the area to make sure Ulscia is gone?"

The wolf nodded. "I'll be within earshot should you need me," he said and then bounded off into the forest.

That wasn't for me, Údar thought. Shaking his head, he channeled Elohai's powers, focusing it to his hands. Once the flames flickered to life, he drew a circle about four feet in diameter. The white flames grew higher until they were licking the leaves above.

"Won't the tree catch fire?" Trinia asked from behind him, deep circles under her eyes.

He looked up. "The White Flame only destroys evil, and unless the trees have a mind of their own, they will not be harmed."

"You serve the White Flame?" Jayden asked, walking about the circle.

"I serve the One who is in the flames," Údar replied. "Now watch."

Taking a breath, he stepped into the middle of the blaze.

CHAPTER 13

———

Trinia gazed around the clearing, disgusted by the black smudges and ooze that covered the ground, not to mention the smell, which was enough to make someone queasy. The cabin was now a heaped pile of collapsed timbers with smoke billowing into the sky. What amazed her the most was they were still alive. That, and Údar had walked into a pillar of white fire.

And stepped out clean of any blood, either on his skin or his clothes. It was as if there had never been a fight.

Údar checked himself as if making sure it was all gone before looking at Jayden and motioning toward the circle. "Just step in. You won't be burned."

Jayden cast an uneasy glance her way before bouncing on the balls of his feet and jumping into the fire as well. She looked down at her stained clothing and grimy hands, wishing there was another way.

"It won't kill you," said Údar evenly.

Trinia looked up at him from where she sat on the grass. "You're sure? Doesn't your god hate me as much as you do?"

"Your people were punished for sacrificing their children to your gods," he replied, grimacing. "And do not forget Elohai sent prophets to them for close to seven hundred years before judgment came."

She folded her arms, looking away. "He destroyed my people."

"They destroyed themselves," he retorted. "But to answer your question, yes, I am sure it will not kill you. We've made a pact, remember?"

It seems like all I'm good for is what I can give others. If it is not my body being used, it's my Gift, and if not my Gift, my blood.

Jayden reappeared on the other side of the circle from where he had entered and, like Údar, was clean of dried ooze and blood. "That was amazing!" he exclaimed. "Can you teach me how to create it?"

Údar gave a hollow laugh. "It's not something that is taught. It is something within you if you follow Elohai."

"I do follow him," Jayden countered.

"Not likely," replied Údar. He looked at her, motioning to the circle of white flames. "Your turn."

She wondered if what he said about his god not killing her would be true. After all, he had killed millions of her people and brought about the end of the Empire. Seeing Jayden emerge unscathed was promising, at least. *I guess I'll find out,* she thought.

Standing, she walked over to the flames and closed her eyes, slowly extending her hand until it passed through the barrier. Opening her eyes, she pulled her hand out and saw no burn marks of any kind. *How does a fire burn but not consume?* she wondered. Casting a glance back at the burning skeleton of the cabin and the charred limbs above it, she knew just how powerful fire could be.

Taking a breath to steel herself, she stepped into the circle. Immediately, white light blinded her and she could see nothing around her.

Trinia.

She froze. Had she heard that right?

Trinia.

A voice was coming from all around her, soft and gentle like rain on an autumn day, but carrying with it the power of a thunderclap. "I'm losing it," Trinia muttered to herself.

Trinia.

Squinting against the brightness, she could not open her eyes enough to see who or what was speaking. "Who are you?" she called, her voice echoing around her.

I am Elohai, the voice replied.

The trembling that had settled returned and her palms itched fiercely. "What do you want?"

Behold, I am doing something in your day, and you would not believe me if I told you, said the voice.

"You could try," Trinia whispered. Her legs were shaking so badly she wasn't sure if she could get back out of the fire.

The air around her vibrated with laughter and strength seeped back into her bones. *You will see in time, dear one.*

Suddenly her legs moved almost of their own volition and she was once again standing in the forest. She gasped for air as her eyes adjusted to the dim light. The implications of what had happened, and to whom she had spoken hit her, and she dropped to a knee. *He's real. He's really real.*

She looked around and saw Mandar speaking with Jayden while Údar was busy cleaning the pipe he had discarded before the battle last night. Everything was normal. Except it wasn't.

After years of praying to Vyrni, never once had she seen the goddess or heard her voice. Offering after offering had been answered with only stony silence. Her people believed that Elohai was like their gods—jealous, petty, wrathful— which explained why he had destroyed them. But unlike the carven images her people worshipped, this god had spoken to her directly.

"You alright?"

Trinia startled and looked up at Jayden, who was staring at her. "Yeah, just my first time purposefully stepping into a fire is all."

He chuckled. "Yes, well, I'm sensing there are going to be a lot of firsts along the way."

"What do you mean?" she asked, standing back up and brushing the leaves off her breeches.

Jayden's face grew thoughtful. "I've been avoiding talking about this, but after what happened last night with that monster grabbing you, I feel like I need to say it."

She waved her hands and said, "I don't blame you for that."

"It's not that." He rubbed the back of his neck, gazing up at the tree limbs above them. "I owe you a life-debt because you saved me. I don't like it. I would prefer not to honor it, yet I still have some sense of honor I'd like to maintain."

That is not where I thought he was going with that, she thought. "Can't I just release you of it? To be honest, I'm not comfortable with it either."

His gaze drifted back to hers. "Nope, only the king can release it. Don't ask me who came up with that idea, because if I knew, I would have some words for them."

Trinia smiled. "Fair enough. Just know that I won't hold you to it. Can we agree on that much?"

Jayden nodded, looking a little relieved. "Yeah."

At the sound of footsteps approaching, she looked to see Údar, two bundles on his back, walking toward them. "Time to go. I will head into town and purchase the horses. You two will go with Mandar, and I shall meet you south of town."

Mandar stepped out of the fire, shaking his fur. "Ah, much better."

"You know where the turnout is on the road?" asked Údar, looking at the wolf.

"Yes, I know the place. Don't worry about us. Just focus on the horses," Mandar replied. The wolf motioned to them with his head as Údar took off into the forest at a sprint. "Come along, no time to waste."

Leaving the charred clearing behind brought with it some relief for her. She didn't want to think about what would have happened if Mandar had not saved her, nor what would happen if Ulscia captured her.

The walk through the forest was a quiet one as she and Jayden walked on either side of the wolf. They walked past many trails splitting off, and Trinia did not understand how Mandar found his way.

After an hour of walking, she noticed the ground becoming more and more rocky as it sloped off to the right slightly. When they finally left the tree line, they were on a small rise, with the Olen Mountains to her left and the low hills to her right on the path. In the distance, there looked to be a brownish haze over the town and hills further into Thydu, which struck her as odd.

Perhaps it is from the cabin burning last night, she thought.

Mandar guided them down a smaller offshoot from the main trail that led into the hills and toward what at first glance seemed to be a road. Yet as close as it seemed, it still took another several hours to reach level ground again.

They took a break when they reached the bottom, and Trinia pulled off her leather boots, rubbing the sore spots. *Now I understand why they wanted to get horses. It would be impossible to walk that far on foot!*

"I would put your boots back on," said Mandar, glancing her way. "Your feet will swell up and it will hurt a lot more trying to get them back in."

"Very well," she grumbled, shoving her bruised feet back into her boots. Looking up at the sun, she guessed it was close to mid-day. "How much longer until we meet up with Údar?"

"Soon," replied the wolf, continuing on.

Trinia began to wonder what Mandar's definition of "soon" was after another couple hours of walking through the hills. She was tired, hungry, and feeling more and more irritable with every step.

Movement ahead caught her eye just as Mandar stopped in front of her, crouching low. "Get down," he whispered, moving to a tall clump of bushes.

She and Jayden bent over and crawled on their hands and knees behind him. Trinia then moved some branches to see what it was and stifled a gasp. *It's a helwreck!*

The creature was at least ten feet tall with broad, muscular shoulders and massive arms as thick as tree trunks. It wore a simple loincloth of furs with skulls decorating it in a macabre fashion. The head was almost too small for its body, and its blue-gray skin helped it blend it with the rocky hills.

Trinia watched as it stubbed its foot against a small boulder. The helwreck flew into a rage and brought down one of its fists on the rock, smashing it to pieces. *No wonder where they got their name,* she mused.

Seemingly satisfied whatever had caused it pain was now dead, the helwreck moved off in the opposite direction. She let out a sigh of relief. "That was close. It was what, twenty-five yards from us?"

Jayden wiped the sweat from him brow. "At least. Thank goodness they are not the brightest."

"We will need to be extra vigilant," said Mandar, staring in the direction the creature went. "I don't want to face one."

"But you're, well, huge," said Jayden, looking the wolf up and down.

Not exactly how I would have put it, thought Trinia.

Mandar chuckled lightly. "True, but as you saw with the rock, their fist is not something you want to get hit by, giant wolf or no."

She conceded that point.

As they left their hiding place, Trinia did her best to keep her eyes open for anything else that might be lurking in the cracks and crags around them. Mercifully, another few minutes of walking brought them to a small turnout beside a main road. There was no sign of Údar.

"Where is he?" asked Jayden.

Mandar shook his head as he sat. "I don't know. He should have been here by now."

"What do we do now?" she asked, running a hand through her tangled hair.

The wolf was quiet a moment before replying. "We wait."

-II-

Jayden helped Trinia collect some wood for a small fire to help stave off the cold. Even though it was still early September, the chill in the air threatened an early winter.

Thoughts drifted to home and what his father would think of him reappearing, alive and well. *I wonder if anyone ever told mother about my death.* It was doubtful since she had locked herself away in Fort Sya by the Barren Coast since before he had left for the Academy. Why she had left was something his father refused to speak about. Perhaps he could visit her sometime after everything was done.

Ack, you're going soft, Jayden! he chided himself, kicking a stick in front of him. *Spending time with family is the last thing you want to do. Remember?*

"What are you doing?" asked Trinia, coming up beside him. "You've been kicking that stick for the past five minutes."

He met her gaze, putting on a smile. "I don't particularly care for it."

Trinia raised a brow. "Offended you, did it?"

Jayden nodded. "Its mere presence insults my fine taste in firewood. I aim to choose only the best, and this stick here, well…" he motioned to it, frowning. "It's pathetic."

She laughed and bent over, picking it up and adding it to her pile before walking back to where Mandar stood watch on the road.

Jayden caught himself staring. *Hells, man! Were you flirting just now? Over a stick, no less?* He shook his head, muttering. "I *am* going soft."

He returned after collecting a few more sticks and threw them onto the pile. Looking to Mandar, he said, "Now what?"

"You make a fire," replied the wolf, staring up the road.

Jayden rolled his eyes and stooped down to get it going. He got the sticks and tinder in place and held his hands just above it, focusing on the magic in him. Before long, the tinder began smoking and finally lit. Soon, it was crackling before them as the shadows grew longer.

Trinia sat across from him, and Mandar seemed almost a statue considering how little he had moved since they arrived. The fact Údar had not yet appeared was more than a little worrisome. Walking all the way to Tranâes was the last thing he wanted to do.

Glancing at Trinia, he motioned to her hair as she braided it. "I hate to point out the obvious, but you may want to conceal your hair color again."

She looked to him and then to her hair, pausing mid braid. "I hadn't thought of that."

When she closed her eyes, he could see the point between her brows furrow ever so slightly in concentration. He watched in wonder as color spread from the roots of her hair down the length until it reached the tip with a soft copper color. He averted his stare before she opened her eyes this time, pretending like he was adding another stick to the fire. "How old are you, Trinia?" he asked.

"Sixteen," she replied, inspecting her hair and pulling it out of the braid. "You?"

"Nineteen," he replied.

"Both young pups as far as I am concerned," quipped Mandar from his post by the road.

Jayden sat a little straighter. "Oh? And just how old are you?" he asked.

The wolf chuckled. "You should get some sleep."

"Sleep?" He looked at the sky. "It's not even time for dinner, why would we go to sleep now? I think you're just avoiding the question."

Mandar turned, giving a crooked smile. "If Údar shows up in the middle of the night and we have to ride, are you willing to do so?"

That sounded incredibly unpleasant. "Fine, I'll close my eyes for a little," Jayden replied.

"I suppose I will, too," agreed Trinia, lying down.

Jayden lay on this back, turning this way and that trying to get comfortable. Everywhere seemed to hold some pebble whose sole purpose was to dig into his ribs. He finally settled on his left side, back to the fire, staring off into the brush. A memory drifted to his mind of a time he had spent the night in Kiäxe with a girl his age. They'd made many promises to each other neither could actually keep. The fun night had brought with it an empty feeling in the morning when she was gone. He did not even know her name.

The thought brought an unwelcome sense of loneliness he had not felt in a long time. He just wanted to numb it, make it go away, and be back in her arms if but for a night. He closed his eyes, trying to picture her. "I wish I was with you," he whispered, drifting off.

CHAPTER 14

She was calling to him.

Jayden opened his eyes, seeing the fire had burned low and Mandar lying beside them asleep. Everything else around them was darkness. Rubbing his eyes, he heard the soft call again.

"Come back to bed with me," it said.

The voice was so beautiful, so familiar. He got up, creating a *soläs* to help him see. "Hello?" he whispered.

The voice sounded a little further away as it called again. "Come back to bed with me."

It was so sweet sounding, so alluring. Jayden yawned. *It would be nice to be back in bed. I'm so tired.*

Stumbling into the dark, he followed the voice, feeling a yearning in his heart for the companionship of a woman, the promise of a warm body beside his. Some moments he thought he spotted her, just beyond the light in a robe of robin's egg blue, but then she was gone. Only her voice trailed back to him.

The yearning grew the longer he chased after her, driving him like a slaver's whip to reach her and make love with her. When he finally crested a small hill, he could see her at the mouth of a cave sitting on a linen bed draped in silks. A feeling crept into his gut that there was a wrongness to the scene, but unable to see the harm, he hurried down to her.

As he approached, he could make out the finer details of her face. Her nose was straight, and her high cheeks gave her a regal appearance. Her brows arched seductively over eyes like polished gold, and her full lips sat in a coy smile. Her skin, white as alabaster, revealed itself in the places where the robes parted, exposing long legs.

Jayden's breath caught. *I must be dreaming.*

She patted the bed beside her. "Come to bed with me."

Was it a command? An invitation? Jayden felt his mouth go dry. The feeling that something was wrong returned. He glanced around as a feeling of dread clawed its way into his chest. *Where am I?*

"Come to bed with me," the woman said. This time there was no mistaking the command in her tone.

What was worse, Jayden felt his body move to comply. He tried to speak, but he could not open his mouth, nor could he move his arms as his legs carried him toward the woman. Standing in front of her, he tried to cry out for help as she began unpinning his cloak and then his shirt.

Help me! Someone! Anyone! his mind screamed.

When he was fully undressed, she shoved him onto the bed and slipped out of her robe. Her smooth white body was the most beautiful and horrifying thing he had ever seen. Black veins stood out all over her body like a hideous spiderweb, and her delicate fingers morphed into sharp talons.

A Baobhan Sith.

Jayden closed his eyes, trying to will the horrible sight away, knowing from the stories he had read at the Academy what would come next. First, she would use him for her own pleasures and then slowly drain him of his blood. If he was lucky, she would let him die. If not, she would use her own blood to turn him into a thrall and damn him to everlasting darkness.

He yelped as she kissed his cheek. "It's been a long time since I've had such a handsome man," she crooned.

A tear slipped down his cheek as he tried to keep his mind from fracturing into a thousand tiny pieces. *Elohai, please... save me.*

She slipped into the bed next to him, her body cold like ice. Dragging a clawed finger across his chest, she cut into his skin as she kissed him again. "Mother promised me a young man would come. It's been terribly lonely all these years in hiding, so I will take my time with you."

Suddenly, the banshee screamed, writhing next to him a moment before she rolled off the bed. He tried to turn his head to see what was happening when a white ball of flame shot over him, heading into the cave. There was another scream, shouting, a growl, then the sick snapping of bones and the smell of burning flesh.

Jayden's breath quickened as a figure appeared on the edge of his vision, eyes alight with white fire and wrapped in a green cloak. Did he dare hope?

"Are you with us?"

It *was* Údar! Jayden wanted to shout for joy, but he felt the world tip and begin to spin as darkness swirled around him.

A light floated above him, a single tongue of pure white flame, and he heard Údar speaking. "Follow the light, Jayden. Fight!"

What am I supposed to be fighting? he wondered.

Údar took off his cloak, laying it over his body, and Jayden realized he felt cold... so very cold.

"We have a problem!" Trinia yelled somewhere out of view.

"Údar! To arms!" cried Mandar, snarling.

I thought the banshee was dead? I'm so cold.

Údar disappeared from view, returning a moment later with Trinia and pointing. "Do not leave him and do not let the flame go out. If you do, he dies."

Trinia looked terrified, but she nodded and cast an uneasy glance down at him.

I'm dying?

"And this time, do not leave the light," Údar growled. He drew his sword and vanished from view.

Jayden felt his eyes closing as wild howls and cackling erupted from all around, followed by a wailing cry like a parent who had lost their child. It was feral, vicious, and threatening, and so, so far away.

Pain seared in his chest, and his mouth opened in a silent scream.

Trinia was there, pushing down on his chest as his body convulsed on the bed. "Jayden, you're okay! Breathe!"

He wasn't okay. He was dying, and it was nothing like the stories he had heard of people going peacefully. It was agonizing, torturous, and excruciating. Another wave hit as the wail came back, sending icy waves of pain through his body. *Just let me die!*

Again, Trinia held him down, speaking comforting words he could no longer hear. All he felt was pain.

-II-

"He'll live, even if he doesn't want to," Údar said gruffly.

Jayden groaned, cracking his eyes open and letting the light of day pour in. *Hells, it's too bright out,* he thought. *And how did I get dressed?*

"Ah, speak of the devil," said Údar.

"The what?" That was Trinia.

"Nothing, don't worry about it," the man replied.

Opening his eyes a little further, Jayden could see them sitting at the mouth of the cave, a large fire burning between them all. Outside, he could see black stains and an alabaster body, headless and charred. "I'm not dead?"

Mandar came into view. "Despite your best efforts, it seems Elohai has other plans."

A pain flitted through his chest where the banshee had cut him. Putting a hand to it, he found it wrapped and bandaged. "The banshee..." he started.

Údar waved a hand. "It's dead. If Mandar hadn't heard your scream, you likely would have been too."

Had I screamed? I don't remember being able to speak. Jayden looked at Údar. "How did you get here?"

The man shifted to face Jayden a little better. "I arrived late into the night, for reasons I will catch everyone up on soon enough. When I arrived, however, I found you missing and woke the others. Thankfully, Mandar's nose and hearing still works despite his age."

"Indeed," replied the wolf, whacking the back of Údar's head with his tail.

Údar swatted it away and continued, "We found you just after the Baobhan Sith started the bonding ritual, so you shouldn't be too badly damaged."

Jayden grabbed his head, letting a wave of nausea pass. "I heard a horrible wailing sound," he said.

"That would have been Ulscia paying us another visit with her brood. She flew into a rage when she saw her daughter's body lying bloody and broken on the ground. It benefited us as it sent the celnísh into a frenzy and they attacked one another," Údar replied.

It was Ulscia's daughter? Now the part about "Mother promised me" made more sense. The nausea came back, and Jayden rolled over and vomited what little contents were in his stomach.

"Mandar, help Trinia mount up, please. I will help Jayden."

The last thing I want is anymore help, Jayden thought.

Rolling back over, he saw Údar staring at him intently, fingers interlocked. "You wished for a woman."

It wasn't a question, Jayden knew. He had slipped up and wished for someone, which was what drew Baobhan Sith to people and how they lured them away. There was no bother denying it. "Yes."

Údar nodded. "There may be hope for you yet." He gave a somber smile. "Do not think I judge you, Jayden. You're not the only man who has wished for such things and found themselves trapped."

Jayden sat up slowly, pausing to let the world stop tilting from side to side. "You rescue them a lot?" he asked, glancing at the man.

"No," he replied, standing. "I was one who needed rescuing."

Údar offered him a hand, which he took, happy to be back on his feet. "Did they lure you too?"

Údar frowned, rubbing his hands. "Jayden, Ulscia herself was the one who tempted me, and as a younger man, I gave myself to her with abandon. It was why she never went beyond the bonding ritual."

Jayden couldn't quite believe what he was hearing. "Wait, wait, wait. You're saying you know Ulscia because you *slept* with her?"

"It's… complicated," said Údar, his face becoming more serious. "The reason I tell you is because the bonding ritual had started, so you are now more susceptible to their charms.

It will ever be a thorn in your side, and you must be on guard at all times."

Jayden rubbed the spot where the banshee had dragged her claw across him. *I don't know why I would want to relive that nightmare again,* he thought.

Placing a hand on his shoulder, Údar said, "I do not condemn you. In light of that, do not do it again."

CHAPTER 15

———

Trinia climbed onto the horse, settling in on the strange saddle. *How do people ride on these things?* she wondered. It was far smaller than what her people used, with no horn to grab onto if needed.

"Feel secure up there?" asked Mandar, sitting in front of the horse.

"We'll see when we get going," she replied, still adjusting. She looked up at him. "Why is the horse not afraid of you?"

Mandar's brows rose. "I spoke with her and told her to take care of you," he replied.

"The horse can talk?" she exclaimed, bending over, trying to see if its lips were moving.

Chuckling, Mandar replied, "Unless you are an animal, you won't hear anything."

She sat back up, disappointed. "Oh."

Footsteps came up the narrow path that led to the Baobhan Sith cave, and Jayden and Údar came into view. The first looked exhausted and was rubbing his chest she had helped bandage last night. The second had his usual stoic look. Údar helped Jayden mount his horse, handing him the reins once he said he was good.

Údar then mounted his horse and started off at an easy pace, which Trinia was grateful for. "I don't know if you can understand me," she whispered to her horse, "but I would like to avoid falling off."

The horse whinnied in response.

"So, care to tell us why you were late?" said Mandar, walking alongside his friend.

Jayden came abreast of her on the right, seemingly as eager as she was to know what had happened.

Údar sat straighter, cracking his neck before saying, "Salorim was attacked."

"What?" Trinia and Jayden said together.

He cast a glance back at them both. "It's nearly destroyed."

"Who would attack?" Mandar questioned. "It makes little sense."

Trinia saw the slight break in the hills up ahead Mandar had mentioned would lead to the road when they had talked last night. She pulled her hair in front of her, double-checking to make sure the illusion was still in place, and thankfully, it was.

"It was Thydu," Údar answered. "Though why they would attack is beyond me. In doing so, they have broken the peace treaty and Ungäar will retaliate with force. It will be war."

Trinia remembered back when she woke up on the edge of the forest, she had thought she was in Thydu. The kingdom had been the westernmost part of the Empire and, based on her father's spy reports, now boasted the most coveted horses in the all the kingdoms.

"Ungäar will not stand for war," said Jayden.

Údar reigned in his horse, turning it around and giving Jayden a keen look. "You know this for certain?"

Trinia's gaze shifted to Jayden, who avoided the look. "A guess," he replied.

Wheeling his horse back around, Údar continued toward the road. "We'll see when we speak with Arthfael. Won't we?"

There was not much talk after that, which provided Trinia with plenty of time to let her mind wander. It seemed so much had happened in such a short amount of time. She could hardly believe it. She still was uncertain of Údar and whether he would change his mind about not killing her to get back at her father. While her goal of stopping him was why she left, she didn't know if she wanted him dead.

As for the Voice, well, he could burn in every fiery hell there was for what he had been doing to her for years. She grimaced at the thought of him touching her and tried to think of something else, anything else, to get her mind off it.

Searching for something to think on, it seemed like a thousand and one ideas all flashed through her mind at once. There was the thought of her powers and what it meant to be the first to have such a Gift. There was the startling revelation that Elohai, the enemy of her people, was real. Which begged the question: were the other gods real? She had evidence for his existence, and nothing but stone statues for the others.

Then came whether her plan to rouse the kingdoms was a good idea, followed by wondering if Niren was alright. Did the horse she used make it back safely? And what of Ulscia? Would she show up again with a hoard of other monsters to get the blood she needed to create her own army of Baobhan Sith?

Trinia shook her head and rubbed her face. How much more difficult could it get?

Looking around, she noticed they were now on the road, which sloped down toward the south and their goal. Even from here, she could see a subtle difference in the colors—a shift from the dull grays and drab browns to autumn colors of oranges, reds, and yellows.

At least there's something to look forward to, she thought.

The hours passed, slowly melding into one day, and then another. On the third morning since leaving the cave, it started to drizzle, and by the following dawn it was a steady downpour. The only thing that lightened the sullen mood that had settled on them was when Mandar returned with a large buck for dinner.

Trinia awoke on the fifth day miserably wet and cold. Mandar had allowed her and Jayden to sleep against him for warmth, but now she smelled like wet dog, which soured her mood even further.

Údar, who she had not seen sleep since they left the cave, clapped his hands together, looking more cheerful than she had seen him to date. "Today, we make a hard push to reach Dorämund Mound. Then, it shall be warm beds and a hot bath for everyone."

Bath? Now that got her attention. It had been too long since she had properly bathed and it was beginning to show. Her hair was a ratty mess, dirt covered almost every inch of her, and the smell… she didn't want to think about it. "Can't we just do another cleanse thing?" she asked.

"The cleanse is for removing the taint of evil, not to make someone smell like roses," Údar replied, slightly irritated by the look of it.

"Is it far?" Jayden asked. He was leaning against one of the sparse trees they had used for shelter.

"About thirty miles," Údar responded, running a hand through his dampened hair. "We'll take it easy on the horses for a few miles. Then we'll ride hard until we get there. Let's go."

When Trinia remounted her horse, she realized how sore her backside was. *Hells below! I cannot wait to be off a horse!*

She managed to settle into a good pace behind Údar and Mandar, riding closely enough to Jayden to speak with him. "Can you tell me what Dorämund Mound is, exactly?"

Jayden shook the previous night's rain from his hair. "Well, it used to be a major city on your way up north to Thydu. They centered the city up atop a big hill that rises from the plains."

Trinia tilted her head. "They?"

"The Airgíd, back during the Empire," he replied, looking at her quizzically. "You don't know this?"

She bristled. "I'm not well-versed in every town the Airgíd ever conquered."

After he said nothing further, she sighed. "I'm sorry. What happened to the place?"

He stretched his neck and shoulders, wincing and placing a hand on his chest. "Fiery hells that hurts! Anyway, it was known for its gold and gems during the time of the Empire. Sometime after that, though, less and less gems were coming from the mines. Now, it's a town where the desperate go hoping to find a new vein of gold."

Trinia drilled him with a stare. Here was someone who looked the part of a thief, had a questionable morality, yet spoke like he knew the entire kingdom around him. "How do you know so much about everything?" she asked.

Jayden gave her a grin. "I like to read."

She narrowed her eyes. "I don't believe you."

He laughed and shrugged. "That's probably wise."

She was about to ask him what that meant when Údar called back to them. "We ride now! Yah!"

The rest of the morning and most of the afternoon was a blur of trees, rocks, hills, and even the occasional building that looked to be from the time of the Empire, broken and ruined.

Údar only allowed a couple of stops along the way to water the horses and give them an hour to rest. Then it was back at a full gallop until a dark lump rose from the flat landscape. Relief and a second wind took Trinia's hopes to new heights at the sight and the thought of a promised bath waiting for her there.

They were a mile out when Údar slowed his horse down and Trinia had to swerve around him. Wheeling back, she rode up to the group. "What is it? Why are we not still going?"

Údar cracked his neck again. "Because we can't go riding up to a city gate like a hoard of celnísh are following us," he replied. "We ride at an easy pace from here on out.

Trinia looked around, realizing she no longer saw Mandar. "Where is Mandar?" she asked.

"Making sure we're not being chased by a hoard of cel-nísh," Údar called over his shoulder. "We discussed it while you two were chatting this morning."

Trinia stuck out her tongue at his back, immediately feeling childish for doing so. She looked to see if Jayden had seen and found him with a lopsided grin on his face. *Hells below.* She gave a gentle nudge to her horse's ribs to get it going again, trying to not think about how stupid she had looked.

The rest of the ride was spent listening to Údar sing a song she had never heard of out of tune and in a language that sounded like complete gibberish. *Is this some form of torture?* she wondered.

"If he wanted to keep the monsters at bay, he should have started singing," said Jayden, keeping his voice low.

She snickered.

Mercifully, the ride to the gate was not long enough for Údar to start another song, and they hit the path leading up to the gates of the city. Broken down statues lined the way, all cut in half at the waist and toppled over. The top halves were nowhere to be seen.

Trinia tried to emulate Údar's relaxed posture in the saddle in the hopes she would blend in a little better. When they reached the gate, however, and she saw how short the citizens of the city were, she decided it wasn't going to matter much. From what she could tell, not a single person was over six foot. *I'm going to need to be extra careful here,* she thought.

It seemed to her the poor lived closer to the gates, with whole sections of the town being made up of shanties and makeshift homes. The streets were filthy even though they were made up of rough-hewn stones rather than dirt, and she wondered how much of it was mud. The farther in, the homes went from wood huts to impressive dwellings constructed from stone and far more opulent and grandiose. The strong always squeezed those they deemed beneath them until there was nothing left to squeeze. Like her father did with her people.

Moving through the crowds, Údar seemed at ease here, which surprised her. The man had been living in the forest for who knew how long, yet he blended into a crowd as if he were one of them.

Údar led them through several side streets, finally stopping in front of a weathered building with an engraved sign hanging above it that read, *The Gilded Girdle.* He hopped down off the horse, stretching his back before coming over to take the reins while she got down.

"Wrap your cloak around you to hide your leather jerkin," he whispered. "We don't want anyone asking questions."

She looked down, quickly pulling the edges of her cloak about her and glancing around to see if anyone had noticed.

"Where are we?" asked Jayden, walking stiffly over to them. "And how soon can we get a bath?"

Údar wrapped the reigns around the post, tying a loose knot. "This is an inn, and I used to know the owners."

Trinia gazed at the building doubtfully. *This is where we get a bath? The place looks like it's going to fall apart!*

Following Údar up the steps, she could only pray that the bath water would be clean.

CHAPTER 16

———

Trinia sank below the steaming water, relishing the warmth it brought to her bones. Resurfacing, she inhaled the flowery scent of lavender and some earthy aroma she could not place. *This is divine!* she thought, grabbing the soap and the soft-bristled scrub brush Matilda had brought her.

The innkeeper's portly wife was the sweetest person Trinia had met thus far and she liked her immediately. As she lathered up the brush and began scrubbing, her mind turned to a few hours ago when she had been shown to her room.

"Oh, you poor dear, traveling alone with those men! I know such occurrences happen, but it's not the place for a woman if you ask me," Matilda had said, bustling through the hall.

"It has been a challenge," Trinia agreed.

The woman turned and looked at her with a kindly smile. "Don't you worry, dear, we'll get you a proper hot bath soon enough. I'll even bring you some of my personal oils to help you feel more ladylike again."

Trinia returned the smile. "I would like that very much."

Matilda beamed and continued down the hall until she reached what would be Trinia's room and unlocked it, ushering her inside. "Now then, it will be a couple of hours to heat enough water for you all. Bless me, three baths to prepare!"

Trinia's eyes were on the bed, and thoughts of a good rest before a bath sounded more appealing by the second.

"... and I'll be needing your clothes, dear. You don't want to be walking around in dirty clothes after getting clean."

"What?" she asked. "My clothes?"

The woman nodded. "Mhmm, I'll be needing them to get them clean. Oh, you don't have to do it now! I'll collect them when I come back with the water for the bath."

Matilda left without another word, humming to herself as she went.

Trinia smiled again, humming the same tune and adding her own twist to it when she forgot the rest. Putting a foot up on the end to the small tub, she inspected the blisters from her boots she had received during all the walking and running. Most were already healing up nicely while one or two smaller ones were still tender to the touch. *I'm going to need new boots or some sort of stocking.*

With the brush lathered, and her leg up out of the water, she went to work ruthlessly scrubbing to get the caked dirt off. Once finished, she went to the next leg and then her arms, body, face, finally finishing with her hair. It was hard to tell just how dirty it was since it was not its natural color, but she made do.

When she had finally gotten every particle of dirt she could see, she climbed out, wrapping the towel that had been provided around her, and sat down in front of the fire. Trinia ran her fingers through her hair to detangle it as best she could. *I may need to trim it a little. This will not be practical as we travel,* she thought. A couple of inches to make it shoulder length would probably be best.

Trinia caught sight of her leather jerkin sticking out from under the bed where she had hidden it. Getting up, she gave it a nudge with her foot, pushing it farther back and out of sight.

There was a soft knock at the door. "Are you decent, dear?"

Moving back to the fire and sitting in the chair, Trinia answered back, "Yes. Come in."

The woman stepped in with a bundle of clothing in her hands Trinia didn't recognize, a hairbrush, and some bread. Setting everything down on the bed, Matilda grabbed the brush and walked over behind her. Trinia turned to see what she was doing.

"Don't fret, but your hair is a mess! Even adventuring ladies need to feel like ladies," said the woman, reaching to grab a handful of hair.

Trinia jumped up, shaking her head. "That's unnecessary. It will be fine, I'm sure."

Matilda put her hands on her hips, giving her a stern look. "It is quite necessary, dear, so sit your rump down in this chair."

Trinia's palms started to itch, and she got the feeling the woman would not relent. *I do not want to be touched,* she thought.

Matilda came around the chair and stood in front of her, and Trinia suddenly felt very tall in comparison. The woman was a good head shorter, but her boisterous presence certainly made up the difference. "Listen, I promise you will not feel a single tug or pull as I work out those knots." She smiled and guided Trinia back to the chair. "You'll see."

Trinia tensed a little at the woman's touch and sat down, the itching in her palms increasing. She worked to keep her breathing in check, trying to remain calm as Matilda went to work on her hair. Soon, the woman began to hum the same tune as she had when they first met. The rise and falls of the tune seemed to work their way into Trinia's tense muscles, relaxing them and putting them at ease.

Soon, she found herself humming along with the woman, eyes closed, and feeling a sense of peace she had never known before. And true to her word, Matilda finished brushing without Trinia feeling a single tug. "Well now, you look like a proper lady again."

Doubtful, Trinia thought, but she smiled at her. "Thank you. May I ask, what song were you humming?"

Matilda busied herself with pulling loose hairs out of the brush and throwing them into the fire. "Oh, just a little song I learned as a child," she said. "Nothing the bards would sing of, I will tell you that."

"Would you sing it for me?" Trinia asked. "I'm no bard, and the tune is beautiful."

The woman blushed. "Well, I suppose I could do my best. Forgive me. I am a bit out of practice, dear."

Trinia pulled her hair over her shoulder, her fingers weaving it together. "I don't mind."

That seemed to please her. Matilda drew herself up, clearing her throat, and sang:

Though through shadows dark I go
And fears assail me on every side
I will rest in Your Power and Might
There You will cast out every fear and fright
Though darkness overwhelms me
And threaten to snuff out my life
I shall cling fast to Your love
And the day You make everything right.

The words struck something deep in her soul, a place that ached to be loved like that. Trinia clapped. "That was worthy of the bards."

Matilda's blush deepened, and she waved a hand. "You're too kind, dear. Now then, the man you came with sent those new clothes for you and said to tell you to rest. As for me, can I get you anything else?"

Trinia cast a quick glance at the clothes. *Údar got me clothing?* She turned her attention back to the woman and said, "Do you have any shears? I want to trim my hair a little."

The woman's eyes twinkled. "I do indeed. Would you like some help with it?"

Smiling, Trinia nodded. "Yes, I think I would."

-II-

Údar took off his cloak, hanging it on the peg near the door as Fergus and Aiden, the innkeeper's sons, dumped the boiling water into the two tubs that had been brought in. He unhooked the sword belt at his waist, rolling it around the sheath, and laid it on the bed.

"That should do ya," said Aiden, the older of the two. "Call for anythin' ya need."

"Thank you," Údar replied, clasping the young man's forearm.

Jayden lay on his bed staring at the ceiling when Údar turned around and sat on a chair, pulling off his boots. *It's been too long since I've had a hot bath,* he thought. The stream nearby the cabin in the forest was bitterly cold, even during the summer, so this would be a treat indeed.

The two tubs took up most of the small room, and given that it was the only one in the inn with two beds, it would have to do. Between the rooms, the baths, the food, and the clothes for Trinia so she would look like a native to Ungäar, he was running out of coin. He would need to figure something out later. For now, he would enjoy the reprieve.

He also wanted to make a stop since they were here to check on someone he had not seen in a long time. Hopefully, she had stayed out of trouble.

Údar stood and removed his shirt and breeches, revealing a latticework of scars. His back, chest, and arms, each covered with scars, some more faded than others, but still there. Each served as a testament to what he had survived over the years. Slipping into the steaming water, he closed his eyes and sighed in contentment. *Nothing like a bath to make you feel human again*, he thought.

He heard Jayden getting his clothes off and walking over to his own tub. "Údar, did you know you have a cut on your side?"

"Yes, what of it?"

"Doesn't it hurt in the water?" Jayden asked. "Ouch! Hells, it boiling!"

"Language, lad," Údar replied. "And no, I'm accustomed to pain. Besides, the oils in here will help clean it."

They sat quietly for several minutes before Jayden's curiosity apparently grew to be too much for him. "How old are you, Údar? Mandar mentioned you've been here a long time, and there's that little detail of you sleeping with Ulscia and being the one to imprison her."

Údar grunted. "Mandar says a good many things."

"You didn't answer the question. Are you really the man legends speak of?" Jayden pressed.

He sighed, looking at the boy. "You will not let me enjoy some deserved peace. Will you?"

Jayden frowned. "You managed to fight off a horde of celnísh, slept with the Queen of the Baobhan Sith, you live alone with a talking wolf, and are a literal legend. Do you really expect me to not have questions?"

"Do you really wish to know?" Údar asked, splashing some water on his face.

"Yes!"

"No." Údar laid his head on the back of the tub.

"Look, I'm having a hard time wrapping my mind around events here, and since the cave I've had plenty of time to think about things."

Likely your first mistake, Údar thought.

He pinched the bridge of his nose, trying to calm down before he said something he would regret. Or before he shoved Jayden under the water and held him there. "I've seen the ages of this world come and go. I have loved women, killed men, watched war tear the foundations of the world to splinters and ash! I am old beyond reckoning, sustained only by the good pleasure of Elohai until I fulfill my quest." He paused, looking at him. "So there, now you know, Jayden, son of Arthfael, Crown Prince of Ungäar. *Now* may I have some peace and quiet?"

Jayden looked dumbfounded. "How do you know who I am? I've kept that bit of information about myself hidden away, and for good reason. There is no way you could have known who I was!"

"Oh, I didn't know at first," he admitted. "But when you started blathering on to the girl about this city and showing off your keen knowledge of Ungäar, well, things started to make more sense."

Údar splashed more water on his face and scrubbed his body, careful to not scrub over the cut on his side as he ordered his thoughts. While Jayden was correct, he lived alone with a talking wolf, it didn't mean he was out of touch with the outside world. He had resources even Mandar was not aware of. *Most are probably long dead by now*, he realized.

"Údar, I need to know what you are going to do with this information," Jayden said after several minutes.

He looked at Jayden. "I'm not going to do anything because it is not my business to reveal. It's yours, and seeing as we are heading to Tranâes to speak to your father, I would suggest you tell a certain someone before we get there."

Jayden averted his gaze, staring into the water in his tub. "I know. I've thought about it. If it were up to me, I would not even be going back there, but I'm bound by my life-debt to her."

"A life-debt?" Údar asked, raising a brow. "To an Airgíd?"

The boy nodded, half-heartedly beginning to scrub himself down. "She saved my life by sacrificing a duplicate. It was an accident according to her, but I still owe her my life."

How interesting. "And why does a Crown Prince wish to not return home?"

Jayden grimaced. "Because despite what everyone thinks, I am no ruler. My father sent me off to the Academy when I was sixteen and not long after I arrived, a few months perhaps, I faked my death."

"Seems a bit extreme, lad." Having cleaned up and resigned himself to not getting the peace he had hoped for, Údar climbed out of the tub and grabbed a towel.

Turning back to Jayden, he said, "I don't know what demons you left there, but I suggest you prepare to face them."

The young prince looked distraught at the thought. Not waiting for a reply, Údar placed a hand on Jayden's head, shoving him down under the water before walking away. A satisfying grin tugged at his lips as Jayden came up sputtering water and curses.

"Language, lad."

CHAPTER 17

———

Trinia awoke the following morning before the sun rose, unable to fall back asleep. Thoughts plagued her constantly, and her dreams were troubled. It did not help she couldn't remember them, only their echo.

I may as well get dressed. Údar will probably want to leave soon, she thought. She did not want to leave the comfort of the bed, nor the shelter of the room, which provided at least some warmth. Sighing, she rolled out of bed and looked over the clothes Údar had sent for her.

There was a new shirt, dark brown with long sleeves, light brown breeches, and a new pair of boots that Matilda had brought, apologizing for forgetting them earlier. To finish it, her midnight blue cloak, now clean and dried.

Trinia slid into the shirt, which hung down to her knees. *This is how they were shirts here?* she wondered. She put on the pants, finding them a better fit than she had expected, and then grabbed the belt and wrapped it around her waist. The buckle looked like polished bronze, but she couldn't be sure.

Once that was secure, she tried one of the boots on, finding it lined with soft leather that felt heavenly compared to her old ones. *I may not even need stockings with this*, she thought. Sticking her foot into the other, she felt something in it, and upon pulling it out, found a pair of wool stockings. *So much for that. At least my feet will be warm.*

Leaning over, Trinia pulled out her leather jerkin and slipped it over her head, getting it into place before cinching the straps down on the sides so it would stay in place. She frowned, realizing the only thing missing was a weapon. *I'm going to need to get some new daggers soon,* she thought.

She tossed the cloak about her shoulders and pinned it in place with her silver broach. Her hands stopped. *I forgot to take this off when I gave it to Matilda!* Would the woman know what it was? Maybe it would not matter since they were leaving anyway.

She gave a quick look around the room to make sure she hadn't missed anything, checked the illusion on her hair, and headed downstairs to meet up with Údar and Jayden. She found them sitting at a table in the corner. "Good morning," she said, joining them.

"Morning," said Jayden. He looked like he had not slept well at all.

"I trust Matilda took good care of you," said Údar, taking a bite of food.

Trinia nodded. "Yes and thank you for the new clothes."

He gave her a nod, taking a sip of a steaming drink.

She looked at the food laid out on the table. "What is all of this?" It all looked and smelled amazing, but there were several items she was not familiar with.

Údar handed her an empty plate and went about explaining what everything was. "We have a hash, eggs, bacon, and these." He motioned to what looked like fluffy round discs.

"What are they?"

He finished chewing before replying, giving a small smile. "Pancakes."

She cast a doubtful glance at them. *I suppose they must be good if it puts a smile on his face.* "I'll take some."

Údar spread some butter on two of the discs, set them on her plate, and drizzled an amber liquid on top. "Matilda makes the best in the kingdom, so I've been told."

Trinia cut a chunk off and took a bite, finding the fluffy texture was not unpleasant, and the flavor had a hint of vanilla to it, making it almost irresistible. She took another bite, and then another.

Jayden wore a slight smirk. "Good?"

Trinia grinned. "Dis is amazen," she said with a mouthful. She turned her eyes to the remaining pancakes. "May I?"

"Be my guest. I've had plenty," Údar replied.

"Help yourself," said Jayden. His mood seemed to brighten a little bit.

I can't believe how delicious these are! she thought, quickly polishing off her plate and grabbing more. By the time she had finished, she had eaten eight of them in total and felt as if she would burst—partially from eating more than she'd had in the past few days but also from how happy they seemed to make her. "Can we take some with us?"

Údar took a long sip from the steaming mug. "No, they do not keep well."

She frowned and then looked at the liquid in his mug. It seemed black as a starless night. "What is that?" she asked.

"Coffee," he said, taking another sip. "Want to try a taste?"

Trinia looked at it again. *It smells good.* "I suppose."

He grabbed her a cup and poured a little from a metal pitcher on the table, handing it to her. Taking the steaming cup in her hands, she smelled it again, enjoying the rich scent.

She took a careful sip, almost spitting it back out. Swallowing, she coughed and set it down. "This is awful!" she exclaimed.

Jayden laughed. "It's an acquired taste, to be sure."

Trinia grabbed another pancake, taking bites in the hopes it would rid the bitter taste from her mouth. *Hells, people enjoy this kind of drink?*

Údar finished his mug and leaned back in his chair. "I need to make a stop before we leave. There is someone I need to see."

After finishing up their meal, Údar led the way across the city and into an area that looked to be where markets would be held during the spring and summer. The road opened to a square brimming with activity at every shop Trinia could see. People were selling tools, farm equipment, feed, seeds, and animals. Farther down were blacksmiths forging weapons and haggling prices with people unwilling to pay full price.

Pushing through the streets, she followed Údar and Jayden through the door of a candlemaker. All the different smells nearly overwhelmed her senses, and she had a hard time breathing. *Sweet Vyrni! How do they work in here?*

Údar walked up to a man Trinia assumed was the owner, asking, "I'm looking for someone, a X'phosian girl. She used to work here a few years back."

The owner shook his head, scratching at his patchy beard. "Don't recall anyone workin' here but me."

"She did work here. I know that much because I set her up with the job," Údar replied.

Trinia leaned forward, whispering to Jayden, "I thought he has been living in the forest all this time?"

Jayden shrugged.

"Don't know of any Iomlíad girl workin' here," said the owner adamantly.

From where she stood, Trinia could see Údar's shoulders tense. "I never said she was an Iomlíad." He grabbed the owner by the shirt, slamming him to the wall. "Where is she?" he growled.

"I–I sold her to make ends m–meet," said the terrified man. "Times were hard and I know some fellas who were lookin' for a girl."

Trinia gasped. *This isn't going to be good.*

Údar swore and dropped the man, storming out of the shop past her. She followed him outside, Jayden close behind her, and she hurried to catch up with him. "Údar, what are you doing? Aren't we leaving?"

"Not yet," he replied, "not until I get her out of there."

Trinia glanced at Jayden worriedly. She had seen the look in Údar's eye. It was the same one he'd had when trying to kill her.

The wind started picking up and gray clouds were forming to the north, promising rain. If they did not leave soon, they would be in the middle of a storm.

As they weaved through the crowds, most people moved out of Údar's way, and Trinia felt like she should apologize to those who hadn't as he shoved them aside. It was not long before the buildings morphed from beautiful stone to rough and wooden, with many ladies standing on the corners with lifeless eyes. Some were barely clothed.

Údar stopped and asked after the girl, describing her: a little over five-foot, skin like amber, brownish hair, light brown eyes. From what Trinia could see, there were women of all sorts, some even looking to be her age, many matching the description in some way. *Are they all X'phosian?* she wondered.

Apparently, one of the girls knew the one he was looking for and took Údar's hand, leading him. If Trinia had to guess, the girl was no more than ten. *I'm going to be sick,* she thought, fighting down the bile rising in her throat. She turned to Jayden, surprised to see a burning fury in his eyes. "How could someone ever do to this to a child?" she whispered.

He shook his head, wiping a tear from his eyes. "Because some men are nothing more than animals. Cruel, vicious animals."

That was all too true in her experience with the Voice, an Airgíd who had positioned himself in a seat of power and had her father's ear. And his daughter's virginity. The girl now leading them had likely never known a life outside of the hell she was in. Tears filled Trinia's eyes. *Vyrni, protect this girl.*

"How can your god allow such things to happen?" she asked quietly.

Jayden swallowed hard, his eyes fixed on the girl. "I don't know."

The girl leading them stopped, pointing to a small structure up ahead. "There," she said, looking up at Údar. "She there."

He knelt in the muck, hugging the little girl. "Thank you, little one. May I give you a gift?"

Her eyes lit up, and she smiled, revealing her missing teeth. "Gift!"

Trinia watched as Údar's hand lit with the white fire and he drew a circle on the ground, like he had at the cabin and again after the battle at the cave. The girl watched in awe and jumped into it without invitation, squealing with joy. *He's cleaning her? What good will that do for her?*

A moment later, the girl appeared again, smiling and laughing, and no cleaner than she had been. But something was different about her. Trinia could see it. A light shone in her eyes that had not been there before... nor had the symbol over the girl's heart—a red circle with a white flame in the middle.

"The mark of Elohai," Jayden whispered in awe.

Trinia looked at him and then at the girl. "You mean she follows him? But why? What good has he ever done her?"

"Gift!" the little girl repeated.

Údar nodded, his features unusually soft. "Yes, dear one. Gift. Share it."

"Share!" yelled the girl, taking off back the way they had come. "Gift! Share!"

Trinia watched her go, more confused than ever. *How is knowing him a gift? Nothing has changed for her!* She turned to Údar, who was leaning heavily against a wall, his eyes on the retreating form of their guide. "What just happened?"

His gaze shifted to hers. "Hope was born," he replied.

"Hope?" Trinia asked, motioning around them. "What hope does she have here? Why not just set her free, give her money to leave this place, or better yet, find her parents!"

Údar shook his head. "You would not understand."

She could feel her emotions rising as her hands shook and her palms itched. It all hit too close to home. "She deserves justice!" she said, her voice shaking.

When he met her gaze again, something shone in them she could not put her finger on. "Oh, the girl will have justice. I almost pity the souls upon whom justice will be poured," he said. "It would be better they had never been born."

The conviction in his tone gave Trinia pause, and she found herself unsure of how to respond. Did he mean that Elohai would bring justice, or would it come about a different way? She wanted answers. For the girl. For herself.

Údar gathered himself again, crossed the muddy path to the structure that had been pointed out, and kicked in the door without so much as a knock. There were shouts, and both she and Jayden remained outside, glancing nervously around as several people walked up, drawn by the commotion. *He's not one for subtly*, she thought.

Suddenly, a body came flying through one of the shuttered windows, landing face down in the muck, quickly followed by another who landed on top of the first. Údar came out, delivering a brutal kick to the face of the second and one to the ribs of the other. "I swear by Elohai above, if I ever see your faces again, mine shall be the last *you* ever see," he shouted.

Both men lay groaning in the mud while Údar swept his gaze around the crowd. Those gathered must have decided it was not worth the crazed man's wrath and dispersed as quickly as they had come.

Údar marched back into the building, returning a few minutes later with a young woman cradled in his arms who matched the description he'd given. She looked pale and seemed to be asleep. Trinia noticed a brand on the girls left shoulder in the shape of a sun and a tattoo below it in a language she didn't recognize.

"Let's go," he said, walking past them.

Trinia exchanged a look with Jayden who shrugged. He was just as lost as she was about this whole matter apparently. The only thing she felt for certain, was that they would not be leaving anytime soon.

CHAPTER 18

———

Walking back through the streets, past the many women and young girls, Trinia could almost feel the hopelessness as a physical force around her, suffocating her. She tried not to meet their gazes, unable to bear the knowledge she could do nothing to help them.

Beside her, Jayden seemed to have the same conflict, and it showed in his features—jaw clenched, brows furrowed, eyes set on the ground at his feet. Trinia pondered what was running through his mind and if she could say anything to help.

Shifting her gaze to Údar's back, she wondered what was so special about this young woman to warrant his intervention, yet a little girl he would let fend for herself. *It's not fair.*

Údar led them back to *The Gilded Girdle,* and as soon as Matilda saw the girl in his arms Trinia thought she might faint.

"Oh, the poor dear!" the woman exclaimed. "Let me get you another room to lay her down in. Hold on but a moment."

Barra, the innkeeper, stepped out from the kitchen area twirling his bushy mustache. "Aye, what be goin' on 'ere?" he asked, eyeing Údar.

"We lodged here last night," said Údar, "and a friend of mine has suffered an overdose of *lynsium*. Matilda is arranging a room for us."

The man nodded, wiping his hands on his apron. "Fine, fine. Will ye be needin' more than one room, then?"

"Yes," said Jayden, stepping forward and placing two gold coins on the counter. "That should cover several days."

Barra's eyes lit up and his smile disappeared under his thick mustache. "Aye, that it will," he replied.

Trinia looked at Jayden as he stepped back, as did Údar. He glanced her. "It's a long story, but I felt I needed to help."

She smiled. After seeing the women trapped in a cycle of horror, it was nice to have a little glimmer of kindness.

Matilda returned, motioning them to follow her to the room she had prepared. "Come now, we need to get her in a bed and some new clothes. Tsk tsk, look at these rags she's in! She would catch her death out there!"

The room was larger than the one Trinia had been in and had roughly the same look to it. A bed was set in the corner, a small table with a chair next to it, a hearth for warmth, and a privy for doing one's business.

Údar laid the girl on the bed and turned to Matilda. "I need some lavender, sage, and *rhyllic* brewed in a tea, can you do that for me?"

"Of course, dear, I shall be back as soon as I can," she replied. Matilda hurried from the room, her voice echoing down the hall, "Oh, the poor dear."

Trinia looked at Údar, arms folded. "How is tea going to help?" she asked. "And what is *rhyllic*?"

Údar stooped, fire bursting to life in his hand as he drew another circle on the floor. "*Rhyllic* is an herb that grows in the mountains throughout Ungäar, and it won't help her in her current state." He glanced up at her. "I had to get Matilda out of here so I could do this."

As the white flames grew upward, Jayden moved to close the door while Údar picked the young woman back up. He looked at Trinia again, and she could see the worry etched into his face. "Pray," he said and stepped in.

Pray? To whom? she wondered. *What was the point?*

The minutes crawled by and Trinia paced back and forth in front of the wall of flames. A couple of times she had reached out to touch it, feeling the gentle heat radiating off it, still trying to wrap her mind around a fire that didn't burn anything.

Údar finally stepped back out, the X'phosian still in his arms, and the fire extinguished in an instant. He laid her back down on the bed, sitting heavily on the end and sweating profusely. "She'll live," he said, wiping his face. "She consumed more than I thought, and it was a fight to keep her with us. But she should wake in a few hours."

"What's her name?" asked Trinia. "You never mentioned it, and I was wondering why?"

Údar leaned back against the wall, closing his eyes. "Her name is Batänny. She's from X'phos and she is an Iomlíad, or Shifter." He opened his eyes, looking at the young woman, and Trinia followed his gaze. "I rescued her about six years ago from slavers when I came here to get some supplies."

"I thought you've been living in the forest all this time?" said Jayden.

"I never said I didn't venture out from there," Údar replied, looking his way. "Did I?"

Trinia pulled out the chair from by the table and sat down. "How old was she? When you rescued her, I mean."

Údar thought about it a moment. "I suspect fourteen or so."

Younger than me, Trinia thought, staring at the young woman's face. *At that time at least. She would be a little older than Jayden now.*

Matilda returned bearing tea, dark brown bread, and a wedge of cheese, setting them down on the table with Trinia's help.

"Compliments of the house," she said. "I spoke with my husband and he said you've already paid for the rooms, but it will be a moment before one is ready for you. Will that be alright?"

Jayden nodded. "I paid for the rooms, and we don't mind the wait. Your hospitality has been above and beyond. We are most thankful."

The woman brightened up and left with a pep in her step. Trinia smiled at Jayden, who returned it in kind. *I think he's a better person than he lets himself believe,* she thought.

She turned her attention back to Údar and saw he was asleep. *I guess that's all the information we're going to get. Now we wait.*

-II-

The day crept by, and as it did, Trinia's anxiety increased. They still had to travel another seven hundred miles to reach Tranâes, and it was already the middle of September. At this rate, they wouldn't arrive until November, and that was barring any further obstacles. Which meant they would not launch an army against her father until spring. *Will it be too late by then?* she wondered. Even without her, her father had resources to pull from, ways of getting people to do what he wanted, when he wanted.

Her mind went to the bargain she had made with Údar. She hated her father, that was not in question. There was no doubt Údar could take on her father after seeing his power displayed again and again, but was that was *she* wanted? After all the beatings, belittling, and apathy she has received from her father over the years, was there anything there to be salvaged?

Trinia sighed in frustration, her forehead resting against the table. Something about seeing all the women and young girls on the corners had stirred up a bitterness in her, a feeling of loathing for all who could treat someone like an object. She harbored a flickering hate toward the Voice for everything he had taken from her, over and over again. If anyone deserved to die as punishment, it was him, and should she get the chance, she would not hesitate to slit his throat.

A soft moan interrupted her thoughts and Trinia lifted her head. Batänny stirred. "Ohhh, my head."

Údar snapped awake, searching around until his gaze settled on the young woman. "Can you hear me?" he asked, leaning forward.

"Unfortunately," Batänny replied, groaning again. "Et-delf."

"A simply thank you will suffice, Batänny," said Údar curtly. "This is now the second time I've had to save you."

"Údar?" Batänny lifted her head and cracked an eye open. "Plagues, it is you."

Not exactly a warm welcome, thought Trinia. *Especially since we went out of our way to get her.*

Údar met Trinia's gaze with a wry smile, seeming to read her mind. "*Lynsium* makes Iomlíad more irritable and seeing as she's coming down off an almost lethal dose, she'll be insufferable for a time."

"Et-dian nos," Batänny grumbled.

"What did she say?" Trinia asked.

Údar chuckled. "Nothing repeatable, I assure you." He stood, stretching his back and wincing. "Ah, forgot about that cut."

"Baby," said Batänny, opening an eye again.

Trinia looked at Údar, shaking her head. "You have the strangest relationships with people."

The young woman slowly twisted around to look at her and then Jayden. "Who are they?"

"This is Trinia and Jayden. They are traveling with me for a time," said Údar, grabbing some cheese and bread from the table and taking a bite.

"Traveling, eh?" said Batänny, trying to sit up in the bed. "I'll come with you."

Údar choked on the bread and Trinia handed him a cup of the now cold tea. He downed it in a flash. When he recovered, he waved his hand. "Oh no! No! Absolutely not!" he wheezed.

Trinia didn't exactly like the idea of adding someone else either. It was bad enough Jayden felt like he was forced into going along because he owed her some sort of life-debt.

Batänny managed to sit all the way up and propped herself in the corner, an effort that seemed to exhaust her. "Why not?" she asked.

"We don't have enough horses," Údar said, and even Trinia thought that was a poor excuse. "I plan on getting you set up with Matilda or some other trustworthy person so you can make a living."

Batänny frowned, tucking her arms close to her body. "Because that worked the last time? The candlemaker sold me two years ago, Údar. Do you think I would try to kill myself if I could have escaped?"

Trinia felt her stomach drop, and she could see by the look on Údar's face her words pained him. She even found herself agreeing with the Shifter. To what purpose would setting her up be if people in the city already knew what she was?

"They'll come back for me if I stay here, you know that," Batänny said, eyes narrowed, her tone accusatory. "Besides, this girl traveling with you could use some feminine company. I can't imagine how she's managed to put up with you for any length of time."

Trinia stifled a laugh, hiding a smile with her hand. She had a sneaking feeling it wasn't the drug talking. Rather, this was just Batänny's personality.

"It's not that simple," said Údar, setting the bread down.

"And why not?" asked Jayden from his place by the door. "Are we to do nothing? Just leave and go our way while she tries to not get sold again?" He walked over and jabbed his finger into the older man's chest. "Is that what your wife and daughter would want?"

Trinia's eyes widened. *Uh oh, that was too far.*

Údar grabbed Jayden's finger and wrenched it to the side with a slight *pop*, dropping him to his knees with a gasp. "Don't you ever bring them into discussion," he rumbled. He let go when Jayden gave a nod. "It's not broken, just out of joint."

"What gives you the right to make choices for other people?" Trinia asked, rising from the chair.

He stalked up to her, glowering. "You wanted my help, remember? We made a bargain."

Trinia lifted her chin. "Then I take back my offer."

Údar huffed. "Fine, I don't need your help anyway! I'll leave you here and head to Rionnagan to finish what I started."

From the corner of Trinia's vision, she could see Batänny looking between the two of them. "Wait, who are you killing?"

Trinia clenched her fists to stop the trembling. If she broke the bargain, it might mean he would try to kill her again right here, but in this case, she held the cards. She put on an air of confidence and smirked. "You may be powerful *Green Cloak,* but you're not powerful enough to take on the entire city by yourself."

She saw the defeat in his eyes. He didn't have to say a word. "Your friend comes with us and I keep up my end of the bargain," she continued.

Údar looked as if he would erupt. His brows were pinched together, darkening his already stormy gray eyes, and his mouth was turned down in a mix between a grimace and a snarl. "So be it." He turned and walked out of the room.

Trinia breathed a sigh of relief. She had done the right thing. Right?

Jayden stood and she watched him pop his finger back into joint. The sound alone was enough to make her want to gag, and he looked awfully pale. He met her gaze, giving that crooked smile of his. "Nice work."

She felt her cheeks warm, so she turned to Batänny on the bed, who stared at her with an odd expression. "What?" Trinia asked.

"Nothing, it's just that… no one has ever stood up for me like that before," she replied. "Thank you."

Trinia smiled and gave a nod. As she grabbed the plates of food and handed them to Batänny, she realized it was the first time she had ever stood up to a man over something. Especially a powerful one. *Maybe I do have what it takes to stop my father.*

CHAPTER 19

The girl had bested him.

Not that he didn't care about Batänny's well-being, he did. But throwing her into the mix would bring problems he did not want to deal with. It was bad enough putting up with the other two.

Údar sat in his room, running his hands through his hair. He should have checked in sooner. Should have stressed to her to not use her abilities under any circumstances.

What gives you the right to make choices for other people? Trinia's words reverberated in his mind.

Bah! She is young, naïve, and has no idea of how the world works. What has she gone through, hmm?

Sighing, he recalled when he had rescued Batänny the first time somewhere near the town of Haeding to the south. She was sassing the slavers and giving them quite the verbal lashing. After beating the men, he'd brought her here to The Mound, thinking if she could establish a life here, she could escape. Yet, it seemed it was short lived.

How much worse was it that it drove her to suicide? he wondered. *Have I become so hard-hearted?*

The thought did not sit well with him and he decided to go to sleep even though it was only late afternoon. The cleansing had worked to remove most of the drugs from her system, but when she started fading, he had worked to absorb the rest into himself, which was considerably draining, and not something he wanted to do. But it was either that or watch her die, and he couldn't stomach the latter.

Lying back on the bed, he closed his eyes, letting his mind wander until he finally drifted off to sleep.

-II-

A gentle breeze picked up around him, not cold as it should be in September, but warm. Just breathing it in warmed his chilled limbs. The presence he felt beside him seemed to emanate that same enthusiasm. Údar opened his eyes and saw a summer sun blazing its way across the sapphire sky. He recognized the grove surrounded by fir trees and the smell of sap and pollen. It was where he and his wife went when they wanted time together.

Glancing toward the presence, he nearly fell over when he saw his wife sitting beside him.

"Hello, Údar," she said, a tender smile on her lips.

He froze, his heart twisting in his chest. *It can't be her... It's a trick!* It was her, though. He could feel it in his heart of hearts. She had her long brown hair tied in its typical bun at the back of her neck, and her brown eyes looked over him worriedly.

She reached out, slowly caressing his face, her hand warm against his skin. "You've new burdens, I see."

Rubbing his eyes to make sure they were not deceiving him, he looked again to see her still sitting there beside him. "Nisha?"

Nisha flashed a smile and leaned in, kissing him on the cheek. Her lips were just as soft as he remembered them. "Yes, it is me," she said.

Údar's heart felt as though it would burst! Hopping up, he pulled her into his arms, swinging her around as she screamed in surprise, falling into laughter. "I cannot believe it! Nisha!" He stopped and set her down, studying her, unable to comprehend what he was seeing.

She looked at him, tenderly taking his hands in hers. "Elohai has allowed me to see you for a time, my love. He thought I might talk some sense into you."

Údar stepped back as if burned. "Elohai sent you?" Anger boiled up in his chest. "Does he seek to mock my pain that I should have to lose you twice?"

Nisha tsked, frowning. "Stubborn man. You should know him better than that. If not for you, I would not have known him, nor would our daughter."

The mention of Lyniel sent a shaft of pain straight through him, dropping him to his knees. "Our daughter... she is with you?" he asked, his voice barely a whisper.

Nisha's face softened, and she knelt in front of him. "She is with Elohai even now, telling him of all the adventures you told her when she was young." She smiled. "He never tires of hearing them."

There was no holding back the tears now. All the years of pain and grief boiled over inside him, refusing to remain hidden away and forgotten. He crumpled to the ground, his head lying in his wife's lap, his tears flowing unimpeded.

"Shh," she soothed, running her fingers through his hair. "We are safe. Be at peace."

How could he possibly be at peace without them in his life? What joy was there apart from them?

It seemed strange how his sorrow contrasted with the bright sky above and the soft caress of his beloved. Both were warm and bright while he was cold and dark—a wraith. The shadows called to him like a siren's song, beckoning him back to their melancholy embrace and away from the light and the pain.

"Údar."

He opened his bleary eyes, working to calm his body down, and sat up, meeting his wife's loving gaze. The passion in it was undeniable. "Yes?"

Nisha tilted her head. "Why do you still mourn? Why do you hate?"

The question was ridiculous. She knew why! He wiped his eyes with his sleeve. "You were taken as punishment for—"

"Don't you dare!" she warned, holding up a finger. "You and I both know it was not a punishment, so you have no excuse to hate Elohai, nor the one who took our lives."

Údar got up and started to pace, rubbing his chest. It felt like his heart was being torn in two all over again. "How can you say such a thing?" he asked. "I have every right to hate them!"

Standing slowly and brushing off her purple linen dress, Nisha shook her head. "What was it you taught us? Love thy neighbor?"

He winced. She would bring that up. "This is different."

She crossed her arms and raised a brow, waiting for him to give his reasoning. It was something she had done when she knew he didn't have one, and it frustrated him to no end. He exhaled. "They took you from me."

"I am here, am I not?" She drifted toward him, taking his hand. "Am I not?"

The pain built inside his chest. "Yes and no," he replied. "Yes, you are here now, yet you will not be in the morning."

Nisha smiled at him in that way of hers, placing her hand over his heart. "Am I not *here*?"

His heart beat faster as he caught the meaning. He placed his hand over hers, whispering, "Always."

She nodded. "So, if I am here with you, how much more will Elohai be with you? If you let yourself be ruled by hate, there is no room for either of us in your heart."

Her words pained him. In feeding his hate, had he blocked out everything else, including the one he loved most? She always had the ability to see to the heart of the matter, even when he could not. It was one of the many reasons he loved her. "I…I don't know how to let go," he admitted. "I've grown accustomed to the shadows and nursing my wounds."

Nisha chuckled. "Then let in the light. Let others in and stop trying to keep them at arm's length." She turned and gazed off into the distance, somewhere beyond the grove. "A girl needs you, Údar. And, in some way, you need her, too. She is the catalyst that will set your foot upon the path which leads you to the end of your journey."

He followed her gaze for a moment and then turned back to her. "You know this?"

"Her road is dark, and many choices lay before her," Nisha continued. Her eyes met his. "You are no different. Your greatest trials await you, my love."

"Not a cheery thought," he said, looking at the ground. "Anything else?"

"Yes," she said, waiting until he met her gaze again. "Stop being so cantankerous."

Údar threw his head back and laughed. "You know me too well."

"Of course I do. I'm your wife." She beamed up at him.

Gazing down into her eyes, he could almost believe…no, he would not dwell on it. He would enjoy this moment with her, this gift. "How much time do we have left?"

"Until I am ready to return," she replied, teasingly.

"Ah, is that so," he said, brushing her curls back from her face.

She nuzzled his hand, closing her eyes. "Let us talk of happier things," she whispered.

-II-

Údar's eyes opened to see the stars through the window of the room. The ache in his chest was still there, like a raw wound that had not yet healed. Taking a shuddering breath, he relived the hours he had spent with Nisha, her touch, her smell.

"Not a dream," he whispered to himself. It had been a vision, a very real experience that went beyond words. "Thank you."

Rolling off the bed, he looked to see the fire had been lit and Jayden slept in the chair by it. He got up and nudged the boy until he woke up. "Go get some sleep in the bed. I will take the chair."

Jayden offered no argument and climbed into the bed, falling back asleep.

Údar took a seat, watching the flames and letting his mind drift until the dawn light could be seen through the window. *Time to get moving*, he thought.

The first order of business would be getting Batänny a horse and some clothing, but seeing as he was running out of coin, he decided the young prince could part with some of his gold. Údar checked Jayden's boot, chuckling as he heard the jingle of coin. *I'm going to have to help him hide it better. Way too easy.*

He took out six gold coins, just enough for the supplies needed and nothing more.

Getting everything necessary only took an hour when all was said and done, and he was back in the room before Jayden was up, slipping the remaining coins back into the boot. With that accomplished, he strode down the hall until he reached Trinia's room and knocked.

He heard a shuffling on the other side, and after a moment, the door opened. "Yes?" Trinia asked, eyeing him groggily. The girl was still dressed in her clothes and her hair was a mess.

Údar held out the clothing. "For Batänny. We leave in an hour."

Trinia took the clothes and shut the door.

She needs you as much as you need her, he reiterated in his mind. He sighed, walking back down the hall.

An hour later, he sat on his mount beside Jayden, glancing up at the cloudy sky. "Plagues, where are they?"

Jayden let out a loud yawn and shivered. "Hells, it's cold out this morning."

Údar nodded, adjusting his cloak. "Yes, it is. It may be an early winter this year."

Trinia and Batänny emerged from the inn, the latter looking much better than she had the day before. "Good morning, gentlemen," said Batänny, smiling. "Ready to go?"

"Been waiting on you," he replied gruffly, turning his horse away before she could reply.

Stop being so cantankerous, Nisha had said.

"Easier said than done," he mumbled.

Riding through the gates of the city, he could see Lake Llewyn shimmering in the sunrise, the road a small line running about a mile from its shores. They would follow it for about six days until they hit Lissir, and then another two weeks until they hit Kiäxe where they would need to resupply. After that, it would be on to Tranâes to meet with the king.

"So where are we going exactly?" Batänny asked from behind him. "Will it be a long journey? Údar! Didn't you say something about a city? Riga mortis, or something like that?"

Údar closed his eyes, grumbling under his breath. "Elohai help me."

CHAPTER 20

———

"Your hair is a different color today. How do you do that?"

Trinia glanced at Batänny nervously. She had kept the same color hair for several days before it had drained her, and she had removed the illusion to allow herself some time to recover. When she had reapplied it last night, however, it was a light sandy color. There would be no getting around it.

"It's an illusion," said Trinia, hoping that would satisfy the curious young woman.

Batänny's eyes brightened. "Can you teach me how to do that? It would sure come in handy!"

"Ah, well… can you use magic?"

"Is that a requirement?"

Trinia was at a loss. She thought all use of magic came with the assumption someone could actually channel it. "Um, I think so."

Batänny frowned, looking ahead. "Drat."

Following her gaze, Trinia saw Jayden, Údar, and Mandar a little ahead of them upon the road. To her left, a sparse wooded area blocked the view of the lake and river, which drained out of it on its journey south.

In the days they had been on the road, the thought of hiding was beginning to wear on her. To constantly remember to keep up the illusion, which drained her energy, was getting more difficult. The others knew, but she still felt alone.

Interacting with Matilda at the inn had given her a feeling of what it might be like to let someone in past her walls. The only one who had come close was Niren, and while she knew he would do practically anything for her, she had never opened up to him about what went on within the palace walls. On some level, she was afraid he would do something foolish.

She cast another glance at Batänny riding beside her. *If anyone could understand what I've been through, it would be her... right?* Trinia looked at the back of her horse's head bobbing up and down as it plodded along behind the others, fighting her indecision. *Maybe start with an easy question, just to test the waters.*

"I like pancakes," she said and then inwardly smacked herself. *Question! Not statement! Hells below!*

Batänny looked at her quizzically at first and then looked as if she were thinking about something. "Yes, they are quite delicious," she said after a moment. "It's been a few years since I've had them, but they were amazing."

Trinia's heart swelled. They shared something in common! She took a breath, trying to calm her nerves before asking, "What about coffee?"

"Absolutely vile," Batänny declared, sticking her tongue out. "I don't know how people drink the stuff!"

"Agreed," said Trinia, laughing. "I tried it at the inn and almost spit it out."

Batänny chuckled. "The slavers forced us to drink it, saying it would help keep us awake while we performed."

"Oh." Trinia couldn't hide her surprise.

Wincing, Batänny said, "Forgive me, I don't mean to make light of anything. My mouth tends to speak before my mind stops it."

Trinia shook her head. "No, I… I understand."

Batänny looked at her, eyes narrowing slightly. "You do?" She seemed doubtful.

Well, I suppose we have dived into deeper waters, thought Trinia. "Like you," she started, struggling to find the words, "I have had my body used for other's pleasures."

Just saying the words out loud brought with it a sense of relief Trinia had not expected. There was still the chance it was a mistake with someone she barely knew, but for the moment, it felt good.

She looked at the woman next to her, not seeing the judgment or repulsion, or whatever it was she had been expecting. Rather, it was an understanding. "I'm sorry you've had to endure that," Batänny said solemnly. "It is not something I would wish on anyone."

"I have never shared that with anyone before," said Trinia. "I would prefer if it stayed between you and me."

"And here I thought you were going to ask something hard," Batänny replied, breaking into a smile.

Trinia giggled, feeling like a weight had been lifted off her shoulders. One thing still bothered her, one thing that seemed far easier in comparison. "May I share with you another secret?"

"If you wish. I don't expect you to spill your whole life story," Batänny replied.

Focusing on the illusion, Trinia withdrew the spell from her hair, revealing the silver strands. Opening her eyes, she could see Batänny staring at her, jaw hanging loose.

"Et-delf!" she exclaimed. "You're an Airgíd! I have heard the stories, you know, 'we've come to conquer you' type stuff, but you're *real*."

Trinia wasn't sure how to respond to what seemed like three different thoughts at the same time.

"How did you get here? And with Green Cloak himself no less?" Batänny pressed, seeming more eager for answers than riding back to town and alerting everyone there was an Airgíd nearby.

Rubbing the back of her neck, Trinia tried to figure out where to start. "Do you want the short version or the long one?"

Batänny scoffed. "It's not like we're going anywhere fast by the looks of it, so bring on the longer tale!"

Trinia grinned. "Okay. Well, it started a few weeks ago when my Gift awakened–"

"You're only sixteen?" Batänny gasped. "I thought you were older. What is your Gift?"

The words stuck in Trinia's throat more than she expected they would, and she realized this woman would be the first person she ever told what her Gift was on purpose. She cleared her throat. "I can, um, duplicate myself."

Batänny's jaw dropped again. "You jest! Show me!"

Trinia shook her head. "It's... it is not something I like to do."

"Does it hurt? Is that why?"

Jayden had asked the same thing. Hadn't he? Their talk in the cabin seemed so far away now. "In a manner of speaking, yes."

"In that case, do not feel any pressure from me," said Batänny, smiling. "How about I show you my ability instead? I think you will find it most humorous."

Trinia shrugged. If it meant avoiding talk about her power, she was all for it. "Please do."

Batänny's eyes twinkled in delight. "Excellent. Now, watch Údar."

Although it seemed an odd request, Trinia did so. When nothing happened for a few moments, she went to ask the woman what she meant and found her missing, only her horse remained beside her. *What the?* She turned her attention back to Údar to see him swatting a hand around his head like he was fending off an invisible pest. *What is he doing?*

On the next swing, Batänny's form was suddenly sprawled out on the road in front of him, her laughter heard from where Trinia was. As was Údar's cursing.

"Pox and plagues, Batänny! What are you doing?"

The woman lay on the ground laughing hysterically. "You should have seen your face!"

Trinia rode up, seeing Jayden trying hard to hide a grin and failing miserably. Even Mandar seemed amused. Údar, however, was anything but. "Get back on your horse, or so help me, I will tie you to the next tree and leave you there," he snapped, kicking his horse and moving around her.

Batänny wiped the tears from her eyes and climbed back on her horse, battling fits of giggling. "Ah, did you see it, Trinia? The look on his face was a thing of beauty."

Trinia stared at her in amazement. "Two questions. First, why do you antagonize him? Second, do your clothes change with you?"

"The first one is easy. Because Green Cloak is a softy at heart, and I know he would never leave me tied to a tree." Batänny paused as if thinking. "Scratch that, he *would* leave me tied to a tree, but he would feel bad about it and come back to get me at some point."

I'm not sure that's any better, Trinia thought.

"As to the second question, yes, my clothes change with me."

"How does that work? They are not a part of you."

Batänny wriggled her eyebrows and waved her fingers as if she were doing some mystical spell. "Magic," she replied sarcastically.

Trinia snorted. "Oh, okay then. That clears everything up."

The woman grinned. "I thought it might."

-II-

The days passed by too slowly for Trinia's taste, and one day was as monotonous as the previous. She would ride for hours, making small talk with Batänny and Jayden while Mandar and Údar led the way on the road. Then, they would stop for the night under the trees and get a small fire going while Mandar brought back wild game for them to eat. The next morning, it would start all over again.

Batänny certainly was the most talkative, and Trinia never ran out of subjects to discuss with the woman. A few times, the Shifter had shown off by becoming a bird and soaring high into the sky before diving and nearly hitting Údar. She drew more colorful language from that man than Trinia had heard to date.

Jayden was more silent than usual and seemed like he was carrying a heavy load on his shoulders by the way he slumped in the saddle. It had occurred to Trinia more than once he must feel the burden of the life-debt he owed her, and for the life of her, she couldn't figure out why she could not merely release him of it.

On the evening of the sixth day they passed Lissir, continuing for another five miles before finally stopping for the night.

As she climbed down from the horse, Trinia massaged her legs, trying to get the feeling back into them and already dreading the next day's ride. *At least the weather has held off,* she thought. It seemed the only blessing they had enjoyed this whole journey. She flipped her hood up against the wind, trying to keep her ears warm.

"I'm hungry," said Batänny, walking up and sitting beside her. "I could eat a horse."

One horse whinnied and Mandar glanced their way before looking toward Batänny. "They said they would appreciate you not using that reference."

The woman glanced at him and then to the horse. "The horses talk?"

"Only if you're an animal," said Trinia matter-of-factly.

Mandar winked in her direction and then walked off into the tree stand. Batänny looked at her, confused. "Is he serious?"

Trinia nodded, trying to keep a straight face.

"Huh. Who would have thought horses could talk? That interesting tidbit aside, I had a question for you, Trinia, if I may."

"Uh, sure?" *What goes on in that mind of hers for it to change directions so quickly? Lingering effects from the lynsium, maybe?*

"Your people live a long time. Right?"

Wow, that was a leap in conversation. Trinia grabbed a stick, snapping one of the smaller branches off it and tossing it into the fire. "The eldest can live up to five hundred years or more," she said. "Back during The Flourishing, it was said they lived for a thousand or more."

"That long?" The young woman gave a low whistle. "Longest an Iomlíad has lived to my knowledge is a hundred. Not sure I want to make it that long though. I'd be insufferable!"

"You already are," Údar mumbled behind them.

Trinia laughed, and she thought she caught a small smile tug at Jayden's lips.

Crack.

They all turned in unison toward where the sound had come from. It was hard to see anything in the fading light. All the shadows seemed to blend together, which only added to the feeling of being watched. Trinia turned to ask Údar what he thought and saw him lying on the ground, a dart in his neck.

"Et-delf!" Batänny cried.

Trinia looked to her right to see Jayden drop as well. A single dart hit Trinia, and she yelped in surprise as she watched Batänny shift before her eyes into a helwreck, quickly dispatching three of the five men who emerged from the shadows with one sweep. Another swing took out the remaining two before they could react.

A dart hit Batänny in the leg and she shifted back to herself, staggering on her feet before collapsing to the ground.

No, no, no! Trinia thought, leaping to her feet. *Think! Think!*

A figure dressed in black clothes stepped into the light, hood thrown back to reveal a hard, feminine face. Her black hair had a single thick braid down the middle and her eyes were cold. Her hand rested easily on the hilt of a dagger. "Well, well, look who we have here," said the woman.

"Who are you?" Trinia asked, edging closer to Batänny.

"The Raven," replied the woman, looking her over with a keen interest. "I'm a slaver, love. Now then, will you come willingly?"

"The fiery hells I will!" Trinia exclaimed, throwing back her hood and reaching for her daggers. Only they weren't there. *Hells!*

The Raven's eyes went wide. "An Airgíd!" she breathed, her lips quickly twisting into a smile. "You would fetch a fine price." Her eyes narrowed. "Why didn't the drugs work on you..."

Trinia's heart slammed against her ribs and she pulled the dart out of her arm, throwing it into the fire. Realizing she was out of options, Trinia took a deep breath, feeling the prickling in her palms rising. *Forgive me.* She shot out her hands on both sides as the Raven took a few steps toward her, and two duplicates appeared on either side. There would be no running this time.

The woman's jaw dropped as she swore. "Et-thid! What is this?"

"The reason you shouldn't have hurt my friends," all three Trinii said in unison.

The woman looked visibly shaken as she took out two daggers. "Don't matter how many of you there are, love, you'll die just the same."

"Not likely," Trinia replied, the duplicates echoing her statement and taking a fighting stance.

The Raven jumped, swinging the dual daggers at them, but Trinia and her duplicates dodged around her, each landing a blow of their own. The woman swore again, throwing a blade as she turned and hitting one of the Trinii in the chest. The force threw it backward.

Trinia cast another and another until five of her total were dancing around the woman, circling, waiting for the right moment to attack. For the first time, she could feel a surge of energy connecting the duplicates to her, and every moment seemed perfectly synchronized even though she could not read their thoughts. *How am I doing this?*

The woman feinted and slashed at the face of one, wheeling on one foot as her momentum carried her. She brought her foot up toward the other as the Trinii moved in at once. The kick landed home, sending the Trinii flying.

Two of the Trinii finally grabbed hold of the Raven's arms and Trinia moved in front of her, glaring. She drew back and landed a hard blow to the side of the woman's head and she went limp. Shaking out her hand and flexing it, Trinia looked around at the four duplicates around her.

"Now what?" she whispered.

-II-

Batänny heard yells and the sounds of fighting through the fog of whatever drugs they had hit her with.

Forcing her eyes open, she turned her head and saw five Trinias standing a couple of feet away from her, all crowded around a dark lump on the forest floor. *Great, I'm hallucinating.* She lifted her hand to her face, rubbing her eyes and trying to refocus them as the effects of the drugs wore off. Yet there were still multiple Trinias, and now they were looking at her in concern. *Okay, that's a little creepy.*

"Are you okay?" one of the Trinias asked, kneeling by her.

"Why are there five of you?" Batänny asked. "Is this your Gift?"

"Are you hurt?" the Trinia repeated.

"My head hurts." The lump on the ground came into focus and she could see it was the Raven, the head slaver in Dorämund Mound. She glanced up at Trinia, trying to focus. "What happened?"

"Long story. Just lie back down and try to rest. Alright?"

She laid her head back on the ground. "Sure, that sounds good." Unsure of what was going on, Batänny kept one eye partly open, watching as the Trinia stood and turned to the others standing there.

"Thank you for your help," the Trinia who had spoken to her whispered. "I... don't really know what to do about this."

The others looked at each other and then back to the first. "Me either," said one.

"Nor I," said the other.

"This is unexpected," said the third.

The Trinias' shoulders slumped. "I have nothing I can offer you." She reached out her hands, taking theirs. In a flash, they were gone.

"Hells below!" Batänny exclaimed, opening her eyes and sitting up. She held her head as the world swam. "Did you just...Did they...What just happened?"

Trinia—the real one?—looked down at her hands, eyes wide and breathing hard. "I–I don't know."

Batänny almost wished the drugs were still in full effect. At least then she could have an easier time with this. She tried to stand up, pausing as stars burst in her vision.

"I can't believe I just did that," Trinia breathed, still in shock. "I just..."

"Sucked them back up into your hands," Batänny said, rubbing her temples. *Et-delf, this has gotten strange!*

Trinia burst out laughing, and Batänny cocked an eye at her. *She's lost it*, she thought. *Or maybe I've lost it? Either way, I need a drink. A very, very, strong drink.*

The girl sat down, tears running down her face as she laughed.

Údar groaned behind her. She turned as he pulled the dart free from his neck, a look of utter confusion on his face. "What the plagues happened?"

The comment sent Trinia into another fit of hysterics. She was practically rolling around on the ground now.

Batänny shook her head, wishing the world would stop spinning. "Oh, nothing much. Just got attacked by slavers, drugged with gods know what, and captain giggles over there—"

Trinia was gasping for air now.

"There were five Trinias, Údar. Five! And then she just sucked them back into her hands!" Batänny continued. "Like, *poof!* Gone!"

"Six," he said, staring past her.

Batänny followed his gaze and saw Trinia—a Trinia at least—with a dagger sticking out of her chest. "Hells!" she cried, scrambling away.

Trinia's laughter died as quickly as it came, and she stared at the duplicate slumped against the trunk of a tree. Batänny looked between the two, seeing no physical difference between them. It was unnerving.

Walking over to the body, the girl kneeled in front of it, gingerly grasping the hand, but nothing happened. Trinia tried two more times with the same effect.

"Is this not disturbing anyone else?" Batänny asked, looking at Údar.

He gave her a look that told her to stop talking as he walked over to Trinia, gently laying a hand on her shoulder. "You did what you had to do. No one will blame for you that."

Batänny rubbed the back of her neck nervously. *How is it I always find myself in trouble?* she wondered. Rising on shaky legs, she went over and placed a hand on Trinia's other shoulder. "Thank you. You saved my life."

The girl looked up at her, and Batänny gave her a reassuring smile. She turned her attention to the figure still lying on the ground a few feet away. "What are we going to do with her?"

CHAPTER 21

———

"She seems to be stronger than we gave her credit for," said Tyarch, fiddling with the hem of his robe. "No food or water didn't work, nor did the lack of sleep. Now here we are, almost two weeks later and still nothing."

Gods I wish I could kill him, thought Caderyn, hands spread apart, holding down the edges of the maps on his desk. Moonlight shone in through the windows, giving his study a rather ethereal look. "Yes, so it would seem," he growled. Once again, his daughter had delayed his plans.

"I'm sure it will not be much longer until she is clay in your hands, my lord."

Caderyn glanced up from the maps, meeting the old man's gaze. "I've told the guards to throw ice water on her in addition to everything else we're doing. It's a matter of time and patience, both of which I am running out of." He returned to the maps, raking in every detail provided of his enemy's positions and fortifications thanks to his spies hidden among them.

Canämor would be the first logical target, as it was right on the border of the forest. If they could cross the river fast enough, they could take Falraxis Mont before that pompous king, Éowald knew what hit him. Then it would be a straight shot to the capital, Caudor.

Looking over the numbers again, Canämor boasted an army of around fifty thousand strong, which was problematic since he only had twenty thousand under his command at the moment. Which was why he needed the other chieftains to bend the knee.

Further to the south, his army would face Ungäar's roughly one hundred thousand strong. With the combined might of the other chiefs and the forced servitude of Canämor's army, he could level the field considerably.

"What will you do if she does not comply?" Tyarch asked.

"Kill her and accept my losses," Caderyn replied. *Quickly followed by you.*

"What if there was a way to get what you needed? Would you be interested in another option?"

Caderyn sighed in frustration, sitting heavily in his fur-lined chair behind his desk. "Speak your piece!"

Tyarch's scarred face writhed into a smile. "Of course, my lord." He stood, limping over and placed his finger on the map. "The answer to your problems lay in Lúinor Keep."

"With the Baobhan Sith Queen, I presume?" Caderyn steepled his fingers in front of him. "Do tell."

"As you may remember, the night you returned with your daughter was the night I had a vision of Ulscia awakening from her long slumber. She would be a powerful ally to have on your side, my lord."

Caderyn pursed his lips. "Powerful *competition.* I am powerful, Tyarch, but even I have my limits thanks to the ancient kings and their paranoia. Much of the Four Kingdoms has magical wards, else my conquest would be far easier. I do not need a power-hungry banshee fighting me, too."

Truly, there was very little in the way of stopping him, yet the kings of old in their fear of the Empire rising sought a way of protecting themselves and discovered the precious metal, *anthian*. Which, according to his spies, protected the people from Airgíd magic and thankfully had no offensive power. Hence the need to use brute strength.

"I dare not argue with you about your power, my lord," said Tyarch, bowing. "As the Voice of the Gods, I seek to serve you in all things. I merely point out Ulscia could help us."

Caderyn was getting tired of these games. He leaned forward, resting his arms on the desk. "Spit it out, Tyarch. How would she help us? Does she command some army I do not know about?"

The old man rubbed his crooked jawline. "I could set up a meeting if you wish, and you could ask her yourself."

An audience with the Banshee Queen herself? Perhaps it would not be such a horrible thing. After all, "Know thy enemy." "Very well," he said at last. "Go and seek an audience with her, but on one condition. It must be here, in the city. Understood?"

Tyarch bowed his head. "Perfectly, my lord. I shall do so at once."

Caderyn watched the man leave, glad to be rid of his presence. He poured over the maps again, jotting down a plan of attack and then settling in to write up the summons to the other chiefs to come with all due haste with their fighting men. It would take several weeks for the riders to reach them, but it would give him time to break his daughter and prepare to show her off for them.

Then the world would burn.

-II-

Trinia paced back and forth before the fire, her anger apparent. Údar couldn't fault her for that. With Mandar still missing, he worried the slavers had gotten him, and his own frustration was barely held in check. The fact they had snuck up on them at all without his notice was disturbing and showed they were professionals.

Údar stared at the Raven, now bound, gagged, and tied to a tree. In all his wanderings, he had never once run into her, but he knew her reputation. Assassin. Slaver. Killer. Now she had gone and made an enemy out of him.

Batänny kicked one of the bodies she had crushed when she had apparently turned into a helwreck, spitting on it. "It's the man who ran the house I was in," she said. Turning, she glared at the woman. "I could turn into a Götthru and slice her up a bit."

"No," Údar replied firmly. "We'll see if she will cooperate with us and give us the information we need first. If not, perhaps."

She sat down, crossing her arms. "Fine."

"Hells, what happened?" asked Jayden, slowly sitting up.

Údar turned. "How nice of you to join us."

The boy looked at him groggily. "Why do I feel like something bad happened?"

"Because something bad *did happen*," said Trinia, still pacing by the fire. "Slavers attacked, a duplicate died, everyone was drugged and..." she paused and looked at Údar. "A dart hit me. Why did it not affect me? And why did it wear off so fast?"

He thought about it a moment. Whatever they had hit him with had knocked him out cold, and it was the same for Jayden and Batänny. "Truthfully, I'm not sure," he said at last. "It's possible since you're an Airgíd the drug didn't interact in the same way it did for us."

"Thankfully," Batänny added. "Otherwise we would all be in a world of trouble right now."

Údar nodded. "Agreed. As for the duration, it's typically enough to knock the target out so the slavers can tie them up and then force them to walk."

"That's cruel!" cried Trinia.

"Yes, it is," he agreed.

Jayden laid his head back on the ground, throwing an arm over his face. "Why we can't we just, you know, *not* get attacked all the time?"

"You mean this is a regular thing for you guys?" Batänny asked, eyes wide.

"It happens more than I would care for," said Údar. Every delay meant it would take that much longer to reach his goal of killing Caderyn, but since the vision of Nisha, even that was called into question. *Enough waiting, time for answers.*

He got up and grabbed a waterskin off his horse and stood over the Raven, pouring it out on her head. She woke with a start, gasping and pulling against her bonds. Catching her breath, she glared at everyone through the long black strands of hair that clung to her face.

"You're going to answer some straightforward questions," Údar said, drawing the woman's attention as he sat down again. "You must know that I am exhausted, a little irritable about being drugged, and not in any mood to deal with arguments. I suggest for everyone's sake, especially your own, we make this easy."

The woman spat to the side. "I don't think so, love. You see, I don't answer to anyone."

Jayden snorted, sitting up. "This should be interesting."

Údar leaned back against the tree opposite her. "How many men do you have?"

"Can't remember."

"Did your men take down a giant wolf?"

"Don't recall."

He narrowed his eyes. "I noticed when we were tying you up, the marking of the hammer and shackles on your right shoulder. Those speak of tortures far worse than anything I am willing to do. However, some may feel differently."

Her expression darkened, the light throwing harsh shadows across her angled features. "You can go sleep with a sarulid, love. You're not getting anything out of me."

Údar shrugged. "As you wish. Batänny, it looks like you will get your wish."

Trinia looked in horror between him and Batänny, who was smiling. "Wait, what? I thought we *weren't* doing that!"

Batänny stood up, cracking her knuckles. "One Götthru, coming up!"

"A Götthru?" the Raven cried, looking at Údar and laughing nervously. "Look, I'm sure we can come to some sort of agreement."

Údar placed his arms on his knees. "We're past that point, I think. What was it again? I should go sleep with a sarulid?"

The woman's eyes went wide.

In a flash of movement, Batänny shifted, taking her sweet time moving toward the Raven and flexing her claws several times for good measure. Údar could see the terror in the woman's eyes.

Meow.

He caught Trinia's bewildered look, nodding toward the cat. "Götthru means cat. They can be very fierce and deadly when they choose to be. Most Iomlíad are afraid of them, believing they can steal their souls."

"Did you hear that? I'm here for your *soul*," the cat said.

Údar rolled his eyes. *Leave it to her to be overdramatic.*

The Raven looked up at the stars, away from the cat perched on her lap. "For the love of the gods," she whispered. "Get this thing off of me!"

"Not until you answer my questions," Údar replied. "You've taken our friend and I need to know where he is."

"I'm not going to answer anything," she bit off.

The cat put its front paws on the woman's chest, leaned in close, and licked her face. Then it rubbed its back on her chin.

"Alright!" she screamed. "Et-thid! I heard you roughed up my boys, so I followed you out here with the men you killed! We were going to take the Shifter to Kiäxe for the games! Jenero pays the most!"

Nodding, Údar said, "Thank you, Batänny. That's enough for now."

The cat looked at Údar, flattening its ears, and growled. He glared back. "Batänny."

It rolled its eyes and hopped down as she shifted back to her human form. "I didn't even get to claw her!"

Údar stood, rubbed his face, and walked over to the Raven, kneeling in front of her. "If those men you came here with were all that came with you, who would be left to take the wolf to Kiäxe?"

A smug smile crossed her lips. "Got me there."

He stood and leaned against the tree, feeling the worried looks from the others. *How many men would they need to take down Mandar? What if some of them circle back when the others don't show up with us in tow?* They were still weeks out from Kiäxe, so why attack now? What was the advantage? Did they really expect Mandar to not fight back on the road? *Unless,* he thought, *they are not going to take the road!*

The river flowed in a steady stream from Lissir with few rapids along the way, and the nearby town would have enough rafts to transport people in half the time it would take on horseback. *Plagues! There are no good options! We could try to outrun them, but they would only show up again, and if we stay to fight, I cannot fend off every dart.*

"Face it, love, there's no winning this fight," said the woman behind him.

"Shut it!" Batänny yelled.

He turned around to see the Shifter land a blow, sending the Raven's head colliding with the tree. Her head lolled to the side. "Batänny!"

She stopped, scowling at him. "What?"

"Get off her. Beating her fixes nothing."

"Made me feel better," she replied, flexing her hand. She met his gaze again. "You look like you're about to do something reckless."

Údar grunted. "Possibly." He looked at Trinia. "I need to speak with you… in private."

"Shouldn't we all hear the plan?" Jayden asked.

"You will," replied Údar. "At the moment, however, I need to speak to Trinia. Come on."

Trinia cast a quick glance at Batänny, who shrugged. He headed away from the fire with her following in his wake. When they were out of earshot of the others, he stopped and faced her. She had her cloak wrapped tightly around her, hood back, and silver hair reflecting the little light from the stars.

"Trinia, I'm going to be honest with you. We're in trouble," he started. "There are more men out there who will probably come looking for their boss when she doesn't show up. We are weeks away from Kiäxe and outnumbered. Do you see where I am going with this?"

"Not really," she said.

He sighed, rubbing his beard. "I'm saying if we try to fight, we lose valuable time, and I will not leave Mandar. If they come back, they will hit us with darts again and we'll have no hope of escaping. I've got no other choice... I need your help."

"Me? What could you possibly need my help for?" she asked. "You're Green Cloak!"

Údar smiled grimly, knowing she wouldn't be able to see it in the dark. "Now you know a secret of mine. I'm only human. Will you help?"

She was quiet, and he knew she had no reason to help him in this. Should she refuse, he would have to fight.

"What do you want me to do?"

CHAPTER 22

—

This is madness, thought Trinia, sitting next to a small creek meandering its way through the trees toward the river the others would likely be on soon.

Údar's plan, if one could call it that, was to allow themselves to get captured. All but her. He had sent her riding on ahead last night, telling her how hard to push the horse and for how long before giving it rest.

"It's over a hundred and thirty miles via the road, and only ninety by river. The current is swift, and we would reach the city in three days. If you do what I say, you can do the same," he said. He extended his hands, holding two daggers. *"Got these off the men. May they protect you."*

She took them, sliding them into the sheaths at her sides. "Thanks."

"This is crazy. You know that?" said Batänny.

"And risky," Jayden added. "But I agree, out of all of our options, this is the best one." He looked at her. "I believe you can do it."

"I still don't understand why it's the best option," she said, wrestling with the thought of being alone.

"Because while the drugs don't affect you, they will simply make sure to secure you even more than they will us,"

Údar replied. "They won't expect anyone to try and come to our rescue."

Trinia wasn't sure why they had so much confidence in her. She had made it out of the forest the first time because of Mandar. She made it out of Salorim because of Jayden. Mandar had rescued her again when the celnísh attacked. What had she done that was worthy of their trust?

The September sun was casting lazy shadows on the ground, and all around her a stillness was eating at her. Trinia bent down and looked at her reflection in the water—silver irises, shoulder length silver hair, cheeks slightly thinner. She was changing, hardening, becoming something new. Not to mention learning she could reabsorb her duplicates. Well, the ones still alive, that is.

The escape from Rionnagan seemed so far away now. Being chased through the streets by her father's men, the dead duplicate she had sacrificed to save herself, the one she'd stabbed several days before...

She shook her head. *You didn't know,* she told herself. *It was too dark, and the power had not manifested yet... you didn't know.*

No matter how much she tried to convince herself, she could not bring herself to believe it. Trinia broke down, unable to restrain her emotions any longer. Tears slid down her cheeks and she covered her mouth to mask her sobs. Every duplicate gone had been a piece of her, never to be replaced. And now, she was more alone than ever.

Letting her grief take her, she stayed there by the brook for several more minutes before the sobs subsided and she could catch her breath. It felt good to mourn their loss, as if in some small way there had been a sliver of herself restored.

Gathering herself, she concentrated on the illusion for her hair, envisioning Batänny's hair color to make it her own. The random colors would no longer work, and she needed something more consistent. Opening her eyes, she saw her reflection in the water and saw Batänny's face staring back at her. Trinia looked behind, but it was only her.

She reached up and touched her face while staring into the water, seeing her hand touch what looked to be her friend's face. *I can mimic faces?*

Leaning closer to the water, Trinia could see little things that were off about the illusion, but unless someone knew every detail, it could be passable. *I'm going to need to practice this more. It might just come in handy!*

Having rested up, she returned to her mount, checking the two bundles on the back. Údar had asked her to keep them safe, and now looking them over, they were two swords. It seemed a lot of effort to go through for something.

She sighed, walking around the horse, a sturdy dapple gray mare, and petting it as she did. "We've got a long way to go. Are you ready?"

The horse whinnied and bobbed its head.

Trinia smiled. "That makes one of us. Let's go."

Remounting the horse, she guided it out of the trees back to the road, setting an easy pace to let the beast warm up before urging it to a gallop.

Two days of hard riding had left her and her mount exhausted as they rode into Haeding, a little town thirty miles due west of her goal according to Údar's directions. As she moved through the streets, she noticed the town bore a similar look to The Mound with its stone buildings, low walls, and a myriad of people wearing checkered pattern clothes and plain tunics.

Trinia avoided eye contact, trying to appear like a confident traveler. The sign of an inn caught her eye, and the temptation of a bed was so appealing, but the lives of others hung in the balance. The thought struck her because she did not understand why it was being left to her. Jayden was a mage, Batänny was a Shifter, and Údar was literally a legend. What was she? The daughter of doom. Harbinger of death. No matter where she went, both seemed to follow her.

Stopping to pick up a little food and water, she saved as much of the coin Jayden had given her to get a room in Kiäxe and lodge the horse. There was no telling how long it would take her to find them, and she needed a safe place to rest her head at night. The inn down the road from her seemed to taunt her as she headed out of town.

She decided to spend the night on the outskirts without a fire, awaking the next day to make the last leg of the journey. This would be the biggest test.

After six hours, she came within sight of the bridge that led over into Kiäxe. She looked at the walls, and everything seemed much more daunting. It was an impressive sight—from its sturdy stone blocks, thick iron portcullis, solid oak doors, and its many machicolations, all of it spoke of strength. Many guards lined the top of it, their spears glinting.

Crossing the bridge, she passed through the gate, emerging on the other side in what she guessed was a market district based on the copious amounts of stalls and venders. The sight reminded her of home.

At least I made it into the city, she thought. *Now it's a matter of not getting caught or being asked too many questions.*

Finding an inn, *The Bard's Hearth*, she paid for a room and a stall and then stored the swords under her bed. Her eyelids were heavy, and she rubbed the sleep out of them. *Got to keep moving.*

Heading back outside, she blended into the crowd. While she couldn't be sure, she guessed there were easily several hundred people in this one area alone.

She marveled at how different these people were from her own kind. While the Airgíd, those within Rionnagan at least, were tall and thin, these people were stocky and broad. While her people had the silver hair from which they got their names, the folk here were mostly reddish brown with blue eyes. They wore colored tunics of blues, greens, and reds, with brown or gray breeches. Her people wore tunics of white or light blue, with strips of brighter colors reserved for special occasions only, and those were few.

Looking around until she found a spot in which she could get out of the crowd and observe, she hurried out of the steady flow of people. Once situated, Trinia looked out over the sea of faces, hope sinking with each passing second. *How am I going to find them? Think! Where would you hide an underground fight ring?*

Her mind drifted back to what Údar had said before leaving.

"When you get there, ask around about these games the Raven spoke of. I'm sure someone there will know where they are. Be careful, though, and always keep your eyes and ears open for danger."

"The woman mentioned a man, Jenero I think it was. Should I ask for him?" she asked.

"You can, just be careful how you phrase it. We don't know how far his reach might be."

If she could find him, she would find her friends. Peering out, she saw nothing unusual. Re-entering the flow of foot-traffic, Trinia followed a man in rich robes out of the market and toward a nicer part of town. They stopped at a merchant's shop. The sign above the door read, *Old Fergus Wares.*

She perused the small shop under the watchful eye of the man she assumed would be Fergus, a rather tough looking brute of a man with a scar across the bridge of his nose and down his cheek. Feeling like she had looked long enough to be polite, she walked up to the counter and tried to play the part of a dumb traveler, which wasn't too hard. "Wonderful collection you have here. I'm just in from Canämor and I was wondering if I might ask a question."

The man scratched his neck, a frown permanently plastered onto his face. "I've not known many X'phosians to travel to Canämor. Anyways, I suppose I could answer a question."

Hells! I still look like Batänny! Switching up her tactics, Trinia leaned forward on the counter, lowering her voice a touch. "I'm looking for a man named Jenero. He owes me and I've not heard from him in a long time. Last I knew he'd been in Canämor."

Laughing, he said, "Jenero owing a X'phosian, and a woman to boot! Now I've heard everything." The man wiped a tear from his eye.

"Do you know where to find him?" she pressed, doubling down on her story. *Sweet Vyrni I hope this works.*

"Aye, lass, I know where he be, though I wouldn't expect to collect. More likely you'll end up in the fights on account of you being an Iomlíad and all."

He knows about them? She tried to imagine what it would be like to live under such a constant threat. "Fights? What fights?"

"Ah, I suppose you wouldn't have heard about it down in X'phos." The man pulled out a trinket from beneath the counter, spat on it, and began to polish it before continuing. "It's the worst kept secret in the city. Iomlíad fights going on right beneath our feet day in and day out, even some slaves from neighboring kingdoms, people who won't be missed when they've gone missing, you see?"

Trinia nodded, working to hide her anger. "And you've seen them?"

"Ack, no, I'm not an animal!" he said, shaking his head. "Plenty do, though."

"And is that where I could find Jenero? At the fights?"

"Aye, very likely." His frowned deepened as he gave her a hard look. "He doesn't take kindly to people holding things over him, lass. You may not be walking out of your meeting with him if you do find him."

She straightened, trying to not act as scared as she felt. "I have my ways of being convincing. Where can I find the games?"

The man rubbed a burly hand through his thinning hair, squinting an eye as he thought. "He's got a home over in the Merchant Quarters. Across the street from that will be an alley. Head down there and take a left. You'll see the guards." He shook a thick finger at her. "Don't tell them you're there to try to strong-arm their boss. I don't think they will take it well."

Trinia smiled. "No, I don't think they would. I shall keep that in mind. Thank you for your help." She headed toward the door and paused. "I didn't catch your name," she said, turning around.

"Heb," he replied.

"I thought you were Fergus?"

The semblance of a smile crossed his face. "I liked the name better."

She chuckled. "Fair enough. Thank you for your help, Heb."

"And, lass?"

"Hmm?"

Heb reached under the counter and produced a small knife with a polished wood handle, offering it to her. "A lass your age shouldn't be going into a place like that without protection, Iomlíad or no. Take it."

"I have—"

"Just take it," he insisted.

Returning to the counter, she took the knife and said a quiet thank you before heading out the door and slipping the knife into her boot, sheath, and all.

She followed the signs until she reached the Merchant Quarters on the far side of the city. By the time she got there, she was tired and irritated, and the sun was making its slow arc toward the horizon. *Hells this has been a long day.*

After asking numerous people, Trinia finally found Jenero's house, a magnificent mansion with marble walls, gold-leafed gates, and statuary that could be seen over the walls. The alley Heb told her about sat between two other homes of lesser grandeur, though they were no less impressive.

Finding a nook out of sight from the street, she took a moment to dispel the current illusion and reapply it to only her hair this time. If X'phosians were brought in for the fights, it wouldn't make sense to walk up to the guards looking like one. When she was done, she crossed the street and headed down the alley, taking a left at the end and finding four guards standing in front of a wooden door with iron bands.

"Who are you?" asked one of the guards, stepping forward and standing between her and the door.

Breathe, breathe, breathe. "A spectator here for the fights," she replied dryly, putting her hands on her hips.

The guard crossed his arms. When she didn't back down, he glanced back at the others and gave a subtle nod. One opened the door, and he beckoned her in.

Picking up her courage, Trinia walked by them confidently and into the darkened passage that led downward. The smell of stale beer, urine, and blood filled her awareness, and she tried to breathe as little as possible.

Down a long hallway and two flights of steps, she entered a large bowl-shaped area surrounded by people yelling, screaming, swearing, and calling out bets. Below, two Iomlíad fought in the ring, shifting from one form to another while trying to figure out the other's weakness.

Trinia watched in rapt attention as one fighter turned into a giant snake, coiling itself around the other and squeezing. Even from where she stood, she heard the sickening crunch of bones breaking.

Sweet Vyrni, help me!

CHAPTER 23

———

How could someone take part in such an awful thing? Trinia wondered, watching in horror as people dragged the crushed body of the Shifter out of the area. The sight made her sick.

Looking around the room at the hundreds of people sitting on the stone seats, she tried to spot a door or passage that would take her down into the lower levels. If they kept the fighters there, her friends were probably being held there too.

Following her gut, she pushed through the crowds heading counterclockwise around the arena. Up ahead, she could make out what looked to be a tunnel, so she adjusted her course and made for it as quickly as she could through the throngs of people.

"I 'erd they got some new blood in the lineup fer fights," said a rather ugly-looking fellow to her left and down several seats.

Trinia froze.

"Aye, a man, a mage, a shifter, and the biggest wolf you ever did see!" exclaimed the one next to him. "I think Jenero is savin' them for last."

Hells! She had to hurry. Pushing forward, she arrived at the tunnel only to find it led to a festering latrine. Frustrated, she moved away from it and kept making her way around the arena, looking for any entrance she could find that might take her to her goal.

She was halfway around when she spotted a viewing box at the other end of the sandy pit, situated roughly thirty feet up from the floor of the arena. It was empty, though she suspected it would be where Jenero would sit for the last fights. Once she had made a mental note of where it was, she pressed on.

Ignoring the leering eyes of the drunkards and the obscene gestures toward her, Trinia spotted an opening carved into the seating and made for it, heading into the darkness. After several long minutes of bumping into people, she emerged into a huge cavern held up by massive pillars of stone. The red stone seemed to cast an eerie glow over the entire area, which was swarming with men and women peddling rather unwholesome services.

Making for the back wall, Trinia finally caught sight of another tunnel guarded by two men who looked rather bored. *This has to be it. Now, how to get them away from their post?* Searching around, she saw nothing that could aid her. About to give up, an idea hit her. It was insane. There was no way it would work.

She smiled. *But it might.*

Ducking behind a small tent, she concentrated on the image of the Raven from what she could remember, hoping that it would be enough to fool the guards. After several long minutes, she got up and found a piece of glass to check her reflection, seeing an image similar to the woman looking back at her. She grinned. The image grinned back. It was going to work.

Okay, now to act smug and like I'm better than everyone else, she thought. Stepping back out into the hustle and bustle,

Trinia squared her shoulders, took confident strides, and wore a rather irritated look on her face as she approached the men.

As soon as they saw her, the guards straightened up and suddenly looked like they loved their jobs. *Perfect.* "Slouching on the job, eh, love?" she said, glaring at the pair. Admittedly, while her voice sounded close, it was a bit off.

The guards exchanged uneasy glances. Trinia, not wanting to get stuck in a conversation with the men, feigned annoyance and shoved them both aside as she walked into the tunnel. They were either too stunned or too terrified to say anything, and they didn't follow her. Farther down the tunnel, she tried to stop her heart from beating out of her chest. *I cannot believe it worked!*

As she moved deeper into the tunnel, her hands began shaking. *It's not over yet. Calm down. Breathe! Find everyone. Escape. Have a meltdown. How on earth have I made it this far? I'm going to get caught.* The thoughts bombarded her one after the other until she felt like she was going insane.

The darkness finally gave way to a hallway dimly lit by torches with doors on either side stretching as far as the bend in the path. Walking up to the first door, she peeked through the iron bars to see a room with several rows of cells. Lifting the lock, Trinia entered the room, quickly glancing into each one to see if her friends were there, only to find they were all empty. *Hells, this is going to take forever!*

Trying as best she could, she checked room after room, and only found other Shifters either sleeping, pounding on the walls, or cursing her because they all thought she was the Raven. It relieved her to know her illusion was so convincing.

Standing in the middle of the hall looking down the many rows of doors, she was half tempted to create duplicates to help her in the search. Unsure of whether an illusion this complex would pass to them, she decided against it and pressed on, continuing to move from room to room and falling into a pattern.

Open, scan, repeat.

"Well, well, well, look who stopped by," said a familiar voice as Trinia entered a room nearing the bend in the hall. Batänny was leaning against the back of her cell, looking none too pleased.

"Batänny!"

Running over to the cell, Trinia smiled. "I found you! I can't believe it! I did it!"

Batänny raised a brow. "Is this you messing with your captives?"

"It's me, Trinia," she hissed, casting a glance at the door.

"Et-delf, you hit your head on that tree harder than I thought," said the woman, shaking her head.

"Batänny!" Trinia didn't mean to sound so irritated, but the woman talked way too much. She dropped the illusion. "Údar sent me ahead. Remember?"

The Shifter gaped at her. "Trinia? Is that you?" She rushed back over to the bars, looking her over closely. "Why did you look like—"

Trinia put a finger to Batänny's lips. "Seriously, not the time for questions. How do I get you out of here?"

"Oh, um, no idea," the woman replied.

"Can't you shift into something and squeeze through the bars?" Trinia asked.

Batänny smacked her forehead. "Of course! I wish I had thought of that!" She gave Trinia an annoyed look. "Notice anything about the bars?"

Trinia stepped back. The bars were...bronze? Seemed like an odd choice. "They're bronze?"

The woman rubbed her temples. "Bronze weakens and nullifies our powers," she said dryly. "Did you learn nothing where you grew up? This is basic Iomlíad lore."

"Again, really not the time," said Trinia. *Too bad it doesn't affect speech, too.*

Looking around the room, she could see that Batänny was the only one in here with three other empty cells. "Where are the others?"

"No idea. They locked me in here sometime yesterday and left with everyone else."

"Hells! I must have checked over forty room rooms already. How many could there be?"

"Too many."

From out in the hall, Trinia heard footsteps approaching. Panicking, she moved behind the door moments before a guard entered and walked up to Batänny's cell.

"Time to eat up," he said. "You fight in a couple hours."

"Not hungry," Batänny replied.

Holding her breath, Trinia moved out of the shadows behind the door and slowly came up behind the man. "And just what are you doing, love?" she asked, impressed that she had sounded more like the Raven that time.

The guard turned in surprise, dropping the food, and she could see Batänny's eyes go wide over his shoulder as Trinia's heart dropped. *Oh, hells...* She had removed the illusion.

Before she could run, the guard grabbed her arms and threw her against the bars of the cell behind her. White light flashed before her eyes. His hand was on her throat and she tried to get to the daggers, but he beat her to them, tossing them across the room as he pressed his body against hers.

"Who are you, eh? How did you get in here?"

Trinia could smell stale beer on his breath and she gagged while trying to pry his hand from her throat with her one free hand.

"Leave her alone!" Batänny screamed, grabbing the bars and recoiling.

The man's eyes were glazed over, but Trinia could see a growing hunger in them that she was painfully familiar with. *Please, no! Vyrni! No!*

"You're a pretty thing. Aren't you?"

Trinia tried to scream as the man pressed himself against her harder, kissing her neck. She wanted to gouge out his eyes, to claw his face, to create a duplicate, but one arm was pinned painfully behind her and the other was desperately trying to get his hand away from her throat. "Let's say you and me get to know one another," he whispered in her ear.

"Let her go! Leave her be!" Batänny threw herself against the bars, her eyes meeting Trinia's.

The man lifted her and tossed her into a cell, locking it behind him as she struggled to get air back into her lungs. She felt time slow down as she reached for the knife in her boot, and as before, the man grabbed it. He placed it up against her throat, wagging a finger in front of her as he held her down.

Tears streamed down her cheeks, panic seizing her as her mind screamed in terror. *Vyrni! Help me!*

But no help came.

CHAPTER 24

——

She hurt.

Her body. Her heart. Her mind. Her soul.

All of it hurt.

Trinia lay in the cell curled up in the corner, staring at the wall. Her tears had stopped flowing hours ago after the guard had left. Not even the Voice had been so cruel.

"Trinia? Trinia, talk to me."

What is there to say? she wondered. A deep numbness was replacing the pain, leaving her feeling cold and empty. Darkness swirled at the edges of her vision and she closed her eyes, letting it envelope her in its tender embrace.

Flashes of what happened sprang out of the blackness at her and her eyes flew open, a scream tearing from her raw throat. Her heart throbbed in her chest and her breathing came in ragged gasps as the sobs returned full force.

"Trinia! Look at me."

Her back was to the bars, face in her hands, paralyzed.

"Damn it, Trinia! Look at me!" Batänny cried.

She slowly turned, looking at the woman through the bars, her figure blurred by the tears. Batänny's face was red, and Trinia could see her trying to hold it together.

"Look at me, Trinia. I'm here. It is going to be okay. Alright? We're going to make it out of this," she said, nodding as if it would add conviction to her words.

Keys jingled from outside the room, and Trinia heard the lock click as the door was thrown open. The Raven stepped through, looking between them before settling on her. "Gods below," she muttered angrily. "She's a mess! How am I supposed to present her to Jenero looking like this?"

"Your man did this," snarled Batänny, grabbing the bars and gripping them until her knuckles were white. Her face twisted in pain and rage.

Let go, thought Trinia. *Stop hurting yourself.*

"He wasn't my man," said the Raven, not looking away. "He was one of Jenero's men, and he is receiving his punishment at the jaws of a skaäsa for damaging my property."

"She is not property!" shouted Batänny, stalking back and forth in her cell. She pointed at the Raven. "This is on your head!"

"Think what you want, love, but that's not how we do things," the Raven snapped back. "And congrats. You're next up in the fights so she won't be your problem anymore."

Two guards walked in, going to Batänny's cell. "Put these on, and no tricks," said one, handing bronze shackles to her through the bars.

Batänny complied, never taking her eyes off the Raven. "When I get out of here, I'm going to take my time killing you."

"Not likely," replied the Raven.

Trinia didn't flinch as the woman opened her cell and squatted down in front of her, pulling out a pair of bronze shackles. "You going to fight me on this, love?"

She gazed up at her, holding out her hands.

The Raven hesitated and then clamped the shackles around her wrists. "What is this?" she asked, picking up the silver broach of Vyrni and turning it over in her hands.

Trinia glared at it. "Nothing of importance."

The woman looked it over and put it in her pocket. "If you say so, love. Come on, get up."

Emotion choked her as she said, "I... I need help."

"Oh, very well," said the woman, hoisting her to her feet.

Trinia collapsed against the cell, grabbing hold of the bars to steady herself. Her legs ached and her hips felt like they were on fire. After a few minutes, she attempted a couple of steps and faltered. The pain was excruciating.

"For pity's sake!" Batänny exclaimed, pulling against the guard's grip. "She was raped! How heartless are you?"

Trinia stared at the floor numbly. Just hearing it said made her sick. It was not as if it hadn't happened before; the Voice had been doing it for years. But this was different. There was a savagery to it that ripped her soul out of her and shattered it into a million little pieces.

"Ardúss, go get two more to carry her. We don't have all day. Jenero is waiting for us," said the Raven.

The guard left and returned a few minutes later with two more guards who held Trinia under her arms and led her out into the hall. She kept her eyes trained on the ground. In front of her, Batänny walked between her guards, constantly glancing back at her. Beyond her walked the Raven, leading them toward the doors into the arena. Absently, she realized her cloak, the last piece of home she had, was back in the cell.

Reaching the arena, the group stopped, and the woman turned around, smirking. "Now's the time, love. Ready for your debut?"

Batänny squared her shoulders, holding her head high. "I'm not going to attack anyone for your sick entertainment."

Tsking, the Raven snapped her fingers, and the guards knocked Batänny to her knees. Trinia watched helplessly as they yanked the woman's head back as the Raven closed in, removing a vial with a swirling pink liquid from some hidden pocket under her black cloak. "This is *psynodram*. I created it to bring the fighting instincts of an Iomlíad to a heightened level. You won't know your friends when you get into the arena and you *will* kill them."

"No," Trinia whimpered, watching as the Raven emptied the vial into Batänny's mouth. "No!"

The guards dragged Batänny to the bronze cage, unshackled her, and threw her in where she lay writhing and trembling. Tears freely flowed down her cheeks as the *psynodram* took effect and she began foaming at the mouth.

The Raven turned to Trinia. "You're coming with me, love. Jenero has promised me a rather sizable sum of money for you. Hopefully he can see past all of the bruising."

Trinia glared at the woman. "You're going to pay for this," she whispered through her tears.

They weaved through the narrow passages, coming out where Trinia had first entered. They made their way into the arena. It all passed in a daze until they closed in on the box she had seen earlier. People in rich robes sat chatting idly with each other or eating. As they approached, one of them, a tall man with short cropped blond hair and trimmed beard to match, rose to meet them. "Ah, the lovely Branwen returns home."

"And I come bearing a gift for you, Jenero," Branwen said, nodding at Trinia. "One of the Airgíd, as promised."

Jenero's icy blue eyes turned to her. "My, my, it's been a long time since we've had one of your kind with us." He stepped up to her, smiling. "I'm sure we'll have plenty of time to get to know each other."

Trinia recoiled but was unable to back away with the grip the guards had on her.

The man grinned, revealing white teeth. "She is feisty! I like that. Olag has your money, Branwen, as usual, and since one of my men damaged the goods, I've added a little extra to the price for you. Please, stay and enjoy the fights before collecting."

"Generous as always. I think I will," said Branwen, walking over and giving him a light kiss before taking a seat.

The guards dropped Trinia into a chair and the roar of the crowd drew her attention to the area. Sitting up, she wiped away the tears to see Údar standing in the middle staring up at the box. It looked as if his fear of being drugged hadn't played out. Not that it mattered. They hadn't even given him a sword to protect himself.

Jenero moved to the front of the box. "Stranger, I've heard you abused my Raven. What have you to say for yourself?"

Údar cast a glance toward Branwen before looking at Jenero. "A lie."

The crowd booed and hissed, slinging vulgarities and calming only when Jenero raised his hands. *They are eating out of his palm,* Trinia thought, disgusted.

The man laughed. "Any last words, stranger?"

"Yes." Údar turned, taking in the hundreds of faces before speaking.

"You've come to see a spectacle!" Údar's voice boomed through the arena. "You crave blood and death at the expense of others! Why?"

The people in the arena booed and jeered at him, trying to drown out his words.

"Like children crushing an ant, you play with lives that are not your own!" His keen eyes raked the crowd.

What is he doing? Trinia wondered. Looking around, there wasn't a single friendly face.

"You serve the Old Gods! You believe they have power over life! But I tell you, there is only one with that power," he continued. "And now you will see His power."

White flames burst to life in his eyes and hands as the doors to the cage at the other end of the arena opened, and a Trifell emerged from the shadows. Trinia gasped along with the crowd, and even Jenero looked afraid.

The creature was easily the size of a horse, and its three scaly heads were filled with razor-sharp teeth. It pawed the ground with its enormous claws, eyes fixed on the man in the center of the arena.

Even though Trinia knew it was Batänny, she couldn't help but feel Údar was as good as dead. No one who met a Trifell lived to tell about it.

She looked at Údar standing there, calmly watching the beast as it charged him. Its claws dug into the sand with the three hungry jaws snapping as it ran. It closed the distance fast, and Trinia shut her eyes, unable to watch.

"Peace."

Trinia opened her eyes in time to see the Trifell stop dead in its tracks, an arm's length away from him. The crowd stared, dumbstruck.

"That's not possible," said Jenero, leaning on the rail of the box.

Trinia watched in growing awe as Údar placed his head against one of the beast's heads while he scratched the others. He whispered something in the Trifell's ear, and it lay down, calm as a newborn lamb.

He turned his attention to the crowds. "You see before you the power of Elohai, the One True God. If any of you wish to test the power of your gods, please, come and try. Though, I don't think it would be wise."

Jenero motioned to the guards around the arena. "Release the others!" he cried.

Doors all around the arena opened and Iomlíad, fourteen in all, poured out, shifting into a variety of creatures. There was a hauntingly beautiful telgost, with its ghostly wings and burning eyes; a skaäsa with its many legs and powerful jaws; a helwreck with its clubbed fists; and Mandar, mouth foaming with teeth bared.

Branwen laughed. "Still feeling confident, love?" she called down at Údar.

Trinia watched as the creatures closed in on him as he stood staring at Jenero. The man turned his back, as if Údar wasn't worth his attention any longer.

Coward! Trinia thought.

The Trifell noticed the newcomers but remained lying down, as if waiting for something. Údar took a deep breath, calling out in the loud voice as he struck the ground with his fists. "Bí saor!"

Be free.

White flames spread across the sands, and as it touched each of the creatures, they seemed to melt away until only the human forms remained, collapsing to the ground.

Jenero whirled around, gripping the rails. "No!"

In all her life among her people, Trinia had never seen power like this before, not even by her father. She watched as the Iomlíad picked themselves up off the ground, looking around in confusion and then with joy, Batänny and Mandar among them.

"These games are over!" Údar called out.

"Guards, seize them! No one leaves!" Jenero cried. But the guards made no move to obey.

"You are blind, Jenero," said Údar, like the name left a bad taste in his mouth. "But you will be blind no more. See? Already your lies fall like scales from their eyes."

Trinia looked around and gasped. All over, people were rubbing their eyes, and flakes like the scales of a snake fell off them. Cries of alarm rose around them, the closest being Branwen. The woman gave a shout as she rubbed her eyes furiously. Trinia noticed that Jenero did not experience this, nor did many others in the crowd.

Údar called for quiet, and everything fell silent. He walked toward the box. "Do you renounce these fights, Jenero?"

"The fights are part of this city," he sneered. "They will never be gone! Even if you take me down, someone will rise in my place!"

Údar shook his head. "No, they won't. Do you renounce them?"

"I will continue to run these fights, and you will not stop me!" he raged.

Trinia could see Údar sigh, and through the white flames, she could almost feel his sadness at the man's answer. Why? The man was a horrible excuse of a person!

"Then you shall be the example," Údar said. He stretched out his hand, and a jet of white flame shot out, wrapping itself around Jenero and lifting him out of the box to the ground.

He screamed as his body contorted and morphed into a slimy, slug-like creature. After it was done, the white flames disappeared and left Údar's eyes.

Trinia gaped. *He turned him into a sarulid!*

Now she really could see the sadness in Údar's eyes, even from where she sat. He looked around one last time, holding out a hand toward the pathetic creature slowly inching away. "Here is what will happen to any who start these fights again. Tell everyone you see that the Green Cloak told you this."

Everything erupted into chaos as people scrambled to get away or were dragged off into the dark tunnels by the mobs executing their own version of justice. Amid it all, Mandar bounded up into the seats near her and made his way to her. "We need to go."

She tried to stand, but the pain was still too much for her. Trinia shook her head. "I can't."

He lay down in front her. "Grab on. I won't let you fall."

Trinia grabbed fists full of fur and held on as he carefully got back up. She caught a glimpse of Branwen slumped in her chair, beads of sweat on her brow, her hands trembling. Her gray-green eyes, filled with terror, met Trinia's gaze.

May you rot, thought Trinia, hugging Mandar's neck.

"Hold on," he said. "We're leaving."

CHAPTER 25

Trinia clung to Mandar like a person clinging to flotsam in a storm to keep from drowning. As the world passed by her, she felt detached, apart—there, and not there at the same time. It was a surreal feeling.

Údar had gone off with Batänny to find Jayden and returned a short time later with him in tow. The crowds, along with the Iomlíad fighters, had dispersed. "We can't leave through the front entrance as Mandar will not fit," said Údar, buckling his sword around his waist. "The river entrance shouldn't be far, and with Mandar's sense of smell, we'll be out of here in no time."

"I have a room in the city," said Trinia, lifting her head. "It has my horse and the swords you sent with me."

"Which inn and what room?" asked Údar, finished with the belt.

The noise of the buckle sent more flashes through her mind, and she shuddered. "The Bard's Hearth," she said, gasping.

"We'll find it," said Batänny, laying a gentle hand on her arm. "Don't worry."

Trinia nodded, laying her head back down against Mandar's warm fur.

"I'll take her outside the city," Mandar's voice rumbled.

"I'll go with you," added Jayden, coming into view. He gave her a half smile, which she returned in kind, though she could see in his eyes a barely hidden concern.

Do I look that bad?

"Very well," said Údar. "Batänny, follow me. Mandar, we'll see you outside the walls in a few hours near the forest."

Holding on tightly as the wolf walked, Trinia's gaze stared off into space. Every tunnel, corridor, and passage all blended together until she eventually heard the sound of water. Along the side of the river, there was just enough room for them to skirt the edge of it as they left the tunnel. It opened to a view of countless stars above.

The stars look different here, she thought, staring up at them. She still noticed the Mother Bear and the Hero of Old, only they were in different places and at different angles. *They are so beautiful.*

Mandar followed the river until they were well within the woods and circled back around, returning to the road and crossing to the other side of it. He stopped and lay down, allowing her to slide down his side. "Thank you, Mandar."

"Stay close to me and I shall keep you warm," he said. "Jayden, you curl up on the other side. I shall keep watch."

"I won't argue that," said Jayden, walking around and out of Trinia's view.

She did not have the strength to argue with the wolf either and leaned into his fur. With her head against his side, Trinia could hear his heartbeat pounding in a steady, comforting rhythm that she used to ground her in reality before finally falling asleep.

-II-

Údar pushed past the drunkard blocking his path as he made his way toward *The Bard's Hearth* with the directions he had gotten from the tavern owner. Batänny had been unusually quiet and Trinia had looked... hollow, not counting the horrible bruises on her face. *What had they done to her? How was she caught?*

The inn finally came into view and he picked up his pace, not wanting to remain in the city any longer. What he had witnessed at the arena had shaken him. *Have so many fallen away?* he wondered.

It brought to mind what Ulscia had said. *No one follows him anymore. The world is changing, Údar, and as far as you are concerned, it's not for the better.*

And it terrified him she might be right.

Passing through the door of the inn, he approached a scrawny, rather ill-tempered looking fellow behind the counter. "Excuse me, I'm looking for a friend of mine," said Údar. "She rented a room and put up a horse in the stables."

"Aye, what of it?" asked the man, eyeing him.

"I'm looking for her," Údar repeated. "Do you know what room she is in?"

The man's gaze shifted toward Batänny and then back to him. "Nope. Unless you want a drink or a room, I suggest you leave, stranger."

Suddenly, Batänny partially shifted, her left arm morphing into one of a helwreck's, and grabbed the man by the neck. "What. Room?" she demanded.

"Batänny, what are you doing?"

She squeezed slightly. "Getting answers."

The man's face was starting to turn blue, and he pointed down the hall. "Twenty," he wheezed. "Room twenty."

"See, that wasn't so hard," she said, dropping him and heading where he had pointed.

Údar jumped over the counter, checking the man to make sure he wouldn't die. When he was satisfied he would live, he took off down the hall after Batänny. *She's lost her mind!*

He rounded the corner to see her kick in the door of room twenty. *Plagues! What is she doing?* He rushed in as she turned with two bundles he recognized in her arms. "Batänny, are you out of your mind?" he shouted.

She shrugged, attempting to go around him, but he blocked her way. "No, you need to explain to me why you just attacked that man."

"He is a disgusting man," she spat. "He needed the encouragement, and you weren't going to do it."

"You cannot go around attacking people, Batänny. We're still in a major city!" he said.

"And why not?" she shouted, throwing the bundles to the ground. "Were not my people attacked and used for blood sport?"

Údar sighed, his frustration dissipating. "I'm not saying you're not right in how you feel, but abusing an innocent is not the way to go about it."

"Abused?" she said, her voice becoming shrill and her eyes filling with tears. "You mean like how they abused Trinia? How they raped her in front of me as I watched helplessly, listening to her screams? Or how I have been brutalized for the past two years?" She pointed a finger at him. "Do not speak to me of abuse, Údar!"

Her words hit like a punch to the gut. "What?"

Batänny was borderline hysterical now. "You heard me!" she screamed. "Trinia tried to rescue me and she got caught. The guard threw her in the cell across from me and raped her! And it's all my fault!" She collapsed, and he caught her as she sobbed into his chest. "It's my fault!" she said, her voice breaking.

Elohai... tell me this is not so. He felt sick. *I sent her on her own. Oh, Elohai, forgive me!*

-II-

Jayden opened his eyes, giving up on getting any sort of sleep. So many questions plagued him, things that made little sense, and he could not understand why. First on his mind was Trinia.

Something was off. They had beaten her, that much was apparent, but it went further than that. A darkness was in her eyes that was not there when he last saw her a few days ago. It was hauntingly void of emotion or the light he had seen in her.

The second thing that bothered him was Ulscia. Since the cave, there hadn't been so much as a cackle in weeks. If she was after Trinia's blood, why had she not continued to attack them on the road? There were more than enough places to do so. *It doesn't add up,* he thought, wrapping his cloak tight about him. *And how did her daughter know I would be among them?*

Third, he wondered if his father knew about the games held in Kiäxe. Supposedly, Ungäar was welcoming of all peoples and cultures, but what he had witnessed in there spoke the opposite. Even in Dorämund Mound and the little girl... how were such things allowed to continue?

So much for trying not to care about anything or anyone but yourself, he chided himself. *Too much longer in this merry bunch of misfits, and you'll convince yourself to take the crown!* He snorted at the absurdity of the thought.

"Sleep evading you?" asked Mandar quietly.

Jayden stood, moving to stand in front of the wolf and glancing up at the moon through the branches. "You could say that."

"A lot on your mind, then?"

He nodded. "Too many things."

Mandar tilted his head a tad. "Such as?"

Jayden stared off into the surrounding trees, seeing his breath billowing in front of him. It was so quiet, the perfect time for an ambush from a hoard of celnísh. "Do you wonder why Ulscia hasn't attacked again?"

"I have not," Mandar admitted. "But it seems you have. Any thoughts?"

Shaking his head, he said, "Nothing I can say for certain. All I know is that she said she wanted Trinia's blood, but she has not pursued us since the cave. And what of the duplicate whose bodies we left behind? Would not it have sufficed?"

He looked at the wolf. "It doesn't add up."

"You make a good argument, and I agree with you, it is odd given her personality. She's not one to leave things alone," said Mandar. "Have you brought this up to Údar?"

"I don't even know what I would say," said Jayden, laughing quietly, and rubbing the bandage on his chest. "Your murderous ex-lover is up to something no good?"

Mandar shook his head. "I probably would not lead with that, no."

Jayden ran a hand through his hair. "I've seen more evil in my kingdom than I ever expected to find. And now Thydu is attacking, and only we know? What of the innocent?"

"Your kingdom?" asked Mandar, eyeing him.

Hells below! "I, uh… my father's kingdom, technically." He met Mandar's gaze. "My father is Arthfael, king of Ungäar."

The wolf nodded. "I assumed as much from what you said. A prodigal son returning home."

Jayden rubbed his neck, staring at the ground. "Reluctantly. If not for my life-debt, I would be in Thydu right now working to become a horse breeder."

Mandar chuckled, and Jayden saw him looking up at the moon, eyes closed. "Ah, yes, Elohai does work in mysterious ways."

Elohai? "What does he have to do with it?"

"Everything," replied the wolf. His golden eye turned to him. "Did it not occur to you, son of Arthfael, that had you gone into Thydu, they would have killed you, labeling you a spy? Your debt kept you from it."

"Okay, but I don't see how that connects to Elohai," said Jayden, rubbing his arms for warmth.

"Elohai saved you through Trinia via the life-debt," said Mandar. "And who is to say if he did not lead you up there to meet her in the first place because he has a purpose for your lives."

Jayden scoffed. "So, I'm a pawn in some game. Is that what you're saying?"

"I am saying there is no such thing as coincidence when you believe in a sovereign God," replied the wolf. "Knowing him like I do, I believe he's growing you up to fulfill the purpose he created you for, as shown through your Gift."

Trinia stirred, whimpering, and muttering something Jayden couldn't make out. Mandar moved his tail, laying it over her, and after a moment, she calmed.

"I don't know what my Gift is," Jayden replied, lowering his voice so he didn't disturb Trinia again.

"Perhaps it's because you do not ask," said Mandar, gazing past his shoulder.

Jayden turned, seeing two figures in the road. "Is that them?"

A warbling whistle broke the silence, followed by Mandar returning a low howl. The pair veered off the road, making straight for them, and soon Jayden could hear Batänny's voice.

"I see them, over there."

Údar stepped into the moonlight a few feet away from Jayden. "Where is Trinia?" he asked.

"With me, sleeping," said Mandar.

"Did you get what you needed?" asked Jayden.

"We did, but we didn't get the horse as we had... complications," he replied.

Complications? Jayden wondered. *As if we need any more of those.*

Batänny walked over and lifted Mandar's tail, settling next to Trinia. Jayden watched her for a moment. Something in her movements, the tilt of her head, the concern etched into her face, told him something was wrong. Very, *very* wrong.

"Jayden, tomorrow I need you to go into town and get us some horses," said Údar.

"I only have enough for two, at most," said Jayden, turning his attention to him. "If you don't have any qualms about how I find some extra coin, I can get more."

He watched the conflicting emotions play across Údar's features in the light. "Do what you must," he said at last.

Jayden nodded. "Done."

CHAPTER 26

Caderyn stood on the balcony outside his chambers, breathing in the cool morning air. The summons he had sent out eight days prior should have arrived three days ago, which meant it would take another week before the other chieftains would arrive. He had instructed them to come with their best men, prepared for a winter assault on the kingdoms, a time when they would not expect a full-scale attack.

Stepping back into his room, he adjusted the furs about his shoulder, slicking his hair back with oil and looking himself over in the mirror. Yes, he looked the part of a mighty king. He summoned every bit of power to himself until the aura about him exuded something akin to godlike. Caderyn refused to be cowed by Ulscia in his own palace.

He left for the Hall of Echoes, eyes up, jaw set confidently. Every servant who walked the halls bowed before him before hurrying away, as was right. *I am the rebuilder of the Empire. All will bow before me.*

Tyarch met him at the doors to the Hall, giving a nod. "You look like the ancient emperors of old, my lord."

Caderyn sniffed. "I know. Let's get this over with."

The doors opened before him and he strode straight to the throne, taking his seat and resting easily in it. *This is where I belong*, he reminded himself. *Let the histories mark this day, October 1st, as the day when I solidified my power.* At least, that's what they would say when he was done here.

At the other end of the Hall, the massive entrance doors opened slowly, revealing a lissome woman with fiery red hair. A younger-looking woman followed behind, her hair golden like the sun. They approached the throne, flanked by guards, stopping at a respectful distance and bowing. "Hail, Caderyn, Future Emperor of the risen Airgíd Empire," said the woman.

A flush of pleasure coursed through him at the sound of the title, and he smiled. "Greetings to you, Ulscia, Queen of the Baobhan Sith, Mistress of the Night."

The woman stood, her red-violet eyes meeting his with a teasing smile on her lips. "It's nice to know not all have forgotten me."

"You're not easily forgettable," said Caderyn, eyeing her. "You are even more beautiful than the stories give you credit for."

"A common trope in stories, I'm afraid," she replied, wrapping a lock of hair around her finger. "We're always the ugly hags, terrors of the night with cloven hooves for feet after lonely men."

"I don't doubt the last part," he replied evenly, captivated by her eyes. "The others are harsh untruths, it seems." His gaze flicked to the younger woman. "And who might this be?"

Ulscia turned, motioning for the woman to approach. "This is Áine, the last of my daughters. I present her to you as a gift of good faith between us."

"I'm happy to be of service to you, *my king*," said Áine, looking up at him through her dark lashes.

"Indeed," replied Caderyn, rubbing his chin thoughtfully. "And how could I refuse such an offering? I accept. Tyarch, take this young woman to my chambers and make her comfortable."

The Voice bowed, extending a gnarled hand to her and leading her out of the Hall. When he was gone, Caderyn waved his hand, dismissing his guards. "Leave us, I wish to speak with the queen privately."

Once they were alone, he stood and walked down the steps, extending his arm to the banshee. "Walk with me."

She dipped her head, weaving her arm through his as he led her toward his study. When they were behind closed doors, he offered her a drink. "I'm afraid all I have is brúan. I don't think you will mind its strength."

"I won't mind a bit," Ulscia replied, smiling.

"A woman after my own heart," he said, filling a glass with the amber liquid and handing it to her. After he poured himself one, he sat across from her, taking a sip. "Now, Tyarch tells me you have a proposal, a sort of alliance, yes?"

The woman took a delicate sip, eyeing him over the rim of the glass. "You and I want similar things, my lord," she said.

"And what is that?"

"Power." She smiled knowingly. "But we both have things that stand in our way. For you, a daughter. For me, a man."

Caderyn scowled. *How much has Tyarch told her?* he wondered. "My daughter has a strong will, but it will not last much longer."

"Perhaps," Ulscia admitted, crossing her legs. Her emerald robe slipped to the side, revealing her thigh.

He took another sip of drink, keeping his eyes locked with hers. *I shall not be seduced so easily*, he thought. "And what of the man?"

"A past lover of incredible power," she said, swirling her drink. "The most powerful man I ever had the pleasure of bedding."

Caderyn narrowed his eyes. She was baiting him. "Lucky man," he replied, feigning disinterest. "But what does that have to do with me? Surely you could handle him without issue?" he added.

He saw a flash of anger in her lovely eyes. "I would that I could," she said, voice tight. "As for you, I believe you know each other. He goes by Údar, but you know him as Green Cloak."

Caderyn choked on his drink. "Green Cloak?"

She smiled and laughed softly. "Yes, I thought you might remember. After all, he left his mark on you. Didn't he?"

"Yes, yes, he did." The room seemed to shrink around him as his heart raced.

Ulscia leaned forward, her robe leaving little to the imagination. "What if I could offer you revenge?" she asked, her voice light and sultry. "And in taking care of this problem for me, I would grant you whatever you asked."

Caderyn leaned back in his seat, unable to take his eyes from her partially exposed bosom. *She would owe me a favor. My, my, this is unexpected.* His gaze flicked up to meet hers. "What did you have in mind for him?"

She leaned back, draining the rest of her drink. "I will bring him to you, and when he arrives, you will kill him."

"If he is as powerful as you claim, just how do you plan to do that?" he asked, raising a brow. He could kill him—that much he knew already—but would Green Cloak willingly come to Rionnagan?

"You needn't worry. I have already started that process," she said standing and slipping out of her robes. "Now then, shall we seal the agreement?"

Caderyn stood, moving over to her, drawn by that intoxicating gaze. He pulled her close, kissing her.

I have her right where I want her, he thought.

-II-

Hours later, he lay on the floor, her body close to him as they lounged before the hearth. *It needed to be done*, he told himself. She would owe him, and she would help him establish his new empire. *Perhaps she can rule beside me as queen? I could hold the favor over her as leverage. Yes, that would work. Then I will be unstoppable with her beside me.*

He could hear shouts of alarm in the hall outside the study, and the doors suddenly burst open. "My lord!" cried a guard, stopping when he saw Caderyn.

Caderyn swore. "How dare you burst into my study!"

"Forgive me, my lord, but your daughter, she is dead!" said the guard, eyes wide.

"What?" Caderyn roared. "How is this possible?"

"We don't know–"

The guard's pleas were cut short as Caderyn shot out a hand, sending a jagged stone into the man's chest and propelling him out into the hall.

"What is it, my lord?" asked Ulscia sleepily on the ground.

Caderyn threw on his clothes, ignoring her. He ran through the halls barefoot until he reached the steps to the dungeon, taking them two at a time as he descended. Shoving the iron door aside, he marched up to the bars to see his daughter lying in a pool of blood, a makeshift shiv sticking out of her chest and a maniacal smile on her face.

The room spun, and he felt his anger building. Focusing on the bars, he watched as they heated up, glowing red hot, and then melted before him. *How is this possible?*

There was only one way in and one way out of this area, monitored at all times by guards. He looked at the shiv in her chest and then noticed the deep slices on her arms. Someone had given her the weapon and allowed her to kill herself. It would not have taken much, knowing what they had put her through to break her, which meant only one thing.

A traitor was in his court.

CHAPTER 27

Údar found the town of Reldor a welcome reprieve after the two weeks on the road. The beauty of the town seemed to be its many bubbling fountains fed by underground springs, providing crystalline waters for the residents. The backdrop of the mountains did not hurt.

Lighting his pipe, he leaned back in the chair on the porch of the inn. He hadn't asked Jayden how he'd gotten the horses, nor the extra bags of coin, and he didn't really care. The words Batänny had said back in Kiäxe continually echoed in his mind, like the tolling of a bell.

She was raped.

He swallowed hard, forcing the emotions back down. As a father, he could imagine all the horrible things he would have done to anyone who touched Lyniel in such a way. It would be slow and agonizing. From what Batänny had said, the man had met a cruel fate—though, not nearly cruel enough, in his opinion.

Exhaling, he blew out a smoke ring and watched it float away to vanish. *I should have never sent her. Elohai forgive me. I should have figured something else out.*

Batänny sat down in the chair next to him, gazing out at the main square in the town, her face unreadable. His stomach twisted into knots, thinking of how he had failed her, too. Another count against him.

She said nothing for the longest time, simply staring out toward the main fountain. "May I ask you a question?"

He side-eyed her, blowing out another smoke ring. "Of course."

Batänny folded her hands in front of her. "I've had a lot of time to think since leaving Kiäxe," she started. "And try as I might, I cannot shake it."

"Speak your mind," he said, trying to read her.

She looked him square in the eye. "Did you plan on freeing the Iomlíad? Before you sent Trinia off alone, I mean. Was there really a purpose, or did you just hate her that much?"

Údar lowered his pipe in surprise. "Why you would ask such a thing?"

"Please, I need an answer from you," she said, tears welling in her eyes.

The question made him nauseous, even more so to think she thought he was capable of such a thing. Given his actions toward Trinia, however, he supposed he couldn't blame her. He looked at the ground. "The truth? I was afraid."

"Afraid?" she echoed, confused.

He took a deep breath, rubbing his face. "Batänny, I know the legends about me, but I am still only human. Yes, I was afraid. They had taken Mandar, they outnumbered us, and I knew I couldn't protect you all if we tried to fight."

The emotions he had kept stuffed down started seeping through the cracks in his walls. "I didn't know if they would keep me drugged and drag me out into the fight as a meal. I didn't know if Trinia would make it to Kiäxe alive or if Ulscia would attack her on the road once she was outside of my protection." He wiped his nose and sniffed. "I didn't know she was there until I saw her in Jenero's viewing box, and since they had not used any more of their drugs on me, I saw an opportunity to save more than just ourselves."

He met Batänny's gaze. "If I could go back to spare her, I would do it without hesitation."

She nodded, wiping the tears from her eyes. "So would I," she whispered, her lip quivering.

Údar stood and set the pipe down, kneeling in front of her and taking her hands in his. "I would do the same for you, Batänny. I should have done more, checked in sooner, but..." he choked on the words. "But I was selfish. I was too wrapped up in my troubles to care about others. I cannot... All I can do is ask for your forgiveness."

Batänny threw her arms around him, weeping into his cloak. Údar closed his eyes, tears slipping down his cheeks. She was so young, and had so much life left to live, yet it had been marred by pain that no woman should have to experience. "I'm so sorry," he said.

The walls broke into a thousand shattered pieces as he hugged her close, wishing more than anything he could mend the brokenness but knowing he could not.

-II-

Trinia lay in the seclusion of her room, staring at the ceiling. While her body no longer ached like it had, she felt like her mind was torn in two and at war with itself.

Go to sleep and rest. Lose yourself to dreams, one side seemed to say.

Nay, we can't. He finds us there, said the other.

Back and forth they argued.

We should have used our power to stop him, said the first voice.

He pinned our arm, and we couldn't breathe, the other replied.

She covered her face and then ran her fingers through her hair. "Stop it. Stop it. Stop it!" she hissed. But the thoughts would not stop.

Around and around they went, playing out all the things she could have or should have done to stop it. It was driving her mad. Trinia sat up, seeing her ragged reflection in the mirror across from her. She got out of bed and stood in front of it, a hand going to her face. *Is that you? Are you the Trinia who left her home?*

Her eyes were slightly sunken in, her hair was in disarray, her lips were pale and chapped, and the bruises from the guard's grip still colored her neck and face. Taking off her shirt, she looked at her body in the mirror. Bruises, some faded, others not, covered most of her skin in purples, blues, and yellows.

Seeing them brought with it a torrent of emotions, and the thoughts came back.

You're broken.

Ruined.

Dirty.

Worthless

A means to an end.

Trinia grabbed her head, hot tears flowing. "Shut up!" she growled at her reflection.

The thoughts stopped.

She grabbed her shirt and slipped it back on, sitting on the edge of her bed while rocking back and forth. She needed to do something, anything, to keep her mind busy. The emotions were too volatile. The shame too real. *Always a means to an end*, she thought bitterly.

Her skin crawled with the guard's touch, and she physically wanted to escape, but there was no escaping from herself. She was trapped. Her gods had abandoned her to banshees, monsters, and men.

And oh, how she hated them all.

-II-

Mandar sat at the edge of the woods overlooking the sleepy town and enjoying the beauty of it—a sharp contrast to the ugliness of what happened in Kiäxe. He shook his head and scratched behind his ear. They were so close to their goal. He could only pray the Maker would provide them with safe travel from here on out.

Which reminded him of his conversation with Jayden the night of their escape. He had mentioned Ulscia not attacking again and how he found it odd. Since then, the more Mandar thought about it, he did as well. *What is she playing at?*

A rustle of the wind around him carried a soft voice Mandar knew right away. *She is searching. One mile northwest. Go to her.*

The Maker. Elohai.

Who is searching, I wonder? Trinia? Mandar made his way, letting the wind guide him toward his destination. Seeing smoke rising from up ahead, he slowed his pace, walking carefully until he saw a familiar face sitting by a pitiful-looking fire.

He stepped out of the brush and sat, his presence seemingly going unnoticed. "Hello," he said.

The Raven startled, looking at him. "Et-thid! Where did you come from?"

"I could ask you the same question," said Mandar, glancing around. "Anyone else here I should know about?"

The woman shook her head, her attention back on the fire. "Only me," she muttered.

The leaves on the trees waved back and forth as the breeze blew through in a sign that he was supposed to talk with her. *You know I do not question you, Maker,* he thought, *but I must admit, this is strange.*

He padded over to the fire and lay down across from the slaver, paws folded over each other. She looked haggard, with dark circles under her eyes and her black clothing ripped in places. "What are you doing here?"

She huffed. "I have no bloody idea, love."

Mandar tilted his head. "What are you searching for, then?"

Glancing at him, she said, "Answers."

"Aren't we all? Now, why don't we start off proper, hmm? I am Mandar, and you are?"

She hesitated, eyeing him for a moment. "Branwen."

"Ah, it means 'beautiful raven,' does it not?"

"It does," she said. "I found it less intimidating than 'the raven.'"

"Hmm, I can see what you mean," said Mandar, nodding. "It's nice to meet *you*." He added emphasis at the end, hoping she would understand he saw *her*, not the façade she wore.

Branwen shook her head, her brows knit together. "Why are you here? How did you even know where to find me?"

He smiled. "Elohai sent me to you. That is why you have come. Is it not?" The memory of Údar in the arena and the white fire flashed through his mind. "Or perhaps you have *seen* and you seek what you saw."

She stood, backing away quickly, a slight trembling in her hands. "How do you know what I have seen?" she asked.

"Because I have seen it," he replied. "Because I *know* it. And I see in you the same thirst I once saw in a little boy a long, long time ago. The question is, do you want to know?"

"You have the answers I seek?" She stepped back to the fire, sitting down.

Yes, much like the boy, he thought. "I can show you the one who has all of them. First, why don't we start with why you are here."

Branwen pulled her black cloak tighter. "Two weeks ago, at the arena. Something was in the fire," she said, eyes distant. "It called me by my name. I was terrified of everything that was happening and hid outside the city. A few days later, the voice from the fire told me to find you in Reldor. And here I am."

Mandar nodded. "And here you are. Anything else?"

The tremor in her hands increased. "It said, 'Follow me.' But I don't know what that means! Where? How?"

"Do you want to learn?" he asked, sitting up on his haunches.

She shook her head. "Learn what, love? I do not even understand what is happening to me!"

Mandar closed his eyes, listening to the wind, for the voice of his Maker, and found him silent. *So, this is a test for me as well*, he thought. Opening his eyes, he started drawing a circle on the ground with his paw, watching as white flames trailed behind until he closed it. He looked at Branwen who sat wide-eyed, staring at the flames. "You have killed many, enslaved countless others, and have committed horrible acts against your people. Yet in that, Elohai has forgiven you. You need but accept it and be baptized by flame."

Her gray-green eyes met his. "Then what?" she asked, voice quivering.

"Then you are his child," Mandar replied.

She shook her head, frowning. "No, I've not earned something like that! You just listed off everything I've done!"

Mandar walked over and sat beside her, looking at the flames and thinking back to the day Údar had said something similar. The truth was the same as much today as it had been. He faced her. "That's why it's a gift. It is a mercy we do not deserve and a grace we did not earn. All that is left is to accept it, or not." He lowered his voice. "Fire purifies and removes the stains on our souls. It makes us clean."

"But… everything I've done…"

He smiled and whispered. "Forgiven."

Branwen choked on a sob, jumping up and running into the fire without a second thought.

Mandar nodded and breathed deeply as the wind swirled around him.

CHAPTER 28

———

Jayden stood at the corner of the inn, listening to Údar and Batänny's conversation, amazed at how broken the man seemed. Not once had he ever seen his father cry or admit to being wrong about something, and never, ever asking forgiveness.

He peered around the edge, seeing Batänny push Údar back a little so she could look at him. *Hells*, thought Jayden, *he looks terrible.*

"Six years ago you saved me," she said, holding his face. "I grew careless and ended up in a similar place. That was not your doing. In fact, you rescued me again when you could have left me there."

Údar tried to look away, but Batänny held his face steady. "I do not blame you. You ask me to forgive you, and I do. That is not a burden you need to carry."

The man broke down again and Jayden put his back to the wall, fighting back his own emotions. Not a single man he knew had ever been so vulnerable, nor so honest. What was stranger was he did not see it as a sign of weakness but one of incredible strength. *How does that even work?* he wondered.

Not wanting to risk getting caught, Jayden headed back the way he had come toward the rear of the inn. He hadn't meant to eavesdrop on them. He had enough problems of his own to worry about and plenty to think on without creeping around corners and watching others. When he reached the back, he turned, heading down an alley to a main road and walking further into town.

He wandered for hours, making at least two laps around the town, plagued with anxiety about home. They were a little over a week out from Tranâes and seeing his father again—the father who thought he was dead. The one he had wanted to spite. *You can still run,* he told himself. *But you won't.*

The words Mandar had spoken back in the forest about serving a sovereign God and not believing in coincidences had stuck with him, and he could not shake the truth in it.

Jayden stopped his aimless walking and sat down on a bench that faced one of the five fountains he'd counted on his walk. It was smaller than the rest and not nearly as pretty, but there was a rustic quality to the way the stones were stacked and how the greenery was arranged around it. If he had to guess, he'd bet this was the first fountain built in the town.

Elohai, if you're there, give me a sign. Show me what the bigger picture is.

No magical lights. No voice from the sky.

Nothing.

That's what I thought.

He heard footsteps coming up the road and watched as a young man, probably close to his age, with black hair and light umber skin approached the fountain. The youth took out a coin and flipped it into the fount before coming to sit on the bench a few feet from him.

Casting a sidelong look at him, Jayden thought the behavior a little strange. *Must be a X'phosian passing through.* His clothing, however, didn't fit that idea as he only wore a brown tunic with a wide leather belt and breeches. Given the weather, he was poorly dressed, to say the least.

"It's a beautiful day out, isn't it?" said the youth, looking up at the sky.

"I suppose," Jayden replied, following his gaze.

The youth looked his way, smiling. "I'm El. If you don't mind me saying, you seem like you've got a lot on your mind."

Is it customary in X'phos to make awkward conversation with strangers? Jayden wondered. "I have a lot on my mind, yes. It's why I found a quiet spot to be alone."

El nodded. "It is good to take time to think in silence. Doing so forces us to face things we do not often like looking at."

Jayden glanced around, seeing no one else near him. *Is this guy lost?*

"No, I'm not lost," El replied, a little amused.

Jayden stood and backed up toward the fountain. "Who are you?"

Leaning forward, El rested his forearms on his knees. "I am Elohai, and you are Basil, son of Arthfael, Crown Prince of Ungäar, and you asked for a sign."

I'm losing my mind! That's it. My sanity is gone after everything that has happened, and I've gone crazy. If not, that meant he was standing in front of the God he served but did not really follow. "How do you know my name?"

El chuckled, shaking his head. "That is what you are most worried about?"

Jayden gulped. "I hate the name Basil. It's why I go by Jayden."

"'Thankful' or 'he will judge,'" said the youth. "That is what your chosen name means."

Sinking down to the ground, Jayden ran his hands through his hair. "I thought it meant 'good looking.'"

El laughed, and Jayden wasn't sure whether to feel relieved or terrified. After a moment, the youth quieted down before speaking again. "You've seen the wickedness in your land, Jayden, and so have I. It is ugly and cancerous, yet no one will root it out." His eyes watered up. "So, I have passed judgment on Ungäar, and destruction will come upon it swiftly. In two years, I will fill the land with sorrow and the peoples shall weep."

Jayden was trying to wrap his mind around what was happening and what Elohai was saying. *Judgment? Sorrow?* "But..." What was there to say? He had seen firsthand the prostituting of children in Dorämund Mound and exploitation of Iomlíad in Kiäxe. More than a few nobles had mistresses, and the corruption of the courts was a way of life.

"Through you, Jayden, these things shall come to pass, and like your name, through it will come a thankfulness and a returning to their first love," said El, standing. He lingered a moment. "Do you know what Basil means?"

Unable to speak, Jayden simply shook his head.

"It means king."

Jayden blinked, and Elohai was gone, leaving him alone at the foot of the fountain, his fingers clawing at the dirt as his heartbeat thrummed in his ears. There could be no doubt of who he had spoken to, which made everything that had been proclaimed all the more horrifying.

He turned to get up, pausing at the sight of words carved into a stone, so worn and faded that he would not have seen them from the bench. It chilled his blood as he traced a shaking finger through the letters, removing the moss.

Elohai has heard me.

"There is no such thing as coincidence," he whispered.

-II-

Mandar waited patiently by the fire for Branwen to emerge. It had been several hours, and he did not mind the waiting. She had many questions to ask the Maker.

A flicker in the flame caught his eye, and he saw her step out, swaying on her feet. A glowing red circle with a white flame on her chest already beginning to fade. She focused on him. "I spoke with him."

"I've no doubt," he replied. It was in her eyes, the light of the redeemed.

Branwen put a hand to her head, squeezing her eyes shut. "He said... He said I need to go back to Kiäxe, but they will kill me if I go back."

Mandar stood and stretched, shaking himself and reliving the stiffness in his joints. "If he has called you there, he will not abandon you. That does not mean it will be easy, however."

She snorted, running her hands through her inky black hair. "An understatement, love. Most of the people there want me dead."

"Will you go?" he asked, trying to read her face.

Sighing, she squinted up at the sky. "He said, 'Follow me.' I'm not used to listening to anyone else but myself, but yes, I will go."

Mandar walked over to her, giving her a warm smile and putting a paw on her shoulder. "Then follow."

Branwen patted his foot awkwardly, and he could sense something else bothering her by the way she shifted back and forth on her feet and fidgeted. "Is there something wrong?" he asked.

"I... No, just trying to grasp everything," she said softly.

He wasn't convinced, but he decided not to push her. "Understandable. Now, I must go. I'm meeting with Údar soon to discuss the next leg of our journey."

"Are you going to tell him I was here?" she asked, seeming worried.

"No," Mandar replied. "Go with Elohai, Branwen, and perhaps we will meet again someday."

She smiled, nodding. "Perhaps. And thank you." Stepping back, she shifted into a raven and took to the air, circling a few times before flying back toward Kiäxe.

So that is how she caught up to us so quickly. Mandar turned and headed back into the forest, taking his time and enjoying the sunlight filtering through the tress. Autumn was his favorite season because of the colors it brought with it. The air was crisp, carrying a smell he could not place yet felt so much like home.

Returning to his place overlooking the town, he found Údar already waiting for him. "Where the hells have you been?" he asked. "We were supposed to meet an hour ago."

"I went for a walk and lost track of time. I apologize." He eyed his friend. "You look terrible."

Údar folded his arms and glared for a moment. Then he sat on a rotted tree stump. "So much is out of my control now," he muttered, clasping his hands in front of him.

"You are the same little boy you were eighteen hundred years ago," Mandar answered, sitting next to his friend. "Always running from what you cannot control."

"It was always easier than the unknown," Údar replied.

"Yet, after all these years, you wrestle with the same things as you did back then. So is it really easier?" he prodded.

Údar seemed to consider it, a smirk tugging at his lips. "I probably should have listened to you more often, eh?"

Mandar moved his tail, whacking the back of his friend's head. "It would be a start."

They settled into a comfortable silence, a sense of peace descending over Mandar. They had been through many trials together over the years, and through it all, their friendship had stayed strong. When Nisha had died, it had strained it because Údar had focused on vengeance while Mandar had tried to counsel his friend to seek Elohai.

"Mandar?"

He looked at Údar. "Hmm?"

"Thank you for being my friend and sticking with me. I know I haven't been the easiest to live with."

Mandar barked out a laugh, putting a paw on his shoulder. "You are a most difficult human, without a doubt, but it's a privilege to stand by you."

Údar gave a wry smile and Mandar shoved him off the stump, bounding several paces away as he laughed.

"You mangy mongrel!"

CHAPTER 29

"Ready to go?"

Trinia nodded. "I'll be right there, Batänny."

She could hear her leave the room, and the weight of the guilt settled on Trinia all over again. A part of her knew distancing herself was not the right thing to do, but she couldn't help it. She didn't want another voice added to the cacophony in her mind.

There was a knock on the door. "I said I'm coming," she snapped, turning around to see Údar standing in the doorway. He was carrying a bundle in his arms and had a surprised look on his face.

"I'm sorry. I don't mean to intrude," he said.

Idiot! Why did you snap at him? "Sorry, I thought it was Batänny again," she said, wringing her hands.

Don't let him get close!

He can't be trusted!

She winced, rubbing her head. "Focus," she muttered.

"Are you alright?" he asked.

"Fine," she said, putting on a strained smile. "What did you need?"

He took a few steps closer, and she edged herself off the bed as he laid the bundle down, unwrapping it to reveal a sheathed sword. Lifting it off the cloth, he drew it, presenting it to her laid out across his palms. "This is Berach. It was my daughter's sword, and I would like you to have it."

Trinia stared at the weapon and then at Údar. "Why are you giving this to me?"

A means to an end. A means to an end. A means to an end.

He cleared his throat. "I don't know what dangers lie ahead and thought it would provide some extra protection for you. I gave Batänny my wife's sword for the same reasons."

He wants something!

There's a catch!

She leaned over, taking it from him and admiring the blade and the wavy pattern forged into it. The hilt was a hardwood she didn't recognize, with etched lines as decoration, and two burnished bronze pieces on either side of it. "It's lighter than I expected," she said.

Údar nodded. "What it lacks in power, it makes up in swiftness."

While she was more accustomed to daggers, and preferred them, the sword felt good in her hand, already feeling like an extension of her arm. She caught her reflection in the blade, unnerved by the hollow eyes staring back at her. Sliding the sword back into its sheath, she took a calming breath. "Thank you, Údar."

"May it serve you well." He turned and walked out.

Trinia ran her fingers over the hilt again, unsure of how to take the gift. He said it was just that, but she could not help feel there was a catch somewhere. The whole reason they were here was because they had a bargain. Was there a deeper meaning to it?

He gave his wife's to Batänny, so there's nothing to read into it.

Probably made a deal with her, too. Has to keep her happy.

Thoughts, thoughts, thoughts! Always with the thoughts! She was so tired of feeling her mind going a thousand different directions at once, contradicting itself and taking her from one emotional extreme to another. It was like she was slipping from reality into an oblivion with nothing to stop her from sliding.

Taking another breath, Trinia slid the belt around her waist and got it into position on her right hip. She drew it a couple of times with her left hand and it felt fluid and natural. *Maybe it was just an act of kindness,* she thought.

Pulling on her boots, she laced them up and stepped out of her room for the first time in days, making her way to the front. Outside, Jayden sat on his chestnut-colored mount, Batänny on her dapple-gray, and Údar was mounting his dun. Trinia walked up to her new bay mare. "Sorry I haven't visited you," she said, leaning her head against it.

It nibbled at her hand, and she giggled. "I don't have anything, sorry." She put her foot in the stirrup and carefully drew herself up. She met Jayden's gaze, glimpsing something in his eyes before he threw on a fake smile. She could tell it was fake because it was the same one she now wore when people talked to her.

"Alright, we have a week of travel ahead of us," said Údar, keeping his horse in check.

Batänny groaned. "Why is the world so big? Who thought that would be a good idea, huh?"

Údar rolled his eyes, turning his horse and heading toward the end of town. Batänny followed after him. "Think about it. Everything is hundreds of miles apart! That is horrible planning if you ask me."

"Which no one did," he replied.

Trinia shook her head. At least it seemed like Batänny was back to her old self.

"Come on," said Jayden, riding by her.

She gave a slight smile. "Right behind you."

A mile or two outside of town, she could see Mandar waiting for them on a small rise, and as they drew close, she could tell he was watching her. After greeting everyone as they passed, he fell into pace beside her, and it amazed her again just how big he was. Standing shoulder to shoulder with her horse, he was an intimidating sight.

"How you are, Trinia?" he asked, moving around to her left side so he could look at her with his good eye.

Why must everyone keep asking me that? "Fine," she replied.

"Mmm."

"What?" She looked at him, her brows drawing together.

"Do you want to know something I have learned about people through the centuries?"

Trinia shrugged. "I suppose."

"When people say they are fine, they really aren't."

She broke from his gaze and focused on Jayden's back. The road. The bird in the sky. Anything to avoid Mandar's knowing eyes. *What does he expect me to say? That I feel dirty and used up? That there's nothing left in me to be taken? Will that make people feel better? Or maybe how I want to end it all because it means I would stop feeling the echo of hands that I never wanted to feel in the first place?*

Anger burned in her chest, and she grew frustrated with herself. Mandar was worried about her, which meant he cared. He had protected her and saved her life multiple times. She should be thankful.

The mountain range on their left ran on for miles before dwindling in size and then disappearing altogether. To their right stood lush forest. It was a beautiful country with its vibrant colors as autumn slowly crawled toward winter, and she wished she could enjoy it. But she knew it was a mask that hid an ugliness.

An ugliness that had tainted her.

"You don't have to be broken alone, Trinia," said Mandar gently, pulling her out of her thoughts.

The anger burned away into despair and her heart felt like it would crumble in her chest. Unable to speak, she nudged her horse to a trot to pull ahead of him and away from his questions.

-II-

The smell of the sea filled the air, and Trinia wished she could see it. Eleven days of nothing but the dreary blandness of the fog-socked coast was all she had, and she was tiring of it. She was tiring of a lot of things.

She was tired of being afraid; tired of nightmares every time she slept; tired of her Gift; tired of riding and fights and running and death…

Dragging herself from the warmth of her blanket, Trinia began preparing to break camp. She hoped tonight she would be sleeping in her own room with a nice bath far away from everyone else. Pain twinged in her chest and she rubbed the spot, wishing it, too, would go away. Ever since they had left Reldor an ache had sometimes come without warning. Sometimes it would take her breath away while others it was nothing more than annoyance.

"We'll reach the city today by mid-day," said Údar, addressing the group. "With any luck, the fog will break before we get there, and you'll see the city in all its glory." He looked at her and added. "You'll need to conceal your hair until we reach the king."

Yet one more thing she was tired of. "Alright, give me a minute."

Once finished, her hair was a dull brown, and she left the shelter of the trees and entered a world of dim white as the fog fought to keep the sun from shining through. She could not see more than a dozen yards ahead along the road, which didn't help her unease. *Anything could be lurking out there...*

The fog seemed to mute everyone, too, and there was little in the way of conversation. It was as if speaking would disturb the silence. She was okay with not talking, though; it was easier.

After several hours, the fog finally thinned, with shafts of sunlight filtering through. Trinia lifted her head, eyes closed, letting the pale light warm her cheeks. Opening them, she took in the sight before her. In the distance stood the towering stone walls of Tranâes. Even from where they were, she could see it was imposing. The walls had to be at least fifty feet high!

"Wow," Batänny breathed, coming up next to her.

"Tranâes is the stronghold of strongholds," said Údar, pulling his horse to a stop.

"I can see why," said Trinia in awe.

From where they sat, she could make out at least eight walls layered within the outer one and a grand palace perched atop a sea cliff. The city itself spread out from there like a blanket from the cliff to the sea.

Soon they began passing by farms and country manors, and she took it all in, noting the people out working with hardly anything on. *Slaves, slaves, and more slaves*, she thought, disgusted.

The road became smoother, the stones more tightly fitted together; the homes became taller, the stonework more notable; the houses that had been here and there started getting closer together, forming into neighborhoods in which people went about their duties in preparing for the snows.

Trinia peered over at Jayden, ready to ask him a question, and saw he had his hood up. Batänny was beside Údar and Mandar had taken on his human form and was walking on the other side, leaving her and Jayden in the back. "What are you doing?" she asked.

He glanced at her and she saw that look in his eyes again—the one he hid so well. Only now, he wasn't hiding it at all. "Trinia, there is something you need to know before we meet with the king."

Danger! Her mind screamed. She shut out the thoughts, trying to focus on what he was going to say. "Yes?"

Jayden guided his horse closer to hers, lowering his voice. "There's a reason I didn't want to come back here, and I should have told you sooner but… Well, I never thought I would need to." He sighed, rubbing his face. "Trinia, Arthfael is my father."

She burst out laughing. When his cheeks turned red, she realized he wasn't joking. "Jayden, what are you saying?" she asked, suddenly feeling woozy.

"I'm saying I'm the Crown Prince of Ungäar. My father is the man you're going to be talking to, and the same one who shipped me off to the Academy." He paused, taking a breath. "Údar told me to tell you—"

"Údar knows?" she asked, shocked.

"He figured it out back in Dorämund," Jayden replied, looking ashamed. "He told me to tell you because of the life-debt. I was wrong for keeping it from you this long, and I am deeply sorry."

Trinia set her gaze forward, fixing it there to keep the world from spinning. So many things made more sense. How he knew so much about Ungäar, its cities, other countries, all of it.

"I knew I needed to tell you beforehand because he thinks I'm dead," he continued, faster now. "I thought about it in Reldor, but you were locked in your room and—"

She held up a hand, cutting him off. "Just stop. All this time you knew where we were going and didn't bother to tell me, and now that we're here, in *your city*, you bring it up?" Trinia shook her head, wrestling with the building emotions. "I can't talk about this right now."

Jayden reached out a hand. "Trinia, I didn't mean—"

"Don't touch me," she snapped, glaring at him through blurring eyes.

He recoiled like he had tried to grab a skaäsa. The hurt was clear in his face as he urged the horse forward, leaving her behind. She tried to calm the emotions, shoving them back down and forcing herself to look at the growing city around her.

Passing through the first gate, she noted that people were everywhere, thousands of people of all shapes, sizes, and colors. It was by far the most diverse place she had seen in Ungäar.

From what she could tell, the city was easily two to three times larger than Rionnagan in both size and population. It was truly awe-inspiring.

The people wore thick fur cloaks to keep the chill of autumn at bay with heavy boots and fur bracers on their arms. The women had their hair done up in a variety of styles, some plaited in many braids, while others wove in leather straps to keep it together. Others kept theirs down or had cut it short to make it more manageable.

Likewise, the men had their hair pulled back and strapped with leather or a single braid. Many decorated their beards in the same manner.

Soldiers patrolled along the wall high above and in the street below, but to Trinia, it seemed there was little need for them to do so. Many of them looked to be younger and quite handsome, dressed in their armor with swords on their hips.

"Try not to gawk too much," Údar said, coming up next to her. "They are likely married, and it is not uncommon for a wife to challenge a woman who stares at her man to a fight."

Trinia immediately broke eye contact with a young man who had looked her way as she stared.

As they moved deeper into the city, she could almost feel the energy buzzing through the air. Everywhere she looked she saw people working alongside each other, and very few seemed to be the slaves she had seen in the countryside. Languages she did not recognize mingled with the common tongue the Airgíd established during the Empire. Almost every person she'd met thus far spoke the common language, albeit with a tinge of the local accent.

It seemed like everyone on every corner was speaking in excited tones. *I wonder what the fuss is about?*

Each gate they passed through brought new wonders. From what Trinia could see, the first gate held shops, markets, and a road leading to the docks. The second gate, a little smaller than the first but just as thick, opened to more shops of finer scale, no doubt for the rich.

People milled about everywhere, coin exchanged hands, goods were purchased or traded, and a thief was caught in the act. Trinia looked on, mesmerized by the sights before her.

All about her, life carried on with a simplicity that painfully reminded her of home. Watching children play in the streets took her back to a time when she and Niren tried to break into the treasury in the palace and had run when the guards spotted them.

It also reminded her of the little girl in Dorämund who had never known what it was like to play. Trinia gripped the reins tighter at the memory.

She noticed with every gate they passed through, the number of guards patrolling it increased. As they reached the seventh one, the guards stopped them. By the look of the opulent homes on the other side, the seventh circle was where the nobles lived. Trinia counted no less than thirty-six guards including the ones on the gatehouse.

"Who are you? State your business," demanded one of the guards.

Trinia glanced at Údar. He seemed like he was trying to decide how best to approach him. "I'm looking for an audience with King Arthfael. We seek his counsel on an urgent matter."

Several of the other guards laughed as the first who'd spoken answered, "The king doesn't give out counsel to any who seek it."

"He may consider it when he knows who I am," Údar replied coolly.

"Oh, so you think you're special. Is that it?" The guard glared at him.

"No," Údar replied, irritation in his voice. "But what I have to say the king will want to hear."

"Doubtful," the guard replied. "Now be off! You—"

"Genär!"

The guard stopped, and Trinia shot a glance at Jayden, who was riding forward. She looked back at the guard, who glared until Jayden flipped back his hood.

"Holy fire!" the guard exclaimed. "It's Prince Basil!"

CHAPTER 30

———

No going back now, thought Jayden, looking down at the guard. "These people are with me, Genär, and my father will want to hear what they have to say."

The guard bowed low, as did all the others. "Prince Basil! Forgive me. We thought you were dead!"

"Yes, that was the point," retorted Jayden. "Take us to my father."

"Yes, Prince Basil!" said Genär, motioning to the other guards to move out of the way. "Hail Prince Basil! He is alive and has returned!"

Jayden cringed inwardly. *Hells below, I hate that name.*

"Wait a second," exclaimed Batänny. "Jayden's name is Basil?" She burst out laughing.

"In case you missed it, he's also the Crown Prince and could have you executed for mocking him," said Údar, tapping the side of his horse.

Batänny stared at Údar. "He wouldn't do that though." Then to him. "Right?"

"I hate that name," he replied, trying to keep a serious face. He would never kill someone over it, but if it meant he had to put some fear into her to avoid endless hours of teasing, well, he didn't mind.

She paled a little and bowed. "I'm sorry, forgive me, Prince Bas—I mean—Jayden, your lordship, sir. Údar, wait for me!"

Jayden smirked and looked to Trinia, but she refused to meet his gaze, her face stoic. He fell in line behind Batänny with Trinia and Mandar following at the back.

Nothing has changed since I left, he noted, gazing around at the homes and their white stone walls. Nobles, some of whom he remembered, stood on their balconies, pointing and staring.

"All hail Crown Prince Basil!" called Genär as they passed through.

Turning around in his saddle, he could see the crowd gathering behind and following them. Soon the whole city would know.

They entered the palace grounds as they passed through the eighth gate, and the palace itself rose at least a hundred feet into the air, lined in marble and quartz on the outside with accents trimmed in gold. The likeness of the first king of Ungäar was carved around the entrance, his sword pointed at the ground as if claiming it. Jayden gazed up at the statue, feeling its empty eyes staring back at him, as if challenging him. To what, he didn't know.

Pools of water spread about the courtyard where fish would be kept for viewing come spring, and most of the trees stood naked without their leaves. The coastal winds tended to sweep them away faster than they could be enjoyed.

I cannot believe I'm back here. He dismounted and walked over to Genär. "Go tell my father of my arrival. I know my way around and will lead my friends to the Hall of Stone to meet him."

The man bowed low and rushed toward the palace. Jayden turned to Údar. "I feel ill."

"If you can survive a Baobhan Sith, I think you will handle this just fine," Údar replied, handing the reins to a stable boy who had come running up. The boy paused, throwing Jayden a look before scampering off with the horse.

Jayden shivered. "Let's make a point to avoid that during our conversation. At least the part with me."

"As you wish."

Batänny and Trinia dismounted with Mandar's assistance and handed the horses over to the care of the stable hands. They were unable to take their eyes off the palace. Jayden supposed he couldn't blame them, but for him, the old sight had lost its luster a long time ago.

Jayden saw the crowds catching up to them and he motioned to the others. "Quickly, let's get inside before we are surrounded. Follow me."

Taking the lead, he ushered them through the entrance and paused to tell the guards to lock the doors behind them and to not let anyone else in until he had spoken with his father. They stared at him in shock and nodded dumbly. "This way," he said to the others.

The immense halls carried their voices as he showed them to the Hall of Stone. Jayden noted the long rugs lining the main walkway were new since he was last here and new paintings and tapestries hung from long ropes tied to the rafters above. Sconces, each with a *soläs* lined the walls, dim until evening, allowing for the massive windows to let in the natural lighting.

Memory after memory resurfaced as they passed by gawking servants who whispered and pointed at him as if he were a foreigner, which he very much felt like. *Three years living in different cities and under the stars can change a person,* he thought ruefully. *Add to that a life-debt and slew of other experiences condensed into little over a month, a person is bound to change in some way.*

There was a low whistle behind him. "I've never seen anything like this in all my life," said Batänny. "Have you, Údar?"

"I've been to Tranâes on many occasions," he replied. "It has been a long time since my last visit, however."

Jayden paused and turned to him. "Is that how you know my father? You met him here?"

"It was before you were born, lad. I was traveling through Ungäar near Nolordale on the border of Canämor, and bandits surrounded him and his guards. I helped dispatch them and he offered me a boon."

He saved my father? "How did you know who he was?" Jayden asked, folding his arms.

Údar chuckled. "I didn't. He was not flying his banner at the time. As for the boon he offered, it is an option to call upon if needed."

"You're using your boon for me?" Trinia asked, stepping up. "I thought you were just going to talk with him, not call in a favor."

Jayden looked between the two of them, sensing a tension there. *Did I miss something? Wasn't the point of coming here was because Údar had some clout with my father?* It struck him that his father owed Údar a life-debt in the same way that he owed Trinia. *Hells, what if she does the same thing to me?*

Údar looked at her. "Trust me, the mind of a king is not easily swayed. It is a last resort."

Jayden started walking again, the weight of the debt he carried burdening him more than ever, especially knowing it could be held over a person until they satisfied it. *Trinia did offer to forgive it,* he told himself. But how would it look if his father, the king, kept his and his son did not? *This is why I ran in the first place! Expectations!*

He gulped as they reached the doors to the Hall of Stone. The two guards outside saluted, putting the flat of their blades to their foreheads. The doors swung inward, and Jayden lifted his chin and squared his shoulders. His father was a hard man and demanded much, so there was no telling what kind of punishment might take place.

As the doors came to a rest, the Hall of Stone was shown in all its glory. A long red rug lined the path to the throne, which sat at the far end of the hall. The dark marble floor absorbed the light from the afternoon sun, which created a halo around the throne itself. Banners of the lords hung on either side from the second level of the room and two braziers sat on either side of the steps up to the throne.

Behind it, an enormous banner of the king, a ten-pointed star with a sword stabbed through it, hung from the lofty ceiling. And in the middle sat Arthfael, King of Ungäar, Lord of Tranâes. His father.

He looked just how Jayden remembered him. Dark brown hair that was almost black, neatly trimmed beard, keen gray eyes.

Arthfael stood and Jayden braced himself, but whatever he had expected, it was not seeing his father rushing to him with tears in his eyes.

"My son!" his father cried, embracing him. "You are alive! Bless the Flames! You're alive!"

Jayden stood dumbstruck as his father pulled back, kissing his cheeks and embracing him again. This was not the man he knew, had grown up with, who had sent him off to the Academy. "Yes, I'm alive," he said, hearing the uncertainty in his own voice.

Arthfael held him at arm's length, looking him up and down. "You've grown! You are a man now, and a fine one at that." His father's gaze went past him to the others. "And who are these people with you?"

"Uh, this is Batänny, Mandar, Trinia, and Údar," he said, motioning to each one. *I am dreaming. That is the only possibility. I'm dreaming.*

His father nodded to each in turn, pausing on Údar. "I know you."

Údar smiled and nodded. "You have an excellent memory. You know me as Green Cloak."

Recognition dawned in Arthfael's eyes, and Jayden could see the walls he was so accustomed to go up. "Ah yes, Green Cloak," he replied, his tone more formal. "It has been a long time."

"Indeed, it has," said Údar with a slight bow of his head.

Not wanting to lose the opportunity with his father's unexpectedly good mood, Jayden said, "Father, we need to speak with you on subjects of some urgency." It surprised Jayden how quickly he fell back into the formal talk of the courts. *It's like I never left.*

Arthfael turned to him, a smile returning to his lips. "What could be more important than the return of my son whom we thought had died? Moreover, a return just in time for the Autumn Ball!"

Jayden closed his eyes, kicking himself. *Hells below, that was what everyone was so excited about!* "Father," he said, opening his eyes, "this is something that cannot wait. Thydu has attacked our northern city of Salorim!"

His father waved a hand, dismissing it. "We have heard the reports. It is nothing more than bandits looking to cause trouble."

"Arthfael, I was there and saw it with my own eyes," said Údar, spreading out his hands. "It was destroyed."

"That is not what my scouts have told me," Arthfael replied sharply. "Should I believe you over my most trusted men? We will speak no more on this matter. My son has returned, and we need to finish preparations for the ball. You are all welcome to stay and enjoy yourselves."

"But, Father—"

"Enough! Rest, my son. The ball is in three days and now that you are home, I expect you to help me as we will celebrate not only the harvest but your return too," said Arthfael, clapping a hand on his shoulder. "It's good to have you home."

CHAPTER 31

———

Trinia sat by the window in her shared room with Batänny, staring out over the sea and listening to the roar of the waves below on the cliffs. She was doing her best to ignore the others. Until now, all she had ever seen was mountains, hills, forests, rivers, and cities. But this was something *new. It's endless*, she thought, gazing toward the horizon.

"Is it just me, or did that all seem really odd?" Batänny asked, sitting on the bed across from her.

"It was," Jayden admitted, standing over by the door. "He is not normally so… pleasant."

"Will he hear what I have to say?" Trinia asked, pulling herself away from the view. "About the Airgíd I mean."

Jayden ruffled his hair and shrugged. "Hells if I know. I thought he was going to order a lashing for me, and instead he greets me with a hug and it's back to business as usual." He shook his head. "Something is going on."

"How did he already know about the attack?" Batänny wondered aloud. "Is it possible scouts passed us to report it?"

"It is, but for him to say it was bandits, even with Údar as a witness, is strange," said Jayden, rubbing his chin.

Trinia turned her attention back to the sea, still trying to come to terms with how Jayden, or Basil, or whoever he was, had lied to her—maybe not directly but with half-truths.

Didn't you do the same?

That's different.

Shut up!

She rubbed her temples, feeling the ache in her chest coming back. The pattern seemed to be whenever she got anxious and the thoughts came, but she had not yet figured out a way to keep them under control.

"You okay, Trinia?" Jayden asked.

"I'm fine," she replied, keeping her eyes on the birds drifting on the breeze outside the window.

Broken.

Dirty.

"So, what is this ball your father was talking about?" Batänny asked.

"It's celebrating the harvest. The entire kingdom does different versions. The ball is held here and there is music, dancing, food, you name it," he said.

"Sounds exciting. Doesn't it, Trinia?"

It sounds awful, she thought. All those people pretending they were better than everyone else while others starved or were traded like goods in other cities. "Yes, exciting," she lied.

You're pushing them away, you know.

It's to protect ourselves.

You don't want them to feel uncomfortable.

Looking down toward the base of the cliffs, Trinia wondered if such a fall would kill her. She was so tired of the thoughts and feeling on edge, like the slightest puff of wind would shatter what was left of her soul.

"Trinia?"

She turned back to Jayden, seeing the concern in his eyes. "Hmm?"

"I wanted to speak with you."

"I think she needs some rest," said Batänny, scooting to the end of the bed. "It's been a long day."

He glanced between them, settling back on Trinia. "I understand," he said, giving a quick smile. "If you need anything, let a servant know. You'll want for nothing while you're here."

With that, he bowed and left the room.

Batänny glanced over at her, raising a brow. "I sent him away because I needed to talk with you, too."

Trinia sighed, leaning the back of her head against the wall. "I'm fine, Batänny. You need not worry."

"Trinia, do you take me for a fool?"

Surprised, she looked over we the woman who wore an angry look. "Of course not. Why would you say something like that?"

She's mad at you.

She hates you.

"Because you're acting like you didn't suffer something horrible and are trying to push us away," Batänny countered. "Do you really think I don't know how you must feel? Do you think I can't see the same look in your eyes I had when I tried to kill myself?" Her eyes started tearing up.

Trinia could only stare. No one had dared bring up what happened, and she preferred it that way. To talk about it was to relive it, and that was something she couldn't do.

Batänny's lips were quivering when she spoke again. "I know I'm older than you by a few years, Trinia, but you're the closest thing to a friend I've ever had. I'll be damned if I watch you try to do what I did."

The passion in her voice increased the ache in Trinia's chest, even if she didn't feel the emotions she would have expected. *Why am I not upset?*

Broken.

Damaged.

Heartless.

The woman wiped her eyes. "I'm not going to force you to talk to me, but please know you can tell me anything. I was there, too."

The ache became a throb and Trinia rubbed her chest, trying to process what Batänny was saying. "I... I'm just not ready yet," she whispered. "And I promise to tell you if I'm thinking of hurting myself."

The woman nodded, wiping her nose on her sleeve. "Good. That is all I ask for. Just know you're not alone."

-II-

In the two days since arriving back home, the sheer number of visitors wishing to see him had overwhelmed Jayden. Standing in front of the mirror in his princely garb, he felt even more an imposter than he had over three years ago. Dressed in a royal blue tunic and black breeches with a black leather belt, he knew he looked the part of Crown Prince.

The servant placed the torc around his neck and smoothed out the wrinkles of the tunic before adding the polished leather jerkin to the uniform. The dark walnut color made the blue stand out against it. Once done, Jayden felt like he was staring at a stranger.

"You look magnificent," said the servant, bowing.

Jayden gave a tight smile. "Thank you, Alard. Fine work, as always."

The man bowed lower. "A pleasure to serve you once again, my prince."

Stepping away from the mirror, Jayden grabbed the ceremonial sash and got it in place around his waist. If he was going to meet with his father and the other nobles, he needed to look like them, and he hated it.

"Will you be needing anything else, my prince?" Alard asked, waiting patiently.

"No, thank you."

Alard bowed again and slipped out the door, shutting it quietly behind him.

"Time to play politics," Jayden muttered.

Heading out a different door, he made his way down the endless maze of hallways, his feet finding the way on their own. It amazed him how it all came back so quickly and how it seemed as if he had never left. Along the way, servants and guards greeted him and bowed, acknowledging his return with smiles and kind words. If they only knew how much he hated this place.

Arriving at the meeting room, he took a breath to calm his nerves before pushing open the door. He noted at least fifteen other nobles seated around a long table. All eyes turned to him.

"Ah, there he is!" his father's voice boomed. "My son, Prince Basil, returned home to us!"

The other nobles stood and clapped as Jayden made his way to his seat at his father's right hand. At Arthfael's command, they returned to their seats. "Thank you for joining me in welcoming my son home. It is a relief to this father's heart to know the rumors of his death have turned out to be just that. I wish to celebrate his return at the Autumn Ball tomorrow."

"An excellent idea," declared Lord Baldwin, a man whom Jayden had great respect for. He was now in his sixties with graying hair and a beard to match.

"Here, here!" called Lord Dromm, a man in his late thirties with a penchant for unsavory women. How he had ever become a lord was beyond Jayden.

Others followed the expected course of agreeing with the king, and Arthfael smiled brightly. "Good! Then we shall make the announcement at the same time."

Jayden glanced at his father. *Announcement?* "Father, what announcement?"

Arthfael turned to him, laying a hand on his shoulder. "Since your return, I did not want to waste a moment and sent word to the emissary from Canämor who arrived a few weeks ago on diplomatic relations that we sought a marriage alliance with them."

"What?" Jayden exclaimed. "Father, you cannot be serious!"

"What better time to announce the betrothal to Princess Enora and bring a lasting peace between our two kingdoms?" asked Arthfael.

Jayden looked around the table and then back to his father. "Canämor has always been envious for the land we have. You have said so yourself. Why would they suddenly change their minds?"

"Much has happened since you disappeared, young prince," said Baldwin, leaning on the table. "Canämor seeks to end the feuding between our kingdoms that threatens the Peace Treaty our forefathers established after the fall of the Empire."

Has the whole world gone mad? Jayden stood, shoving his chair back. "We have Thydu marching into our lands and you speak of marriage to a kingdom that had sought a way to destroy us?" he asked, baffled.

"Basil, there is no attack from Thydu," his father replied, the light in his eyes dimming. "Green Cloak was mistaken."

Jayden shook his head, slamming his fist on the table. "And I tell you he saw it!"

The room went still, and he could feel all eyes on him. Arthfael's face grew rigid in the way Jayden recognized from childhood when he was about to get reprimanded. "Perhaps I was too hasty in bringing you into the planning for things. You clearly have not recovered your strength. Go get some rest, and I shall see you tomorrow evening when I shall announce the betrothal."

Jayden bit back a reply, knowing it would do no good. His father's word was law. He cast an angry glance around the table and stormed out of the room.

Bursting through the doors to the outer courtyard, he inhaled the cool evening air as he walked over to the low wall that overlooked the cliffs. Leaning against it, he closed his eyes, trying and failing to comprehend the logic in his father's decision.

Only there was none.

"Jayden?"

"Hells below!" he cried, spinning around. Údar stood a few feet away, pipe in hand. "Are you trying to stop my heart?"

The light from the pipe lit Údar's eyes, and Jayden could see a hint of mirth in them. "Not intentionally," Údar replied, walking over and leaning on the wall with him. "Something has you troubled."

"A good many things have me troubled," said Jayden running a hand through his hair. "The world has lost all sense and meaning since I left Salorim, and it seems it has reached my home city as well. My father is trying to arrange a marriage for me to the Princess Enora of Canämor!"

"Not an unwise choice," said Údar, blowing a smoke ring. "But a slippery slope knowing Éowald and his lust for power."

Jayden threw his hands in the air in exasperation. "How in the hells do you know so much about the kingdoms? You've been living in the forest!"

Údar turned to him with a wry smile. "I'm almost two thousand years old, lad. I've seen a thing or two in my time, and I know the minds of kings better than they know themselves because I have watched them since their founding."

"Wait, wait. Two *thousand* years? That's impossible!"

"One-thousand-eight-hundred and sixty-four, to be specific," Údar corrected. "And nothing is impossible with Elohai, which brings me back to your issue."

Jayden held his head, looking up at the stars as they sparkled into existence above them. "You mean to tell me you were alive during the time of the Empire? And that you witnessed the founding of the four kingdoms?"

The man nodded, seemingly enjoying the moment at Jayden's expense. A thought struck him, and he met Údar's gaze. "Why are you telling me this now?"

"Ah, now you're thinking. Why indeed." Údar blew out another ring. "I tell you because I believe you are right. Something is amiss and not even I can figure it out. While I do not know your father well, his actions do seem rather hasty, and in my wealth of experience, that means trouble."

"What does that mean for me?" Jayden asked, throwing his arms wide again. "Hells below, Údar, this is why I ran! To get away from all of this!"

"Jayden, may I share something with you?"

The solemnness in his tone gave Jayden pause. "I'm not going to like it. Am I?"

"Probably not," Údar said, laughing softly. His expression sobered after a moment. "I've been running from a calling, a personal journey I started when I was a child. I had moments when I was following Elohai, and others, like when you found me, I was trying to hide from him."

Yeah, not liking the direction this is going, thought Jayden.

"But there comes a time when we can no longer run, and we are forced to choose between two hard things," Údar continued, glancing up at the stars. "Tell me, Jayden, how far would you go to outrun your future?"

"I suppose in some ways, I have already tried," he confessed. "It's what I was trying to do when I met Trinia."

"And it seems she is the catalyst for the decisions we have faced of late." Údar looked down at the pipe, knocking the embers out on the wall. "There is no such thing as coincidence when you serve a sovereign God."

"So Mandar informed me." Jayden looked out over the sea as the moon rose in the west. "You're saying I have to choose, but how do I know which is the right one?"

Údar followed his gaze. "When I learn to make the right choice every time, I'll be sure to let you know."

Jayden cracked a smile. "Some sage you are."

Údar grunted. "Just a man on a journey, same as you."

He nodded, looking at the man, seeing the weight of the years on Údar's shoulders. The things he must have seen and experienced. *No wonder he is so grouchy all the time,* Jayden thought. *I suppose I would be too.*

The silence stretched out as they leaned on the wall, watching the moon rise and cast its milky-white light on the city below them—a city Elohai had pronounced a terrible judgment upon.

A city to be filled with nothing more than stones and sorrow.

CHAPTER 32

———

"Where are they?" asked Caderyn, glowering down from the throne at the messenger who shifted nervously on his feet.

"They have… refused, my lord. They say you do not have the authority to call them together."

"I am Chief of *all* Airgíd," he bellowed, rising. "I am their *King* because I rule the City of Snow and Stars! *I* will rebuild the might of the Old Empire, and I will not tolerate such disobedience!"

The messenger bowed, trembling. "Of course, my lord, er, king. What would you have me do?"

Caderyn took a step down. "I want you to go and bring me every Airgíd chieftain from here to Lyzus."

Step.

"I want you to kill their wives."

Step.

"I want them to watch as we sacrifice their children to the gods they pay lip service to."

Step.

"Then, when I have taken everything from them, I shall permit them to die as traitors," he growled, coming to stand before the messenger. "Now go."

The messenger bowed and backed away slowly before hurrying out of the hall. Caderyn watched him go, cracking his knuckles. The pathetic fools thought they could ignore him, did they? The decision would cost them dearly.

He turned and left the hall, finding himself going back to the dungeons where a few weeks ago his plan had almost been foiled. Descending the steps and standing before the open cell where his daughter had killed herself, he stared at the dried blood staining the stone floor. Someone had brought his daughter the weapon she had taken her life with. The selfish brat knew what it would cost him! Thankfully, the gods had smiled upon him by sending him Ulscia and her daughter. Their power as Baobhan Sith would secure him the throne and the fealty of the others.

But the bigger problem remained. A traitor roamed the city, one who had access to the palace itself, which was not something many had. He had grilled and tortured everyone he could think of for information on it, even that sorry excuse for a guard, Niren, who had let his daughter escape the first time. Nothing. It was as if the traitor were a ghost.

He kneeled beside the dried blood, running his fingers over it. "Even in death you cannot stop the prophecy surrounding you, my daughter. The world shall burn, and the Empire shall rise again despite your attempts to stop it. Because you were too weak to do what needed to be done."

-II-

Trinia and Batänny followed a young servant girl to the baths where they could freshen up and prepare for the Autumn Ball later that evening. If there was one thing she loved, it was a good hot bath. *Maybe this will help lift my spirits.* She also needed to make sure she didn't accidentally drop the illusion on her hair. Not until she was with the king and could talk with him.

A woman by the name of Carys bustled around the room as they entered, tutting as she looked at them. "T'will not do, not at all. Get out of those rags."

Guided by an older servant woman, Trinia went behind a small partisan made of oak to allow some privacy while slipping out of her clothes and into a silken robe.

Carys ordered the other servants about like a general commanding their troops. From what Trinia could tell, she was firm but not harsh.

Coming out from behind the screen, Trinia saw Batänny on the other side, arms folded across her chest, as the female servants rolled up their sleeves. "Um, what's going on?" Batänny asked, looking from the woman to the other servants.

"Come now, no time to waste! We shall help you get clean."

"No one is laying a hand on me," Batänny replied adamantly. "I'll bathe myself, thank you."

Carys' brows furrowed together and Trinia stifled a chuckle. "Listen here, lassie, you will get in this tub, and we're going to get you clean before tonight. Do I make myself clear?"

When Batänny didn't budge, Trinia shook her head and walked over to the tub. They assisted her out of her robe and helped her into it before she sank into the steaming water with a sigh. *It cannot get much better than this,* she thought.

"Would you prefer jasmine or lavender oil?" asked one of the younger girls, showing two glass bottles to Trinia.

"What are they for?" she asked and then pointed at the jasmine.

"It's to help relax you while we rub your shoulders, lass," said Carys, glancing her way.

"You said nothing about that!" Batänny blurted, hurrying over and tossing her robe aside at the foot of the tub as she climbed in.

While Trinia preferred no one touching her, she didn't want Batänny worrying, so she allowed the woman to drizzle the oil on her back.

The smell of it filled the room, and she found her anxious mind able to relax as the servant girl worked out the knots in her neck and shoulders, even down her arms to the tips of her fingers. *This is divine.*

She was not as fond of the copious amounts of scrubbing that came afterward, however, despite Carys insisting it was needed. "The dirt caked on you could build a mud hut."

Once scrubbed and the water had grown cold, Carys ushered them out, wrapped them in towels, and took them to an adjacent room where the headmistress told them to sit. She turned to the servants, telling them to get more oil, brushes, and clothes. Addressing Trinia, she said, "Now, lassie, you must look the part of an honored guest of the prince. Don't fuss. It will only make it take longer."

Honored guest of the prince? She shot a look to Batänny, who shrugged. *He's probably trying to make up for lying.*

As effective as the shoulder rub had been in relieving the tension in her body, having her hair braided undid it. Trinia winced more than once as the deft fingers pulled and tugged to get her hair into place, and she noted a string of colorful words from Batänny. When finished, Trinia's hair was pulled back on the sides, plaited, and tied off with a leather strap at the back, leaving two strands at the front to frame her face. Batänny's hair had a fishnet pattern that started at the front and was held in place by little silver beads where the braids intersected.

The servants applied more oil to Trinia's hair, and she declined the offer to rub her body down with oil. Her shoulders were one thing, the rest of her was quite another.

"I feel like I'm being basted before being thrown on a spit to be cooked," Batänny grumbled as the servants applied the oil to her.

Carys tutted, sending a look her way. Trinia smiled, and Batänny rolled her eyes, muttering curses under her breath.

Batänny had grown on her since their meeting. Sure, she was a little crazy and talked way more than anyone Trinia had ever known, but she had been there to ground her in the midst of what happened. Over the weeks of travel, she had been close by. In truth, Batänny was the closest thing to a sister Trinia had ever had. *And all I have done is push her away when she was trying to help,* Trinia thought bitterly.

The servants who had left returned with two beautiful dresses. Carys grabbed one the color of the summer sun and held it out to Batänny. "This dress should do for you."

Batänny reached out, touching it gingerly and casting a glance at the woman. "It's gorgeous."

Carys nodded approvingly. "I thought you might like it. Quickly now, go with Delyth here and put it on."

As Batänny followed the servant behind a partition on the other side of the room, Carys held out a dress of sapphire blue. "This one is for you, lass."

"It's beautiful," Trinia whispered. Back home, she had formal clothes but nothing as beautiful or as extravagant as this.

"Ow!" Batänny yelped. "Gentle!"

"You'll live," Carys said amused. The older woman leaned in. "I was going to give it to the grumpy one, but I like you better." She winked.

"I heard that!" Batänny called. "Aye! Watch your hands there!"

Carys laughed, clearly enjoying Batänny's discomfort. Turning back to her she said, "Come, lass, I shall help you into this one. Most girls your age probably wouldn't fit, but since you're a wee bit taller than most, you should be able to pull it off."

"I've never worn a dress," Trinia admitted. "Can you make sure I don't trip and fall on my face?"

"Of course! Now, follow my instructions and we'll get you sorted."

It took more than a little help from the woman to get Trinia into it, and once she was in, the dress was a near perfect fit when the straps in the back were tightened.

"There! You look like a princess!"

Trinia chuckled nervously. *That might be a stretch.*

The woman led her around the partition and Batänny was already waiting. Trinia gasped at the transformation. Batänny's dress had long sleeves with a small loop at the end to slip a finger through to hold it in place. The collar wrapped around her neck, with a cutaway at the shoulders.

"How are you supposed to breathe in these things?" Batänny asked with hand over her stomach.

Carys rolled her eyes, walking over and loosening the strings in the back a touch. "Really, lass, it's not that hard."

"I don't see you in one," Batänny retorted.

"Ha! Those days are long over for me."

Trinia turned toward the mirror, seeing the transformation in herself now. The dress had similar sleeves to Batänny's, but her shoulders were bare, and the neckline squared just below the collarbone. Her hair was braided back and still under the illusion, with two tendrils on either side. Her cheeks, softer but a month ago, were now slightly drawn in from life on the road. Thankfully, the dark circles below her eyes were gone. It was as if the horrors had never happened and she wasn't an Airgíd at all. Something she found herself wishing for more than anything.

Batänny came over, resting a gentle hand on her shoulder, and with it, came the thoughts once again.

Fake.

False.

Traitor.

-II-

Údar stood in front of the window as the servants finished scrubbing Mandar down despite his many protests. He cracked a tired smile.

"The sooner you stop fussing, the sooner we can finish," said the elderly woman.

"I can clean myself well enough," Mandar protested. "Údar, tell them!"

Turning, he looked at his friend's pleading face and couldn't help but laugh. "It is their custom, Mandar. I was washed in half the time. Let Mabyn do what she needs to do."

Mandar glared at him, finally relenting to let the woman scrub him. Údar winked at his friend, turning back to the window and looking out over a small garden. Everything was dead now, but in the spring, he knew people would be busy planting seeds and tending to it. He decided someday he would have a garden, some place to work the earth with his hands. It had been a passion of Nisha's and he wanted to honor her in that way.

"Confound it, woman, I'm clean!"

"Shush! Let me rinse your hair."

When Mabyn finally finished scrubbing Mandar down, they brought fresh clothes for him. The shirt was burgundy with silver trim with brown pants and brown leather boots.

Údar's shirt was deep green with the same silver trim as Mandar's, though his sleeves were a little looser.

With Mandar now dressed, Mabyn went about trimming his hair with shears and then pulled it back in a warrior's knot. When the woman left, he stepped up next to Údar, still grumbling. "Humans. You know I shall have a thin spot in my fur now."

Údar snorted. "You don't seem to mind them most of the time, and I always said you could use a trim."

"I'm not a pup who has to be licked clean! Why should I need someone to scrub me down or cut my hair?"

He patted his friend on the shoulder in mock seriousness. "I'm glad you made it out alive."

"Mock me all you want," Mandar replied gruffly, "just remember I know where you sleep."

"All bark, no bite," Údar replied, walking to his chair.

"We'll see about that."

Mandar settled down across from him in another chair, crossing his legs. "Údar, has Jayden mentioned anything to you about Ulscia?"

He raised a brow. "No, should he have?"

"No, it's just that he spoke to me of her outside of Kiäxe. Did it ever occur to you we escaped her too easily?"

Údar stared at the fire in the hearth. "It had not. Though, now that you bring it up, it does seem odd and unlike her."

"My thoughts exactly," said Mandar, nodding.

Údar tugged at his beard in thought, going back to his conversation in the forest with her. The banshee had said she wanted Trinia's blood, and he had been so confident of her motives before. However, at the cave, not once did she try to take the girl. Even the attack had seemed light compared to the one in the forest. *What I am missing?*

Had he been so blinded by rage and vengeance that he missed something obvious? *Why did I want to bring her here? Because Arthfael owes me a debt, yes, and Ungäar has the biggest army of all the kingdoms. If we marched on Rionnagan and I got my revenge, what then?*

Mandar shifted in his seat and cleared his throat. "You have that look, Údar. What are you thinking?"

Údar stared at the flames a moment longer before meeting his friend's gaze. "I'm thinking I missed something, and now everyone will pay for that mistake."

CHAPTER 33

———

Trinia held onto Mandar's arm as they approached the doors that led to the ball. They had already passed many attendees who were gliding about, goblets and ale horns filled to the brim. The smell of the drinks alone brought back flashes of the guard in Kiäxe, which did nothing to help her nerves. *I can't do this. I can't do this. I can't do this!*

Údar led with Batänny on his arm and the doors opened for them, granting a view of the ball. Trinia felt her eyes go wide.

The hall, like the others she had seen, was immense, with vaulted ceilings and exposed oaken beams. Banners and ribbons hung from the walls, and *soläs* floated about in mid-air, creating a magical atmosphere. Tables were lined with meats, cheeses, fruits, and vegetables of all shapes and sizes. Pies, tarts, and other deserts were no less diverse. Across the hall, wine flowed and ale was poured in a seemingly unending supply.

And the people. Everywhere Trinia looked, people moved here and there, some dancing, some laughing, some kissing, and still others engaging in heated debates. She took it all in at a glance, amazed at the splendor.

"Quite the sight," remarked Mandar.

She nodded. "Quite."

They followed Údar and Batänny in the steady procession toward the king and... Jayden? Trinia stood on her toes, trying to see the young man next to the king. It was Jayden! Only he looked different compared to how she knew him. Gone was the ragged clothes of travel, the dirt-stained face, and disordered hair, and in its place stood a prince. He wore a copper tunic with a red sash emblazoned with the mark of his house, the ten-point star with a sword through it. Breeches of earthy brown and black leather boots laced up to below his knee. A silver torc around his neck finished off the regal look.

Trinia could see by the set of his jaw he wanted to be there about as much as she did, perhaps even less. His eyes ranged over the crowd before finding her. A smile, a genuine one, touched his lips and she felt heat rise to her cheeks. For the first time in several weeks, her palms itched furiously.

"Greetings again, Green Cloak," said Arthfael when it was finally their turn. "I hope your stay has been comfortable?"

"Most comfortable, thank you," Údar replied.

Trinia noted Údar didn't bow or address the king as 'my lord,' which seemed to bother Arthfael.

"I want to thank you for finding and returning my son to me," said the king. "It will be for the betterment of Ungäar for this marriage to move forward."

Trinia's gaze snapped to Jayden, whose face flushed a deep red. *Marriage?*

"I would advise against hasty plans and enjoy time with your son."

Arthfael's eyes darkened. "Do you presume to tell me how to rule *my* kingdom, Green Cloak?"

Údar gave a tight smile. "Of course not." He turned and made with his way toward the food with Batänny in tow.

Mandar and Trinia stepped up, and the dark look in the king's eyes disappeared, hiding behind a smile. "Ah, and you must be Trinia. My son mentioned today you wish to speak to me?"

Trinia gave an awkward bow. "Yes, my lord. It is a matter I think you will find of interest."

"Perhaps a time for tomorrow may be arranged. Basil, can you see to it?"

She could see Jayden's jaw clench. "Yes, Father."

"Excellent, now please enjoy the ball!" said the king, motioning for them to continue.

Trinia released a breath, and Mandar laid a callused hand on hers. "You did well. That was the hardest part of the night."

I can only hope, she thought.

They caught up with Údar and Batänny at the tables, and the Iomlíad had a heap of food on her plate. Trinia raised a brow. "You expect to eat all of that in your dress? Weren't you complaining earlier about not being able to breathe?"

"I might bring some back to the room for later," Batänny replied. "It's not often you get to eat in the courts of kings."

"I'll give you that," said Údar, grabbing a goblet of wine from a passing servant.

Trinia grabbed a few bits of meat and cheese and followed Batänny to a corner of the hall, both quietly enjoying their meal as the music filled the air with lively tunes. Údar and Mandar disappeared into the crowd.

Watching the people, all she could think about was how out of touch they all were to the world around them. In Dorämund, people hardly eked out a living, and Iomlíad fought in games underground in Kiäxe. Yet here, there was food enough for all and then some.

Her mind drifted back to the little girl and the look of joy on her face when she had emerged from the white fire. Trinia guessed the girl had spoken with Údar's god like she had. The only difference was the girl had come out marked.

I am doing something in your day that you would not believe if I told you.

The words resounded in her mind. Just what had he meant? That he was letting children starve, be sold off, raped? The last thought made her sick and her palms burned. *Why did you allow it to happen? What god does that?*

Anger flashed in her chest. *Why would anyone serve a god who allowed such horrible things to happen to innocent people?*

And why was there such a contrast in people who followed Elohai? Údar had tried to kill her, Jayden followed whatever rules fit him best, and from what she had been able to gather by listening, the people of Tranâes also worshipped Elohai. If anyone was constant, it was Mandar.

Trinia picked at her food before setting it aside, losing all appetite. *When do we get to go back to our room?*

The music slowed, and the crowd found partners. A man looking to be in his twenties walked over, offering a hand to Batänny. "My lady, you have caught my eye. May I dance with you?"

Trinia glanced at her friend, who had taken a mouthful of food and was quickly trying to swallow. "Um, yes," she said finally, looking at Trinia. "You alright if I go?"

"Yes, go on!" Trinia replied, smiling.

The man led her off and soon the crowd swallowed them up, leaving Trinia alone.

Alone.

Forgotten.

Damaged.

The thoughts hit her out of nowhere, and she rubbed her head.

"My lady, you have caught my eye. May I have this dance?"

Trinia jerked her head up to see Jayden standing before her, hand outstretched.

No! Run!

Not safe!

Get away!

Thought after thought screamed at her, but she was frozen in place.

He lied!

He can't be trusted!

He's not safe!

Trinia felt eyes on her as those around her turned to see who the girl was the prince was asking to dance. What would happen if she refused? Would Arthfael choose not to speak with her if she slighted his son in front of half the kingdom? How would it look if he were to be seen with a girl on the eve of a marriage?

Jayden leaned in closer. "If you do not wish to dance, just say, 'Perhaps another dance, my lord,'" he whispered.

Trinia stood, reaching out a hand. "I accept."

The look on his face was almost worth the discomfort of being close to him. He placed his hand under hers and led her to where pairs of people danced to a mellow song. Once in place, he gave a bow. "May I have permission to hold you?"

Now it was her turn to be surprised. *He's asking?*

Jayden took half a step closer so only she could hear. "I don't know what you've gone through, Trinia, but I can imagine it was not good."

He paused, and Trinia's heart leapt into her throat.

"You have shied away from every touch or hand I have offered," he whispered. "I should like to make amends if I ever made you uncomfortable."

Trinia bit the inside of her cheek as he met her eyes, and she nodded, swallowing past the emotion. "Alright."

She held her breath as Jayden placed a hand on the small of her back and took her hand in his. He gave a warm smile as he led her through the steps, whispering every move before he made it so she wouldn't stumble.

Being so close to him, Trinia picked up the scent of cinnamon as they danced. Her mind screamed to stop, to run away, but her heart kept her in step with him. Tears welled in her eyes and she fought to control her emotions. Without thinking, she whispered, "Jayden... a guard raped me in Kiäxe"

He looked at her, awareness filling his eyes. The rest spilled out, and she could not stop the torrent. "Back home, my father beat me, and his priest would visit my room and sleep with me." The emotions threatened to choke her. "I'm damaged, broken."

Jayden stopped, eyeing her, his emotions unreadable. "Come with me," he said at last, gently guiding her through the crowd and out of the hall.

Where is he taking me? Panic set in, and she regretted her moment of weakness.

A fur cloak hung on a peg and he snatched it, throwing it around her shoulders as he led her down a hall, through a door, and into the cool night air. He fastened it around her, meeting her eyes again. "I didn't want anyone you don't trust to hear those things," he said.

The panic subsided a little and Trinia felt like she could breathe again. He offered her an arm, and she took it, looking at the garden around them. Several trees were jealously holding onto their leaves while others sat naked and unadorned. They walked the path, weaving through it in silence. A few *soläs* sat beside it, giving off a yellow light.

"I do not think you are any of those things you mentioned," Jayden said at last. "And I would be lying if I said I was not seething with rage at those who would do such a thing."

Trinia looked at him, searching his face. "I'm sorry if I—"

"Do not apologize for something out of your control," he said firmly, shaking his head.

She looked away, staring at the cobblestone path. *Easier said than done.* Trinia gazed up as they rounded a corner to an opening, and there, centered in the middle of the garden, was the fountain. She guessed it was about ten feet high with a deep circular pool at the bottom.

"This is why I brought you out here," said Jayden, gazing at the fountain. "I thought it might encourage you."

Trinia followed his gaze to the top of the fountain where there sat a crystal she hadn't noticed. She was going to ask him about it when the moon crested above the palace roof, its light hitting the gem and racing down within the rock itself, peeking out through cracks and holes, finally filling the basin of the fountain with a bright radiance.

She gasped as the area around her filled with undulating ripples of white light. "It's beautiful."

Jayden smiled as he looked at her. "Even with all its cracks and holes?"

Tears flooded her eyes again as she caught his meaning, and she saw something in his eyes change, their intensity growing and reflecting the light. "We're all broken, Trinia, each in our own way. But we can find beauty in it if we look for it."

His eyes drew her in, and she moved into him without thinking, without fear. Heart pounding in her chest, she kissed him.

And he returned it with a gentleness she had never known.

CHAPTER 34

The rest of the night passed in a blur, and Trinia could not remember when she ended up back at her room. It was late, she knew that much, and Carys had been there to help her out of the dress and into something more comfortable to sleep in. And now the woman was rushing about the room.

"Up, up, up. You meet with the king in little over an hour, lass."

Trinia groaned, rolling over and hugging the blankets to her, imagining they were Jayden's arms. The scene in front of the fountain had replayed in her mind again and again as she slept, and she wanted to get back to that place—a moment when she felt absolutely safe.

Carys ripped the blanket off her, and she curled up, shivering. "Hells below!"

"Language! Now get your bottom out of that bed or I shall be forced to drag you out of it myself," said the woman. "You too."

Sitting up, Trinia spotted Batänny over in her bed shooing the woman away. "I'm up. Begone with your threats," she said sleepily.

At least I'm not the only one last night took a toll on, she thought. Her time with Jayden, while amazing, had drained her emotionally and left her feeling raw and on edge. Now, she was left with conflicting feelings for him in light of a marriage announcement. *What was I thinking?*

Carys returned with a modest dress, a light shade of purple, laying it out next to her. "A fine color for you. Now hurry up, we must redo your hair!"

Batänny chuckled, and Trinia threw her pillow at her head. "Hey!" She lifted her face, glaring at Trinia in mock annoyance. "I need my beauty sleep."

Trinia rolled her eyes, taking off the sleeping shirt and pulling the dress over her head. "Perhaps you shouldn't have had so much to drink."

The woman scoffed, taking on an air of sophistication. "I am a lady. We do not guzzle drinks like the commoners; we sip."

"Ha! And do they flirt with every young man in sight?" Trinia retorted.

Batänny waggled her eyebrows. "Only the good-looking ones."

Shaking her head, Trinia adjusted the fit of the sleeves on the dress while slipping her feet into the matching slippers Carys provided. When the older woman left the room, Batänny shot out of bed. "So where did you and Jayden run off to last night? Was everything okay? I couldn't tell if you were upset or not."

Trinia winced. "You saw that?"

"I think a lot of people did, but most were probably too drunk, anyway. But were you alright?"

She was thankful for Batänny's thoughtfulness. "He asked me to dance with him, and I got caught up in the moment and told him what happened. To me, I mean."

Batänny sat on the bed next to her, looking wary. "And?"

"And that is when you saw us leaving. He did not want anyone to hear. He was protecting me." She could still smell the scent of cinnamon lingering in the air. "He took me to a garden and showed me a fountain and..."

Batänny scooted closer, eyes filled with worry. "And what?"

"I kissed him."

"What?" The woman jumped up, looking at her with a stunned expression.

"I didn't mean to! It just happened!" said Trinia, glancing nervously at the door, as if Carys would come back through at any moment. She dropped her voice to a whisper. "Besides, it was only for a second."

"Well, if that's all," Batänny replied, raising a brow. "That *is* all, right?"

Trinia nodded adamantly. "Yes. We returned to the ball after that, there was the announcement of the betrothal to some princess from Canämor, and then I came back to my room. Gods above, Batänny, what did you think happened?"

The woman shrugged. "That's why I asked. Sometimes when we hurt, we seek others out for comfort."

Trinia's jaw dropped. "You thought I *slept* with him?"

Her eyes widened. "I, uh, oh, I didn't think about how that came out."

Unbelievable! How could she think I would do such a thing? Trinia waved her hands. "You know what, I'm going to be late for breakfast with the king. I should go."

Batänny grabbed her arm as she passed. "Trinia, I'm sorry. I didn't mean it that way."

Yanking her arm from her grasp, Trinia gave her a hard look. "Yes, you did."

The look of shame in the woman's eyes spoke volumes, and Trinia stormed through the door, leaving her behind.

After everything I've been through, she thinks I'm going to bed someone just because they make me feel good? Just because she was a whore doesn't mean I am, she thought.

Slut.

Damaged.

Broken.

Trinia paused, rubbing her head. "Stop it! Shut up!"

Turning the corner, she saw Carys returning. The older woman looked her up and down, slowing her pace. "Are you alright, lass? Where are you going?"

Trinia put on a fake smile, one she was used to wearing now. "Fine, I was looking for you, actually. I plan on wearing my hair down, so there is no needed to fuss with it." Her tone left no room for argument. "Please show me to the king."

Carys eyed her for a moment as if trying to read her thoughts. Finally, she relented and motioned for Trinia to follow. "This way."

After many twists and turns, Carys stopped, nodding at the door. "In there."

Trinia gave a slight bow. "Thank you." She pulled it open, seeing several things at once. First was Údar, seated at the end of a long table closest to the door. Second were the nobles also in the room. Finally, Jayden met her confused gaze apologetically.

Jayden walked over, voice lowered. "I didn't know the other lords would be here either." He put on a smile as he pulled out a chair for her next to Údar, who also seemed on irritated.

"I'm so glad you made it," said Arthfael at the head of the table. "I spoke to Jayden after the ball last night, and he suggested what you had to say was a matter of security for the kingdom, so I thought it pertinent for my lords to attend as well."

Trinia bowed her head slightly. "I understand." *Hells, I have to reveal myself to all of them?*

"I must also apologize. We have already eaten, so you may proceed with what you have to say," said the king.

Jayden frowned as he sat back down next to his father, looking unhappy at how things were starting off. Údar leaned in, whispering in her ear. "I suggest you start by removing your illusion. Otherwise, they are not going to take you seriously."

Removing the illusion before the king was intimidating enough, and now she had to do it in front of at least ten other nobles. Her palms itched intensely, and the thoughts thrummed in her mind.

They will not listen.

You are just a girl.

Who do you think you are?

Trinia stood, looking at the king and steeling herself as best she could. "My lord, I bring news from the north, from the Realm of the Airgíd that Caderyn, Chieftain of the Airgíd, is preparing to attack the Four Kingdoms."

Several of the nobles laughed, and the king looked unamused. "The Airgíd?" he asked contemptuously. "And what would a girl know of them and their plans?"

Closing her eyes, she released the illusion, hearing cries of alarm in the room. Opening them, she looked at the king. "Because I am Caderyn's daughter, Trinia of Rionnagan, once known as the City of Snow and Stars."

The nobles pushed back their chairs, drawing swords. Údar was on his feet in a flash, pushing her back and drawing his own sword to stand between them and her. *He's protecting me?*

"She's one of them!" cried a dark-haired man, edging toward her.

Suddenly a barrier formed around her and Údar, and peeking around him, she could see Jayden, his hands outstretched.

"What is the meaning of this?" said Arthfael, looking at his son. "You would protect our enemy?"

Jayden finished casting, speaking to his father while looking at her. "Would your enemy come to your home to warn you of danger, Father?"

"It's a trick!" said another of the nobles.

"It is not trick," growled Údar. "She is Caderyn's daughter, and she speaks the truth."

"Hear her out, Father," Jayden pressed.

Arthfael stared at her a long moment before easing back into his seat. "I will listen."

The other lords glanced between each other and finally followed their king, though Údar remained standing. Trinia stepped out from behind him, focusing on the king. "My lord, I sought out your help because my father wishes to rebuild the Old Empire anew. He would have used me to bring it about because of a prophecy foretelling that I would destroy the world. I do not wish any such thing to happen."

The other lords murmured among themselves, and she pressed on, determined to finish what she started. "I know it could mean the destruction of my people, telling you these things, but I beg of you, help me stop my father."

Arthfael rubbed his chin thoughtfully. "And you say he planned to use you? How?"

"Through my Gift," she replied. Flicking her hand out to the left, a perfect duplicate appeared, much to the amazement of all in the room. Trinia nodded at it and took its hand, reabsorbing it into herself.

"Sorcery!" shouted a nobleman.

"Airgíd trickery!" yelled another.

"Enough!" said the king over the din. "Silence, all of you!"

When the nobles quieted down, he looked at her through narrowed eyes. "You have made an intriguing display, but what would you have me do? Take my army through the borders of Canämor and start a war when we are close to securing peace?"

"Father—"

"Silence!" He turned a withering gaze toward his son. "Your *king* speaks."

Jayden recoiled, and Trinia realized how alike Arthfael and her father were. Each sought always to grasp power just outside of their reach, always for the supposed betterment of others and all while tearing down the ones they claimed to be doing it for.

Arthfael turned back to her, leaning on the table. "You say he is attacking, and for the moment, let's say I believe you. Do you have his plans? Where he will attack first? His numbers and the supplies he has available?"

She got a sinking feeling in her stomach. *I never thought to bring anything with me.* The chances of her making it out of the city alive was, at the time, the only thing she had focused on.

The king tapped his fingers impatiently. "Well? Have you these things, or not?"

Trinia shook her head. "No."

He leaned back, a look of disgust on his face. "So, all you bring are fables? You are no better than Green Cloak and his rumormongering." Arthfael stood. "This has been a waste of time. I don't want to see either of you in my presence again. You will depart tomorrow at dawn and take your lies elsewhere."

What? Just like that? Trinia could not believe it. *How can he be so blind?*

The other lords stood, slowly making their way out of the room and casting dark looks her way. *But I told the truth.*

Trinia sat on her bed looking out at the ocean below as it stretched to the horizon. She was at a loss. *They disregarded me like I was nothing. Like I was playing a game with them!*

It was nearly noon and she hadn't eaten a thing since last night. *They treated me like an ignorant girl and someone less than themselves in importance!*

Birds circled around and rode the air currents near the cliffs, going up and then back down in a steady cacophony. *They call us all liars! They think because they have titles, they are untouchable. All of them are no better than my father!*

She clenched her fists, palms burning, chest aching, as anger and rage surged through her. *I hate them. I hate what they represent. Their lust for power, for women, for all of it!*

Her body shook with pent-up emotion. *They take, take, take until there is nothing left to give. My father did it, the Voice did it, the guard in Kiäxe did it. The lot of them can burn in the fiery hells for eternity!*

Make them pay. Make them pay. Make them pay, repeated the thoughts.

"I should make them pay," she whispered to her reflection. "Make them suffer as I have suffered. Take their precious power and watch it crumble to dust before their eyes."

Make them pay!
Make them suffer!
Break them!

"I'll rip control from their hands," she hissed vehemently, hot tears slipping down her cheeks. "And when they beg for mercy, I will not stop until they are just as hollow as me. Then they will know my pain."

Looking at her reflection, part of her felt like she was staring at a stranger while another part of her felt like it was someone who had been there the entire time. *I'll leave tonight and make for Rionnagan.* She watched her brows draw together in a scowl. *My father will be the first to fall.*

CHAPTER 35

———

Údar could hardly sleep. It seemed as though every dream was plagued by visions of a distant land, dragons, and a boy with a golden tattoo. Finally giving up, he rolled out of bed. *I need to take it easier on the wine next time.*

Mandar was still asleep, and he decided he would take some time for himself—something he had not been able to do in quite some time. Dressing quickly and throwing his cloak over his shoulders, he slipped out of their room and headed down the hall.

Not wanting to explain to the guards why he was up before the sun and roaming the halls, he slipped out through the kitchen. With the door closing behind him, Údar took a breath of the crisp air, feeling invigorated as it filled his lungs. He crossed to the other side of the courtyard and sat down on a stone bench, enjoying the quiet of the morning and the cloudless sky.

Huddled on the seat, he wrapped his cloak tighter about him, relishing the moment. He thought back to his life before, back to when Nisha was alive and they would lie out under the stars, trying to count them all. Even after all these centuries, the pain still was there. It had eased somewhat after the vision. He was trying to weed out the hatred he'd nurtured for over three hundred years, but he was finding it a rather daunting task.

Since he had learned what had happened to Trinia, he had distanced himself from her. The thought of his choice to send her on alone had weighed on him. He wanted to apologize, beg her forgiveness like he had with Batänny, but every time he had the chance, he shied away from it.

No more running, he thought. *I will pull her aside in the morning when we leave, apologize, and ask her forgiveness. For all of it.*

After a little while, he heard the kitchen door opening and saw a figure emerging, hood pulled up and cloak wrapped tightly around them, heading toward the stables. Odd.

A few minutes later, another one followed, dressed in the same manner, also moving toward the stables. Údar shook his head. *Young lovers on a midnight tryst, no doubt. They will be in a world of trouble if they get caught.* He smiled. He had done the same once upon a time.

When the second figure disappeared, he turned his mind to their next course of action. They could head north to Canämor and hope Éowald would listen to reason.

And if not? What then? The lack of an answer to that question bothered him greatly.

When the night air started to seep into his bones, Údar slipped back into the palace, slowly making his way back to his room. *I'll talk with Mandar about it in a few hours.* His friend always seemed to keep a clear head, which Údar appreciated.

Coming to the corner that turned down the hall toward his room, he heard voices talking low. Senses alert, he pressed himself to the wall and peeked around to see six guards standing outside the door.

"You think this is a good idea? The man is a legend!"

⁃ One of the guards nodded. "We've got orders. Either restrain them or kill them if you have to. The king doesn't care which."

Údar leaned back against the wall. Arthfael was betraying them? Why?

He heard the door open, and he quickly shot down the hall as quietly as he could behind them. As he reached the room he heard, "The other one isn't here!"

Stepping through, he closed it behind him. "Looking for me?"

He dodged the wild swing of the squat one and landed a blow to the man on his right, causing him to drop his dagger. Údar caught it and drove it into the thigh of the one behind before slamming a knee into the squat man's chin and knocking him out.

With a feral scream, another attacked from Údar's left, landing a grazing blow to his shoulder with a club. Twisting, Údar punched the man in the groin, dropping him to ground, and ripped the club away. Wielding the club now, he slammed it into the man's skull and then deflected two more incoming blows that sent his opponents off balance.

Ripping the dagger out of the man's leg, he sliced his attacker's throat and stabbed another in the eye while bringing the club down hard on the forearm of the other man's sword-arm with a sickening *crack*! With a swift punch to the liver and another to the throat, the man fell gurgling and gasping for air.

In a matter of a few heartbeats, five lay dead or dying while one was knocked out.

Stepping over them, Údar walked over to a pitcher of water and dumped it on Mandar, who woke sputtering. His eyes landed on the bodies and then on Údar. "What is this? What happened?"

"Arthfael has betrayed us. Hurry and dress, we must see to the others. Quickly now!" said Údar, going to his bed and gathering his things before strapping on his sword. *Elohai, let us reach Batänny and Trinia in time!*

Soon they were rushing through the halls to the girls' room. When they reached it, Údar drew his sword and shoved the door open to find Batänny in her bed. Trinia wasn't there, and his heart sank. "Plagues!"

Batänny shot up, looking around and cursing under her breath. "Et-delf, what are you two doing here?

Údar grabbed her clothes and shoved them into her arms. "Hurry and get dressed, we need to leave before—" He heard heavy boots coming down the hall toward them. "Quickly, lay back down!" he hissed.

Batänny did so while he and Mandar stood behind the door as it began to open. The guards marched in looking around, and as soon as the last of them entered, Údar and Mandar sprang into action. Taking the first two, he smashed the nose of one with an elbow and landed another blow to the other's jaw, sending him to the floor.

Mandar swept the legs out from under a man, grabbing the dagger from the man's belt and ending him before he hit the ground. Now armed, he went to work on the others while Údar got one of the wooden clubs from another. The guards did not know what hit them until it was too late, and they put up little defense.

Batänny sat back up, throwing on her clothes while Údar went over to Trinia's bed and felt it. Cold.

"Can someone explain to me what is going on?" she asked, whispering harshly. "And where is Trinia?"

Glancing around, Údar saw no sign of a struggle, and the girl's pack was not there. Lyniel's sword was missing as well. A terrible reality slammed into him. "She left."

"What?" Batänny and Mandar said in unison.

Údar ran a hand through his hair and down over his face. "She left. I woke up and couldn't sleep, so I went and sat in the garden for a little while. Someone left the palace kitchen, followed by another, but I thought it was just two servants out for a tryst! It must have been her!"

"Who was the other?" asked Mandar, watching by the door.

"Jayden," Batänny said, holding her head.

Údar closed his eyes, sinking down onto the bed. *The life-debt. I am a fool!*

"You couldn't have known, Údar," said Mandar, seemingly reading his thoughts. "It was night, and you had no reason to be on the lookout for such things."

"That is no excuse! I should have sensed the king was going to betray us! Jayden mentioned something was wrong, but I did not take it further than that. A part of me didn't feel right after the meeting yesterday, and I should have done something then."

Mandar shook his head. "You are not superhuman, Údar, so stop thinking of yourself as such!"

Údar glared at his friend. "Did I say I was?"

"The Maker help me! You know as well as I that you are too hard on yourself. What other reason would there be for thinking you could have stopped this? Are you like Elohai to know such things?"

He was silent a moment before responding. "I just... I feel helpless," he whispered.

Batänny, now fully dressed with sword on her hip, placed a hand on his shoulder. "You're not alone in that."

"Elohai is in control of everything, even when it doesn't seem like it," said Mandar, coming over to him.

Údar shook his head. "Sometimes I wonder if that is truly the case."

"I've been around a lot longer than you, my friend, and in the doubting, we come to find the answers we seek. We have but to look." Mandar clapped a hand on his shoulder. "I'm with you."

"Should we form a plan or something?" Batänny asked. "How are we going to get out of here?

Údar stood, throwing his hood up and making for the door. "I'm working on it."

Mandar fell in step beside him as they moved down the hall. "Are you doing something rash and ill thought out?"

"Depends on what you think I am doing," he replied quietly as he peered around a corner. "Clear."

They began marching down another long hall swiftly and silently. Mandar lowered his voice as he said, "Don't be coy with me, Údar. We both know you are no good at it."

"I plan on getting answers, and then we go after Trinia and Jayden. That is my plan," Údar replied. "If the guards took us alive, my guess is they would bring us before Arthfael in the Hall of Stone, so we go there first."

He put his ear up to a door and could hear servants talking on the other side. After a minute or two, the voices faded, and he dared to open the door, breathing a sigh of relief. "Let's go," he whispered.

Mandar spoke up again as they walked. "I could follow their scent once we're beyond the city walls. There is no need for this course of action!"

"I second Mandar on this, Údar," chimed Batänny.

"Arthfael isn't going to know about Trinia, and it's even less likely he knows about his son," said Mandar, grabbing his shoulder.

Údar spun on both of them. "Something bigger is at play here. Thydu attacking, Canämor wanting an alliance, and Arthfael not the least bit fazed by his son showing back up alive? Does that not seem strange to you?" He kept walking. "We are getting answers."

"And what about escaping?" Batänny asked. "Remember that part? The Hall of Stone only has one entrance!"

If it comes to that, Elohai, grant me the strength to do what needs to be done.

"We'll worry about it later," he replied.

Coming around a corner, he saw a large painting of a mountain lake at sunset opposite them on the wall and he smiled. "There you are!" Running up to it, he reached behind it trying to find the latch that had been there. There was a soft *click*, and the painting swung out silently, revealing an entryway.

Údar waved them into it as calls of alarm echoed through the halls. "Hurry!" he ordered.

Once they were inside, he pulled the secret door shut and they held their breath. The sound of heavy footfalls rang through the hall they had been standing in moments ago and proceeded down the hall and out of earshot.

Inside the passage, the dim light of morning filtered through in shafts, barely illuminating it. "Stick close to me. There are many such passages, and it would be easy to get yourself lost in them," Údar whispered.

"How the hells did you know about this?" asked Batänny, eyeing him in bewilderment. "And why do I feel like you're directing that to me?" she added, glaring at him.

"I told you. I've been here many times, and we will not be discussing it further," he replied. "Not right now, anyway."

Dust filled the passageway, and it smelled strongly of mold. It had not seen a lot of use in recent days by the look of things. As he led the way, he could hear conversations filtering through the cracks and spyholes from servants, guards, and even some nobles who were speaking with their mistresses. He shook his head.

Údar came to a stop and pressed his hands up against the wall to his left, which began opening on hidden hinges. The group stepped out into the Hall of Stone. Stepping past the painting to get a clear view of the throne, Údar was taken aback to see Ulscia standing by Arthfael's side.

"Hello, Údar," she said. "How nice of you to come."

"Et-delf, how did she get here?" cried Batänny from behind him.

Ulscia laughed, draping a hand on the king's shoulder. "Poor Údar, always one step behind. You really should choose your friends more wisely."

He looked to Arthfael. "What have you done?"

"What have I done?" said Arthfael, his face twisting into an ugly sneer. "I have secured the throne for my son and his son's son, and every male heir from now until the ending of the world!" He stood, walking down the steps with Ulscia trailing behind, a smug smile on her lips. "Our forefathers imprisoned the Baobhan Sith, saying they were protecting us. Pah! They were afraid!"

"And rightly so," Údar countered. "They feed off loneliness and lust, be it for a warm body or for power. You've played into her hands!"

Arthfael smiled wickedly. "No, you have played into *ours*. Ulscia told me you would come with my son over a month ago, and that you would come with lies of Thydu attacking when *you* destroyed it."

"Is that true, Údar?" Batänny asked.

"No," he replied. "I barely escaped from there myself."

"And escape you did!" said Arthfael. "How you tricked my son into believing your lies, however, is far more treacherous. Using that Airgíd filth to seduce him! Filling his head with temptations!"

Údar shook his head. "You are lost, Arthfael, son of Agalon. You have sold your soul for an empty promise of power and you delude yourself."

"Silence," Arthfael spat. "With Ulscia by my side, my armies will be unstoppable. You are lost, Green Cloak. You are nothing more than a relic of a bygone age!"

Ulscia put her arms around the king, whispering in his ear. He nodded, clapping his hands twice. The main entrance to the Hall burst open with guards pouring through until they filled it. "Now, you will all die."

Údar shook his head, feeling the white fire within surge to life, and he saw a vision in his mind's eye. "You've doomed yourself, and your kingdom, King Arthfael. A great darkness comes. Your kingdom will be the first to fall, not by your enemies, but by your friends. They will cut your body to pieces and display them over the entrance of every gate in this city as a reminder of your betrayal. Your name shall be a curse on every tongue, from now until the ending of the world."

Arthfael's eyes filled with fear and rage as he called out, "Guards! Guards! Kill them!"

"Um, Údar, now would be a good time for that plan you mentioned earlier," Batänny cried.

Údar closed his eyes, focusing on the white flames and he who was in the flames, as a sphere of white fire enveloped the group. *If it be your will, save us. I cannot do it alone.*

A flash was followed by a thunderclap, and then all went dark.

CHAPTER 36

———

The air crackled and sizzled around them as they lay on the scorched grass. Batänny groaned and rolled over, her stomach feeling like it was in her throat. "Ugh, what happened?"

She sat up, albeit slowly, gazing around at the surroundings. "Where the hells are we?"

"I should like to know as well," Mandar grumbled to her right, once more in his wolf form.

She turned around and saw Údar leaning up against a rock, his face pale. "Údar!" Scrambling over to him, she felt for a pulse. "He's alive," she said. "Barely."

"Sorry...for not...warning...you." Údar's eyes cracked open ever so slightly.

Batänny felt like she could slap him and probably would have if he didn't look like he was on death's door. "This is why we make plans!" she exclaimed.

"What did you do?" Mandar asked, coming alongside her. "Where are we?"

Údar took a labored breath, his head lulling to the side. She put her ear to his chest and heard his heart beating faintly. "I think he passed out. Mandar, watch him for a moment, would you? I'm going to have a look around."

She took a running jump and shifted into a hawk, slowly climbing higher and higher on the winds. Thankfully, there were no clouds, and the air was considerably warmer, which only added to her puzzlement. *Where in the name of all that is holy did he take us?* she wondered.

Wheeling left, and with her animal sense of direction, she flew west for several miles before banking around to head back. The land below her was mostly grasslands as far as her eyes could see, with a dark spot toward the south. She veered toward it, flying for close to an hour before she could make out a huge forest that seemed to stretch from horizon to horizon. *Et-delf! That's impossible!*

Turning back, she flew as fast as she could until she finally spotted Mandar on the lookout. Coming in fast and low, she slid to a stop a few feet away from them and shifted back into her human form. "X'phos!" she cried. "We're in X'phos! That's hundreds of miles away from where we just were!"

Údar coughed, a smile playing across his lips though his eyes remained shut. "Elohai... saved us..."

"You better not die on us," she said, feeling his forehead. "Not now."

He chuckled faintly. "Not... yet."

Mandar sat down next to him, eyeing him. "You didn't tell me you could teleport."

"Old dogs... can learn new... tricks, eh?" He coughed again, and this time blood formed on the edges of his mouth. "At a cost."

"Batänny, get him on my back," Mandar ordered. "Swiftly now!"

"I saw a town close to here to the northwest." Batänny shifted into a helwreck to get the man onto Mandar's back and then shifted again. "Maybe five miles."

"There's no time to waste," said Mandar, taking off at a sprint.

She shifted into a wolf, and when she could not keep up with Mandar, she shifted into a bird. As she flew, she felt an eerie sense of familiarity. *I'm home*, she thought. *I can't believe I'm home.* How long had it been since she walked in her homeland? How old was she now, twenty-one summers? She felt a twinge in her chest.

Gazing at the green landscape around them, she could almost feel the lost years settling on her. There was no memory to recall that tied her to this place, no loved ones she knew of, nothing. She could have returned here after Údar set her free, but she realized now, she had been too afraid.

How can we save Trinia if we are hundreds if not thousands of miles away from her? Just the thought of it brought tears to her eyes. *After everything the girl has been through...*

She looked down at Údar's limp form, barely holding on to Mandar's fur. *Is he going to make it? What if he dies? What do we do then?*

Finally, she caught sight of the town. It was bigger than she remembered, but that meant there was a better chance they would have a healer or two to support them. At least, she hoped so.

Arriving a little after mid-day, they entered it seeking a healer, asking everyone they met until one finally pointed to a small house down the road.

Batänny knocked on the door until she heard a voice inside yelling, "I do not offer services during mealtime!"

"Please, our friend is near death!" she begged. "He needs help!"

"No! Now begone!"

Údar began mumbling, and Batänny hurried over to him. "What is it? Údar, what are you saying?"

"Da...dark...ness."

Batänny looked at Mandar worriedly. "Is he going blind?"

"I don't think that's it," Mandar said softly.

"It's coming...for..."

Batänny checked his pulse again... then again. "Et-delf! Údar!" She shook him, but he didn't speak. "No!"

She turned toward the door, her hand shifting into a club-fist, and smashed it down. Marching in amid the protests, she grabbed the man by the collar and lifted him off the ground as tears welled in her eyes. "You're going to save him, or you will die with him. Understood?"

The man, dark-skinned and dressed in a white tunic, nodded and quickly rushed outside to tend to her friend. Batänny glanced at the older woman sitting at the table, two children beside her, clinging to her clothes. A shadow of a memory coming back to her.

"No, you can't have her!"

"It's our right. She comes with us!"

"No! Batänny!"

"Batänny!"

She gasped, backed away from the terrified look on the children's faces, and headed back outside, finding the healer breathing heavily. "What? What is it?"

Mandar spoke first. "Údar's alive, but he needs greater care than this man can provide. He said there is a Master Healer in Ke'grul, the capital. It's our only chance."

"How far is that?" she asked, dreading the answer.

"A week, at least," said the healer, his face scrunched in concentration. "Your friend is weak, very weak. He has maybe two days, three at most."

She looked at Údar, lying pale on the ground, creeping ever closer to death. *You have saved me more times than I can count. Time to return the favor.* Turning her attention to Mandar, she said, "How fast can you run?"

He lifted a wolfish brow. "What are you thinking?"

Taking a deep breath, she shifted into a powerful horse. "Get him on my back." To his credit, Mandar did not argue and told the healer what to do. Once they had Údar secured to her, she nodded to him. "Sorry about your door. And scaring your family."

The healer glanced at the door and then back to her. "Your friend is lucky to have you, but I tell you, he will not live long enough to see Ke'grul."

Batänny stared down the road and pawed the ground once, twice, three times. "Watch me."

CHAPTER 37

Jayden hadn't meant to follow her. He had his own issues to worry about, and yet, lo and behold, he had found her sneaking through the palace halls, stealing a horse, and riding like the king's army was after her.

He had seen something in her eyes at the meeting, in her bearing, that had worried him. His father refusing to listen and nobles nearly attacking her hadn't helped the issue, and his father's blatant disrespect was uncalled for and below him.

That was nearly two weeks ago.

Hidden in a nearby shop, Jayden watched as Trinia tried to haggle with a merchant for a fresh horse, and it was not going well. Should he have revealed himself before now? Probably. His curiosity at the outset had turned to a mounting concern she was going to do something drastic. Now, he was certain of it. At least she had enough sense to have her illusion spell back on her hair.

When the merchant's arms started flailing wildly, Jayden decided it was time to step in. Crossing the mostly empty streets of Reldor, he could hear the merchant yelling.

"Snake! You would try and trade to me this worthless animal?"

"It's a good horse," Trinia countered angrily, pointing a finger at the man. "It's not my fault you're as dumb as a helwreck and can't see that!"

Hells, has she lost her mind? Jayden watched as the merchant's eyes nearly popped out of his head. *Uh oh.*

"You insolent little whelp!" The man raised his hand to strike.

"Ah there you are!" called Jayden, trying to remain composed. "I have been looking everywhere for you, *sister.*"

Trinia looked at him in shock. "Jayden?"

He came up next to her, careful to avoid touching her in her agitated stated, and addressed the merchant. "I'm so sorry. We're not from around here and my sister *loves* horses."

The man looked at him, glancing between them. "You two look nothing alike."

Hells, can't you just take me at my word? Jayden put on a serious face, leaning in. "That's because I'm only a half-brother, on our mother's side, if you know what I mean. Complicated family dynamics."

"So it would seem," replied the merchant, still looking unsure.

He's not going to let this go easily, I see. Time for the next option. "Which of the horses was my sister looking at? A nice one, I presume?"

The man nodded vigorously. "My best! And she wanted to trade me that worn out thing over there," he said, pointing to where Trinia had tied her horse. The poor animal's head hung low.

"May I see the fantastic beast that caught her eye?" Jayden asked, stepping between them and guiding the man over to the fence. "Money isn't a problem."

The merchant's eyes lit up and Jayden smiled to himself. After some negotiation on price, and a few withering glares from Trinia, he walked back over to her, leading her new horse. She snatched the lead rein from him. "What are you doing here?"

"Making sure you don't end up in a local prison," he retorted. "And you're welcome."

"I had it under control," she snapped, taking the tack off her old horse. "Did you follow me?"

Jayden raised a brow, folding his arms. "I feel like that should be obvious at this point."

Trinia shot him another glare and then turned back to what she was doing.

Sighing, Jayden put a hand on the horse, stroking its mane. "I saw you leaving the hall and followed. I was worried about you, and I see I was right to do so."

"I'm fine," she replied.

"No, you're really not. Why would you leave? Did you tell the others? And just where are you going?"

"To finish things, if you must know. I'm going back to Rionnagan to take down my father or die trying." She threw the saddle up the horse's back, strapping it down.

"Hells, you cannot be serious!"

Trinia looked at him. "I made a bargain with Údar, and he said he would get me the help I needed in exchange for my father's blood on his blade. He failed to deliver, and your father made it clear he doesn't believe me, which means I'm on my own. So, yes, I'm serious."

What was he supposed to say to that? Coming around the horse, he said, "I didn't know my father was going to call the nobles. I made it clear it was to be the three of us."

"But that's not the point. Is it?" Trinia stopped, facing him fully. "I'm a means to an end, Jayden. My father, Údar, the Queen of the Baobhan Sith, a drunken guard." She paused, taking a shuddering breath. "I'm not wanted for *me*, only what I can give, and there is nothing left."

Everything in him wanted to hold her, tell her it would be alright, that she was wanted. Except he couldn't. He didn't know if it would be alright or if things were going to work out. Hells, he didn't even know how *he* felt. Her kiss had been the most wonderfully confusing moment of his life, but was it anything more than that?

Trinia shook her head, tying off the last straps. "I'm going north to do what I can to stop him."

"But winter is practically here!" he protested. "The snows will hit before you reach there and you will freeze to death."

She swung herself up in the saddle, adjusting her cloak and sword, and then met his gaze. "I've watched people freeze to death, Jayden. Do you know what happens right before they slip away?"

He shook his head slowly. "No."

Her eyes misted as she turned the horse away. "They become numb and stop caring. So, in a sense, I'm already there." Clicking her tongue, Trinia urged the horse to a trot, following the main road out of the town.

-II-

Jayden found himself sitting in front of the fountain he had met Elohai at weeks ago. It seemed an eternity away now. "I let her go. Just like that," he muttered.

The memory of her saving him, not once, but twice, came to mind, and how everything had changed after that. Three years of being on his own, getting into trouble, drinks, women… what had come of it? Nothing. Yet, he had met Trinia in the same village Cal lived in. She happened to be there at the same time and *happened* to run down the street he had tried, and failed, to kill Cal. Saving his life indebted him to her, keeping him from going into Thydu, which then attacked Salorim. He met Údar, who had saved his father at one point, which in turn put a life-debt on his father.

Jayden ran his fingers through his hair, heaving a sigh as smaller pieces began falling into place in his mind. Údar was connected to Caderyn, who was Trinia's father, because he had killed Údar's wife and daughter, and Ulscia was connected to Údar because he imprisoned her.

He stood up, walking around the fountain.

Batänny knew Údar because he had rescued her, and she had gone through similar things as Trinia. He paused as a picture formed in his mind.

If Trinia had never left, I would have gone into Thydu, Údar would have never left the forest, and Batänny would have died. But she did run, and she stopped me, drew Údar out, and he saved her. I saw what was happening in my kingdom with new eyes, and the little girl found Elohai.

Jayden sat down on the edge of the fountain, breathing heavily as the words of Údar came back to him. *She seems to be the catalyst...*

"There is no such thing as coincidence," he whispered, holding the back of his head. "What about her?"

She was the reason, but why did she have to go through it all? Where was the fairness in it? He leaned forward, putting his face in his hands. "Elohai... I don't know what to do."

All was quiet.

He could no longer deny that there was more than mere luck at play, yet it seemed to come with a heavy cost for one person. And why her?

"Why do you allow this?" he whispered, closing his eyes.

A day will come when you will have to choose between two hard choices… How far will you go to outrun your future?

Jayden opened his eyes, staring at the stones at his feet, noticing an inscription he hadn't seen there before. A wave of emotion hit him, sending him into a fit of laughter. Tears rolled down his face as he glanced back at the stone. "Elohai redeems," he said aloud.

Choose.

He jumped up, taking one last look at the stone.

Then he ran.

CHAPTER 38

———

Unlovable.

Unwanted.

Unworthy.

"You forgot, despised, outcast, broken, and alone," Trinia said aloud, scowling at the road in front of her. The thoughts, voices, or whatever they were, refused to leave her be. "If you're going to remind me of my flaws, the least you can do is cover them all."

You pushed him away.

Now you're alone.

Pathetic.

Weak.

Trinia gripped the reins tighter, wishing they would just stop. Her heart was heavy enough as it was. She had been abused—physically, mentally, sexually, and emotionally—her belief in a benevolent goddess destroyed and her trust in others obliterated. She was a speck of dust, a hollow soul, a broken *thing* to be discarded when its use had run its course.

She was numb. The only thing she had left that she could feel was a burning hatred. It seethed and roiled in her chest like an angry serpent ready to strike the first person to encounter it. If Jayden had not shown up out of nowhere, she would have hurt the merchant.

Another part of her, a part that tried to come to the surface for air, whispered to her to go back to her companions. It told her to not feed the hatred.

But the monster she was becoming, the thing that desired to avenge the pains inflicted to it, continually drowned the other. She had been pushed too far, and now she would push back.

The sounds of hooves pulled her from her dim musings, and she turned around in the saddle, seeing Jayden riding up. *What does he want now?* she wondered.

He slowed to a stop, pulling his horse up short. "I'm coming with you."

Trinia kept riding, turning her back to him. "Go home, Jayden. We both know you don't want to be here."

Jayden rode around, blocking her path. She scowled. "Move."

"No," he replied, jaw set. "I'm choosing to go with you, Trinia."

She shook her head in frustration. "Why? Because of the life-debt? I already told you, I'm not holding you to that! You could have left at any time."

"And yet I didn't!" he shouted, working to keep control over his horse. His eyes held an intensity she had never seen in them before. "I stayed because I chose to keep what little honor I had left, it's true. And I would be lying if I said a part of me isn't running from a forced marriage to a girl I've never met."

"See? There is your answer," she stated, trying to go around him, but he blocked her again.

"You're going down a dark road, Trinia," he said. "And I intend to walk willingly down it with you. I will follow behind you like a wraith if I must, or be a silent yet constant presence beside you, but I *will not* let you do it alone."

Trinia wanted to hate him. To put the hate she had for his father and the nobles on him. The hate she carried for the drunken guard, the Voice, the slavers, Ulscia, her own father. She wanted to send him away, chase him off, push him until he left. To drive a wedge so large and create a chasm so deep that he couldn't get to her.

But she couldn't.

He knew she was an Airgíd, and he had stayed. He knew who her father was, and he had stayed. He knew what had been done to her, and he had stayed.

Through it all, he had been there.

Trinia felt her defenses slipping. "Alright. Silent companion it is then."

He did not smile or make a joke, nor did he try to lighten her mood. He merely nodded, moving his horse out of the way and giving her the road, falling in step beside her and sitting at ease in the saddle, his eyes fixed ahead.

Something has changed in him, she thought, glancing at him with an echo of a smile on her lips. *It suits him.*

-II-

Three weeks. Three long, cold weeks they had been on the road, slowly making their way back to her city. Trinia shivered, hugging her cloak closer about her as the storm raged on. Every day for the last week the winter storm pummeled them, and while the wind did not bite as hard as it did in her realm, its chill seeped deep into her bones, robbing her of all warmth.

She shivered again as Jayden threw another log onto their pitiful excuse of a fire before walking to the mouth of the cave they had taken shelter in to keep watch. True to his word, he had not spoken another word since Reldor. It had made for a difficult first few nights, but they had managed. She curled up and tugged her cloak tighter around her, rubbing the ache in her chest—a constant companion these days. Aside from the cold, it was all she felt anymore.

They had passed Nolordale, a large fortress city on the borders of Canämor, a little over a week ago when the storm had hit as they approached Elmare, a small village close to the Forest of Nex. The irony that it would have been the first place she stopped if everything had gone as planned when she escaped did not elude her.

As night fell, Jayden cast a barrier around them and the fire, attempting to keep the heat contained as he had done every night. Trinia wasn't sure if she was just so cold it didn't matter, or if it would have been far colder had he not. She did not want to find out.

He sat down a few feet away from her, always careful to keep his distance. It was like a knife in her heart. He didn't have to say he cared or that he loved her. It showed in every thoughtful action, and it killed her inside because she could not return it.

She dozed off, drifting in and out of sleep through the night. At one point, she woke up to see the fire slowly dying and Jayden's strained face focusing on it, trying to stoke it back to life with his magic. He did get it going again, but by then, they were both shivering. "J-Jayden," she whispered.

He looked at her and nodded to show he had heard her.

"Come, lay b-behind me. It'll b-be warmer."

Moving around the fire, he lay down behind her, still leaving room. She scooched back against him, pulling his arm around her, holding it close, and drifting back to sleep.

The next morning the weather eased, and the snow slowed to a more manageable level, so they pressed on. Miles passed steadily as they made their way north into Canämor, sticking to the smaller villages as much as possible for shelter now that they had left the mountains near the border. To Trinia, it was much flatter than Ungäar, lacking the beautiful rolling hills, craggy mountains, and lush forests.

They finally arrived in Elmare and Jayden secured a room for them with a hearth. They enjoyed a proper meal and warmth for the first time in weeks. She found no solace in sleep, however. Nightmares plagued her, and she woke up more than once screaming and covered in sweat. It startled Jayden every time, and she hated it. He looked exhausted and worn.

Still here, she thought, trying to go back to sleep.

After breakfast the next morning, Jayden led her back out to the stables. They mounted up, leaving the village behind and slowly making their way toward the eaves of the Forest of Nex. The weather was deceptively beautiful with the sun shining its pale light and the ground covered in about a foot of snow or more. Approaching the edge of the forest, she could see icy crystals hanging from the branches like teeth.

As they passed under the shadow of the forest, she felt like she was in the underworld itself, not because there was a lack of light but a lack of life. It was still and deathly quiet apart from the horses and the clinking of the tack.

From what she could tell, they were on the Old Road that once connected the Airgíd to their empire beyond the borders of the forest. The clearing allowed for at least three carts to travel abreast, and while slightly overgrown, it seemed not much had changed in the millennia since the empire's fall.

Hours after leaving Elmare, she could hear running water, and soon the forest cleared a little at the banks of the Lisdarien River. The head waters were located many miles to the north from Rionnagan, and Trinia remembered playing in it during the summers. Those memories seemed so far away now.

They crossed over the two bridges that spanned the gaps to a small island in the middle of the river and its tributary from Mugros Lake. Once over, they entered the forest proper. From there, based on what she could remember, they would follow the Old Road along the river until they reached the gates of Rionnagan.

Five days after leaving the village, they came to the boundary of the tree line and she caught sight of her home. Before them, the City of Snow and Stars rose from the valley floor up and into the face of the mountain like a cancerous sore. It was fitting since it now looked dead and decaying with its broken battlements and empty towers carved into the mountain face.

Between the forest and the walls lay the open ground she had ridden across roughly three months ago. Now she was back to finish it.

"We will stay here until nightfall," she said, turning to Jayden. "You can still turn back."

He met her gaze, and she held her breath.

"Never."

CHAPTER 39

———

Elohai, I don't know what to do here. You have a plan of some kind, that much I have figured out. Sorry I'm so dense. Please protect us. Jayden paused, taking a deep breath. *Protect Trinia.*

He opened his eyes, watching the light fade. Trinia was asleep beside him, mumbling in her slumber. For weeks, he was silent, at least vocally, and for the first time in his life, he had prayed. Really prayed.

Every night she slept and awoke with nightmares. Every time she talked to herself, condemning voices in her head when she thought he wouldn't notice. Every time she broke down without warning.

She didn't have to thank him for being there or tell him she was grateful he had stayed. It showed in the ways she let him in past her walls or allowed him to hold her. And that was enough.

You can still turn back.

Never.

He smiled. *I'm surprised it took her so long to ask.*

When night finally fell, he nudged Trinia. "Time to go."

She sat up and nodded. He could see the hardness return to her eyes along with the tension in her shoulders. *Elohai, protect us.*

Jayden had his sword and Trinia still carried the one Údar had gifted her, but other than that, they only had their Gifts and magic to bring to bear on the most powerful Airgíd. *I'm sure it'll be fine*, he thought, staring toward the city.

"We ride hard and leave our horses behind once we get within half a mile. After that, it is on foot and through the gate," she said, adjusting the sword belt at her side.

He glanced at her, raising a brow. "The front gate? Just walk straight in?"

Trinia tightened the belt, looking up at him. "Got any better ideas?"

"Front gate it is."

They mounted up and he followed closely behind her as they crossed the mossy terrain. It was such a contrast to his homeland, with its red moss and short grasses peeking through the snow in places. No trees stood beyond the forest, which seemed to be on purpose. Less chance of an army sneaking up to your gate. *Or, in our case, two crazy people on a suicide mission.*

With the moon hidden behind the clouds, there was a smaller chance of getting spotted before they reached the walls—a blessing he thanked Elohai for.

When they were a half mile away, Trinia slowed and hopped off, wrapping the reins around a stout little bush. Jayden quickly dismounted and did the same, running to catch up with her. The city loomed ahead, ominously lit by torches and braziers along the outside of the gate.

Even in its ruined state, it held a wonder Jayden could not deny. *To think this used to be the seat of the Old Empire,* he thought, gazing up at the huge walls and battlements.

Reaching the wall, Trinia stuck to it, glancing up now and again while Jayden kept his focus on the ground level. There was no telling where patrols or guards might be standing watch. The gate itself, he noticed, was the most intact thing in the city by the look of it.

Coming to it, Trinia peered around and then motioned for him to follow. As he moved through, he hid a grin. *We might actually make it.*

-II-

Trinia led the way into Rionnagan and through the gates she had barely made it out of a few months before. They passed the market square and vendors and moved up through the streets she'd sped down, hoping to escape a fate she wanted no part in. It was like a dream—a horrible, horrible dream she could not wake up from.

You can't stop him.

He's too powerful.

You're going to die.

Her palms itched, her chest ached, and her head throbbed. *No, no, no! Not now! I must focus.*

The Voice is there.

He'll take you again.

You'll be his.

Trinia caught herself against the side of a home, clutching at her chest as the memories resurfaced.

The door creaked open, and she hid under the blankets, praying to Vyrni to save her.

"Hello, dear one," said the Voice, gently pulling back the covers.

She curled up as he ran his hands over her, tears sliding down her cheeks.

"Shh, don't worry," he said. "I won't hurt you."

"Trinia?"

She spun, seeing Jayden's worried face. "I'm fine," she gasped. "I'm fine." Turning, she pressed on, grabbing hold of the hate and letting it fuel her, letting it numb the ache.

Revenge! her mind cried.

Revenge!

Revenge!

As memories she had tried to forget bombarded her senses, they only fueled her rage. Her body felt the echoes of each blow, each unwanted touch, as if it were happening all over again. Her skin crawled like it was made of insects, skittering here and there.

Justice! her soul demanded.

Justice!

Justice!

Trinia's hands shook as the anger burned like an inferno within her. *This ends tonight!*

They came to the Middle Quarter and slowed down, sticking to the shadows and away from the torchlight as much as possible. No one was up at this hour, but she didn't want to risk getting caught before they got to the palace.

"Trinia," Jayden whispered behind her. "Why are there no guards? Don't your people have guards?"

She paused, looking around and suddenly noticing their absence. "We do," she replied. "Not many, though, as we have little need since no one has ever attacked us. Well, not in the last thousand years, anyway."

"Do you not find it a little odd?" he asked.

Glancing back at him, she nodded. "I do, but there is nothing to do except move forward."

Jayden gave a firm nod. "Lead the way."

His confidence in her warmed her heart, and she turned away before he could see the pain his kindness caused her.

Finally, they reached the Grand Stair leading up to the palace. Not a soul was to be seen, and all was quiet. Jayden came alongside her, staring at it in awe. "Wow, that's a lot of stairs."

Despite the tension of the moment, Trinia laughed under her breath, a smile tugging at her lips. "Do you think you can make it?"

Jayden gave a wry grin. "My lady, I have fought celnísh in the dead of night, met a talking wolf, survived a Baobhan Sith, and traveled hundreds of miles with the most cantankerous man in all of Wintenaeth. These stairs don't stand a chance."

Trinia rolled her eyes, unable to stop smiling. "Come on then, O' Great Prince, and face your greatest foe."

He winked as he made his way up the steps, and she followed close behind until they neared the top and she took the lead. Getting on her hands and knees, she crawled the last few, peeking over the lip of the stairs to see the doors to the Hall of Echoes slightly ajar and voices yelling. She stood, covering the last distance in a few long strides. When she turned, Jayden wasn't there.

Trinia looked back at the Stair, her heart skipping a beat. In the dim light pouring from the door, she could see Niren with a blade to Jayden's throat. "Niren, no!"

-II-

Jayden hadn't heard the person behind him until he felt the knife at his throat.

"Get up and don't try anything or I will slit your gullet."

He obeyed, slowly standing up as the figure pushed him forward up the last steps and in view of Trinia. She looked behind her and then caught sight of him. *I'm sorry, Trinia*, he thought.

"Niren, no!" Trinia moved from the shadows carefully. "What are you doing?"

"I could ask you the same thing," Niren growled. "You're supposed to be dead."

Trinia shook her head, taking another step. "I had to leave, Niren. My father would have used my Gift to murder our people in pursuit of power. I'm sorry for hitting you with the bucket, I didn't think you would have let me leave."

"She hit you with a bucket?" Jayden asked, instantly regretting it as the knife pressed harder against his throat.

"You don't know what I've been through because of you," Niren replied. "First, they beat me for allowing you to escape, and then your father personally tortured me because he believed I helped you kill yourself in the dungeon."

Trinia stopped, and Jayden could see the confusion and utter terror on her face. "The duplicate," she groaned. "It lived?"

"*Guards!*" Niren bellowed.

The doors swung open and Jayden counted twenty guards as they surrounded them, grabbing Trinia's arms before she could react. She screamed and flailed to no avail, and he could feel the blade digging into his skin. If he tried to use his magic now, Niren would kill him. Then there would be no one left to help her. *Bide your time*, he told himself.

More faces appeared at the door, making way for them as the guards dragged them into the light of the hall. When his eyes adjusted, he took in the sheer size of the room around them. Stone pillars stood like silent sentinels in a long colonnade toward the end where he saw a throne. Here and there, some pillars had cracked and toppled, and statues of long dead emperors watched with hollow eyes, dark and menacing.

All about them were Airgíd, all tall like Trinia. Some were built like mountains while others like willows, their silver hair varied as were the styles. All looked with disdain at him.

I wonder if this is how Trinia felt in my land.

Nearing the end of the hall, he made out a man on the throne, and a tendril of fear snaked its way into his belly. Even from where they were, the man's presence radiated power. His cold silver eyes, firm jaw and high cheekbones gave him a harsh look. *Caderyn.*

To the left of him was a hideous creature with snaking veins across his face, discolored and unnatural. His eyes gleamed at the sight of Trinia, and the wrinkled face smiled in malicious delight. *The Voice.*

Several men stood before Caderyn at the foot of the throne, all with angry looks on their faces.

"What is the meaning of this?" a tall, broad fellow asked, glaring at them.

"A southern spy and Lord Caderyn's daughter," called Niren.

The look of surprise on Caderyn's face quickly turned into a malevolent grin. He stood, and Jayden guessed that if he were standing next to the chieftain, the top of his head might reach his chin. *Hells, he is tall!*

Caderyn walked down the steps, stopping in front of Trinia. "Well, isn't this a welcome surprise," he said, his voice gravelly and grating. "I underestimated you, daughter of mine."

"You may well live to regret that," Trinia replied, pulling against the guards.

Come to bed with me.

Jayden froze.

Come to bed with me, Jayden.

He knew that siren call. *No, no, no!* he thought. There was a flash of golden hair in the sea of silver, a glimpse of a fair figure, the sparkle of hungry eyes.

Jaaaaayden.

His heart started beating wildly, and the scar on his chest burned. A Baobhan Sith!

Caderyn cast a glance his way. "Take him to my study. We'll torture him for information later once my business here is concluded."

"No!" Trinia cried, and he saw her struggling to get her hands free, but the guards had them pinned behind her back.

Jayden could feel blood running down his neck as his captor dragged him from the hall, down a corridor, and into a study. It was lit only by the fire in the hearth, and he saw the golden-haired woman sitting in a fur-lined chair, eyeing him. He felt his muscles relax and the scar on his chest felt as if it were on fire.

Niren removed the knife from his throat, and Jayden tried to turn and blast the man, but his body would not obey. The woman smiled, waving a hand dismissively. "You may go, Niren. He will not be any trouble."

They already started the bonding ritual... you will be more susceptible to them from now on...

Údar's words returned, their full meaning sending a chill down Jayden's spine.

"Caderyn asked me to—"

Jayden blinked, and the banshee was beside him, irises gone and spider-black veins spreading out from them. "I said, you may go."

When the door shut, she turned to him, licking her lips. "What a treat that I shall get to kill the man who took my sister from me." She drew close, her rancid breath gagging him. "I. Own. You. Now, lie down before the fire so I may finish what my sister started."

His body obeyed, and Jayden felt the obscurity creeping in at the edge of his vision. He strained with everything in him, focusing on his magic and trying to do something to break the spell she had over him, but nothing worked.

Lying down close to the fire, he turned toward it, watching the flames dance as the creature's robe dropped to the floor on the other side of him. *Elohai...save me.*

"Mother said you were a handsome man," said the banshee, pulling off one of his boots. "Though I must admit, I had expected... more."

Memories of the women he had slept with, the people he had stolen from, and every lie he had ever told flashed in his mind. He had left behind pain, ignored suffering, and turned a blind eye to all but himself.

Forgive me...

For what? asked a still small voice.

A tear slid down Jayden's cheek as he felt the banshee's clawed fingers taking off his other boot. *Everything.*

"I may just decide to keep you," said the banshee, undoing his belt with her black eyes watching him. "When Mother is finished with her plans, I will need someone to keep me warm at night."

In the fire appeared a single white flame. *Reach into the fire and take hold. Do not let go,* said the voice.

A finger twitched and then another. Jayden moved his hand toward the fire, though his mind and body protested. The heat was intense, and he kept his eyes on the single white flame. With everything he had left in him, he thrust his hand into the fire, grabbing hold of the white fire.

The banshee hissed, grabbing his arm and tried to pull his hand away, but he clung to it as his sleeve caught on fire. "Let go!" she commanded, her voice frantic.

He screamed in agony as the red flames licked his skin and tears ran down his face. Never before had he known such pain.

Follow me, said the voice.

"I will," he wept.

Suddenly the whole fire turned bright white. Jayden felt a surge of power flowing through his body, touching every hidden place and burning away the old. It refined him, creating something new, and yet kept him the same.

The white flames grew in their intensity, and Jayden turned to the banshee. She was writhing on the floor, mouth open in a silent scream. Her skin dripped off her bones, melting like wax into a gory mess until there was nothing left, not even a stain.

Then, the flames were gone.

Go to Trinia, said Elohai. *But do not intervene. What is happening must take place.*

Jayden rolled over, cradling his severely burned arm, and staggered to his feet through the pain. "I'm coming, Trinia… I'm coming."

CHAPTER 40

———

Jayden was gone.

Trinia stared at the door Niren took him through, hoping to see him return.

"I must admit, you had me fooled," said Caderyn, climbing the steps and seating himself on the throne. "I thought I had *you*, not a duplicate."

She turned her attention back to him, glaring.

"Caderyn," said one of the men, stepping forward, "we demand to know why you have killed our chieftains and why you think you have the right to crown yourself king!"

There was a hearty cheer from the others, and Trinia glanced around at them in horror. *He killed the other chieftains?*

"I have *every* right!" Caderyn shouted. "And now that my daughter has returned, my power is solidified. Tyarch!"

The Voice moved next to him. "Yes, my lord?"

"Take my daughter before the altar of Caluvan and scourge her. Then, once she knows her place, bring her back to me," said Caderyn, scowling.

"With pleasure, my lord," replied the Voice.

Trinia jerked against the guards' grip on her arms as the man hobbled down the stair toward her, his eyes gleaming.

Her palms felt like they were on fire and the ache in her chest was like a dagger. The voices in her head cried out.

She screamed, her voice sounding feral, even to her, as the rage built up inside. She stomped on one of the guards' feet, pushing herself away from him in the same motion. The guard lost his grip just enough for her to pull her arm free, flicking it out in front of her. She felt the power of her Gift surge through her, causing rippling pain as pieces of her flesh tore from her to create six duplicates. The crowd shrank back with cries of alarm.

The duplicates, her Trinii, drew their swords at her focused command and attacked the guards. Trinia pulled herself free of the other guard and drew her sword, casting four more duplicates, who grabbed the Voice and held him on his knees. She walked over, looking down on him and his fear-filled eyes. Stooping over, she whispered in his ear.

"This is for everything you took that did not belong to you."

Trinia rammed the sword into his stomach and pulled up, spilling the man's insides on the steps. She felt no relief, no satisfaction, no sense of peace. Only emptiness.

Cold, black emptiness.

She turned her attention to her father, pointing the sword at him. By the look on his face, he seemed almost amused.

"Do you really think you want to face me," he asked, giving her a condescending look. "Not even you have that kind of power."

Trinia focused on the Trinii, drawing them closer to her as she stepped back among them. She concentrated on her father's face, and the angle of his brow, and the hateful look in his eyes, working the illusion in place over all of them. When it was done, she and the Trinii spread out, speaking in unison. "You don't know what kind of power we have."

Caderyn sneered. "Do you think mere tricks will stop me? Very well, let us see what you have." He stood, reaching behind the throne. When he turned around, he held a large battle axe. He jumped from the top of the steps, cleaving one of the Trinii in two.

As one, Trinia and the Trinii attacked, weaving in and out of battle with him. From the corner of her eye, she could see those gathered running for the door, leaving the hall to her and her father. Ducking under his axe as he swung, Trinia sliced the back of his calf with her sword.

He roared in pain as he brought the axe around and caught two Trinii when they moved in for the attack, killing them instantly. Caderyn laughed, lifting the battle axe high and smashing it into the chest of another Trinii on the ground. "You cannot beat me, daughter of mine! Why do you continue to fight me?"

Trinia froze, calling off the Trinii with a thought. Bodies of duplicates lay scattered about, and her father had numerous wounds. Yet he didn't seem the least bit winded or tired, whereas she could feel herself weakening.

He drew in a deep breath, and Trinia felt her power weaken even more, the illusion failing and returning all the Trinii to normal.

He's drawing my power! How is that possible?

Caderyn closed his eyes, spreading his arms wide. "Do you feel it, daughter? Your power slowly draining out of you? Your power is mine!"

Trinia summoned what was left of her strength. "All those years of feeling weak. That was you. Wasn't it? That's why you beat me, abused me… You wanted my power. Well," she said, her face twisting into a snarl, "you can have it!"

She threw her hands forward, shrieking as she mentally commanded the Trinii to attack. They dropped their swords and rushed him, grabbing hold of her father as he tried to throw them off. One plunged its head into his chest, while another's arm absorbed into his side.

"What is this?" he cried, trying to pull the duplicates from him. "What is happening?"

Soon, all the Trinii were gone, and her father grabbed his head, shouting and swinging his arms wildly. "Get out! Get out of my head! Noooo!" He ran, yelling and cursing, and smashed his head against a pillar. He dropped to the ground, blood pooling around him.

Trinia dropped to her knees, heaving a steady breath as an overwhelming giddiness filled her body. She shook as the emotions flooded every part of her. The laughter started low, bubbling up and slowly growing in its volume until it echoed through the empty hall.

-II-

Jayden watched it all unfold, horrified by what she had done to her father. Not that the man had not deserved it, but to see the mass of bodies clinging to Caderyn reminded him too much of the celnish with their misshapen bodies and distorted features.

What chilled him to the core was Trinia's manic laughter ringing in the hall. He approached her slowly, carefully. Suddenly the laughter stopped, and three more of her stood around him. They grabbed him, and he cried out as they took him by his burned arm.

Trinia looked up at him, her eyes black and void of emotion. *Merciful Elohai! What happened to her?*

She stood and walked over, looking at his arm and frowning at it before meeting his gaze. The emptiness in her eyes was haunting. "You came back?" she said, her voice emotionless.

He nodded through the pain. "I told you... I wasn't... wasn't going to leave."

"I killed them."

"I know." He had never seen battle and never fought in a war, but he expected this was what the aftermath of one might look like—chaos and gore.

She glanced around at the bodies lying strewn about, both duplicate and Airgíd. "This is where it all starts," she said. "I'm going to make them pay."

Jayden fought to hold on to consciousness as the duplicates' fingers dug into his wounded arm. "Who... Make who pay?"

Trinia turned to him and drew close, holding his face as she placed a gentle kiss on his lips.

"Everyone."

EPILOGUE

———

Mandar watched out the window of their room in Ke'grul as carts rolled through the busy streets toward the morning market several blocks away. It had been several weeks since they'd found themselves in X'phos, transported by Elohai, according to Údar, though why here and not to Trinia, he didn't know.

A soft groan came from behind him. "Are you still standing there?"

He smiled and turned to look at Údar fully. "It's only been an hour since you last woke, my friend."

Údar groaned again as he tried to reposition himself in the bed. "Only that long?"

"Only that long," Mandar confirmed.

"Ugh. It feels likes days." He looked him. "How long?"

Mandar sighed, moving to take a seat in the chair next to the bed and folding his hands in front of him. "Nearly four weeks."

"*Plagues!*" Údar leaned his head back on the pillow, closing his eyes. "We've failed her, Mandar. I failed."

The defeat in his friend's voice pained Mandar, though he had to admit that it certainly looked that way. "She's a strong girl," he said finally. "She'll—"

"Everyone has a breaking point, Mandar," Údar whispered. "No one can bend forever."

Mandar wasn't sure how to respond to that. In all his years, he'd never experienced the things Údar had gone through, the pains and loss. He was a lone wolf in the service of his creator, and some things he would never understand about humans, even if he could take their form at times. "What should we do now?" he asked. "Give up?"

"Would you think less of me if I did?"

"No," he replied. "But you would think less of yourself." Learning forward, he added, "You lost yourself when Nisha died. Did Elohai give up on you?"

Údar looked at him. "No... He didn't."

He gave a small smile. "So, I ask again: what should we do now?"

Doubt creeped into Údar's eyes and he turned away. Mandar refused to let him wallow away in shame and self-pity. Not when so much was at stake. Pulling from deep within his memory, he found two things he hoped would reach his friend. "If there be only one, I will be there, for that one person is worth my effort," he said, quoting his friend. "And does not Elohai leave the ninety-nine in search of the one? Is that not what you told me?"

Údar nodded. "Yes, I did tell you that."

"Do you still believe it?"

As the silence stretched into minutes, Mandar wondered if he'd pushed too far too soon. Perhaps he should have waited a little longer, at least until the man had healed. But there it was, that spark in Údar's eye that he'd come to recognize when he was determined to see something through.

Údar flipped back the covers and carefully sat up, resting his hands on the sides of the bed. He swayed back and forth a moment, and Mandar was afraid he would fall over, but he steadied himself.

When their eyes met, he could see a thin light in his friend that hadn't been there moments before. Údar reached out, grabbing his arm in a warrior's shake. "As soon as I have recovered, we will leave."

"You and Batänny both."

"Batänny?" Údar glanced around. "Did something happen?"

Mandar snorted. "Fleas and ticks, man! If not for her, you would be dead! She ran from O'pha Tor to Ke'grul in two and a half days, nearly killing herself in the process."

"Is she alright?" Údar asked worriedly. "Where is she?"

"Happily enjoying not carrying your heavy backside. That's where I am," said Batänny, entering the room and taking a seat beside Mandar. "Nevertheless, I'm ready to go when you are."

She held up a finger. "I'm not going to carry either of you, though."

The End

GLOSSARY

Academy of Mages – The Academy was established shortly after the Peace Treaty of 8112 AE, which brought an end to the fighting amongst the Four Kingdoms. Since the use of Gifts was regulated and/or out-right banned for commoners, the Academy became a place to send people of influence to learn how to harness their magic for "the betterment of others."

After Empire – This dates everything after the fall of the empire in 8026 and is the time period in which the story takes place. Referred to as AE on all official documents.

Airgíd – The Airgíd are a race of powerful magic users that lived in close communion with Elohai in their distant past, toward the beginning of the world some 9,000 years ago. Because of their silver hair, they are sometimes called, "The Silver Ones."

Ancient Lands – These lands were once inhabited by the Airgíd and were prosperous. However, when Elohai's judgment came upon them, it became an icy wasteland, especially in the far north, and few Airgíd venture that far now.

Anthian – After the fall of the Empire, the kingdom grew anxious that the Airgíd might try and rebuild. They went mining for different ores and, according to some, Elohai led them to the precious metal, *anthian*, which is supposed to protect the people from Airgíd magic. It had no offensive abilities and it most often is put into armor or used in decorations because of its blue-green color.

Baobhan Sith – These banshees are temptresses of men and use seduction and sexual rituals to bond men to them. This leads to the destruction of those men and typically anything they control. These banshees are the personification of lust in the book and represent the reality of what pornography does to a person.

Before Empire – This dates everything before the rise of the Airgíd, 0 to approximately 5005 BE, and is referred to as BE on all official documents.

Brúan – A harsh tasting drink of the Airgíd made from distilling the red moss found in the region and adding ground skaäsa. It is then fermented for a minimum of eight years.

Canämor – Canämor claimed the northeastern section of the Empire—from the Forest of Nex to the sea. It is slightly more advanced in its armor and weapons than any other kingdom but lacks adequate farming and relies heavily on the sea.

Canämori – Someone who is a native of Canämor.

Caudor – Capital of Canämor.

Celnísh – The demonic shadow-spawn of Ulscia, who refers to them as her "children."

During Empire – This dates everything during the time period of the empire, starting in 5020 DE and is referred to as DE on all official documents.

Elohai – The Maker, Creator of the World, the One True God.

Forest of Nex – Nex means "shadow" and the forest is aptly named as it was infested with celnísh starting in 8130 AE. It is also the barrier that stands between the designated "Realm of the Airgíd" and the Four Kingdoms, and no one save only the very foolish travel through it.

Götthru – This is the term used by the Iomlíad to describe a cat, which, according to their lore, is capable of stealing souls.

Great Southern Forest – The largest in Wintenaeth, the Great Southern Forest stretches for hundreds of miles, covering most of X'phos.

Helwreck – A large creature that stands between ten and thirteen feet tall, with huge arms and hands. They can smash through rocks and beat their way into the sides of mountains with ease. One hit from these powerful creatures will kill a human instantly. They are very dim witted and thus their name is used as an insult when someone does something dumb.

Iomlíad – The Iomlíad were among the first peoples created, and they were gifted with the ability to shift into any created creature (excluding humans). They are called "Iomlíad" or "Shifters," sometimes interchangeably.

Iudran – Brother of Ulscia who killed Caluvan, their father, and fled to the east.

Ke'grul - Capital city of X'phos.

Lúinor Keep – Fortress of Ulscia and the Baobhan Sith situated in the middle of Mugros Lake.

Lynsium – *Lynsium* is a drug used on Iomlíad to placate them. If an Iomlíad has too much, it can lead to organ failure and death within a couple of hours.

Mages – Mages were established shortly after the fall of the Airgíd Empire and rise of the Four Kingdoms.

Mugros Lake – A lake created by Ulscia to create a natural barrier between her and her enemies.

Old Gods – The Old Gods are those worshipped by the Airgíd during the time of the Empire, and many still serve them throughout the Four Kingdoms. They are: Caluvan—king of the gods; Rhaemel—queen of the gods; Hagaet—goddess of fate; Silun—god of the sun; Madol—god of the hunt; Nalogriv—god of the underworld; Tuloth—god of the smith; Yinu—goddess of the harvest; Vyrni—goddess of protection; Sadrua—goddess of the moon

Psynodram – A specialized drug used to send Iomlíad into a blind rage and typically forcing them to shift into more dangerous creatures than they would otherwise choose. Any Iomlíad that drinks it will not know friend from foe and long-term effects are unknown.

Rhyllic – A mountain herb that grows throughout Ungäar and has a very earthly flavor to it.

Rionnagan (The City of Snow and Stars) – Capital of the Airgíd, its walls are said to have reflected the glory of the stars during the height of the Empire, and it was dubbed the City of Snow and Stars not long after.

Sarulid – a slimy giant slug about six feet long. They are harmless unless you are a farmer trying to grow crops.

Skaäsa – A centipede like creature with powerful jaws and an extremely bad temperament. These creatures tend to live in rocky areas or the hills where they can find places to hide and blend in with their surroundings.

Soläs – A *soläs* is an orb of light that mages can create as a light source when needed or as decoration. In some cases, they can be supercharged and weaponized, rendering people permanently blind.

The White Flame – It is the manifestation of Elohai's power dwelling in someone. No one can create the White Flame unless they know Elohai and follow him.

The Flourishing – Refers to the time when the lands were bountiful and all peoples grew and prospered together between o and approximately 5005 BE.

Thydu – Thydu claimed the northwestern portion of the Empire and is inhabited by a hardier people. They are known for their mastery of horses. Their primary source of trade are war horses, which is extremely lucrative.

Thydian - Someone who is a native of Thydu.

Telgost – A hauntingly beautiful she-ghost with wings and burning eyes. They happen when a woman falls to the seduction of the Baobhan Sith and their life has been drained from them. Telgost will attack women in a vain attempt to reclaim the life stolen from them, only to weep and wail when it does not revive their souls.

Tranâes – Capital of Ungäar.

Trifell – A three-headed beast the size of a large horse and covered in scales. They have huge claws and razor-sharp teeth, and no one who has encountered a trifell has lived to tell of it. Thus, their numbers are unknown. Based on reports, they seem to roam primarily in X'phos.

Trinii – The cumulative name for Trinia's duplicates when they are linked as one.

Ungäar – Ungäar beat the others in claiming the heart of the fertile lands that once kept the Empire fed. It boasts Qepho City, home of the Academy of Mages. Combined with their sheer numbers, Ungäar is by far the most powerful of the kingdoms, but it has an ugly side that few dare mention.

Ungäarian – Someone who is a native of Ungäar

Vyrbrake – Capital of Thydu

Wintenaeth – The land of Wintenaeth is vast. Filled with majestic mountains, lush valleys, craggy shore-lines, and wild forests, and is called home to no less than four kingdoms.

X'phos – X'phos made up the southern border of the Airgíd Empire and is home of the Free Peoples who serve no one. Their strength is in the community and their wealth in the vine. It is also the homeland of the Iomlíad, a people with shape-shifting abilities unique only to them.

X'phosian – Someone who is a native of X'phos, typically recognized by their free-loving nature and their Iom-líad abilities.

CPSIA information can be obtained
at www.ICGtesting.com
Printed in the USA
BVHW080008231220
596053BV00004B/11